"You did w[...] [...] [...] at Kadin, not having to explain that he'd melted into the kiss right along with her.

"What did you mean by what you said?"

That he didn't have to worry? That she wasn't the settling-down type? "Exactly what it sounded like."

"I wasn't hitting on you," he said.

Was he worried he'd somehow encouraged her?

"No, silly, I hit on you. And it worked." She smiled.

"Penny...I don't want you to get the wrong idea."

So professional. She bet he hung on to that like a badge, his ready defense whenever a woman got too close.

"I don't have the wrong idea. You kissed me back." Oh, God, was she really doing this? Flirting with fire? This wasn't ordinary flirting. This was war. She stopped and made him face her. "Look, whatever happens, happens. There are no rules when you're with me.'"

***

Be sure to check out the next books in this series.
Cold Case Detectives:
Powerful investigations, unexpected passion...

"Did I do what you expected?"

A WANTED MAN

BY
JENNIFER MOREY

MILLS & BOON

Published in Great Britain 2015
by Mills & Boon, an imprint of Harlequin (UK) Limited,
Eton House, 18-24 Paradise Road, Richmond, Surrey, TW9 1SR

© 2015 Jennifer Morey

ISBN: 978-0-263-91747-5

18-0915

Harlequin (UK) Limited's policy is to use papers that are natural, renewable and recyclable products and made from wood grown in sustainable forests. The logging and manufacturing processes conform to the legal environmental regulations of the country of origin.

Printed and bound in Spain
by CPI, Barcelona

Two-time RITA® Award nominee and Golden Quill Award winner **Jennifer Morey** writes single-title contemporary romance and page-turning romantic suspense. She has a geology degree and has managed export programs in compliance with the International Traffic in Arms Regulations (ITAR) for the aerospace industry. She lives at the feet of the Rocky Mountains in Denver, Colorado, and loves to hear from readers through her website, www.jennifermorey.com, or Facebook.

For Mom,
who loved a good murder mystery.

Chapter 1

Penny Darden saw the old, rickety barn through the arch of tree branches and cold nostalgia gripped her. She stopped walking. Tall wildflowers swayed down the center of the curving one-lane dirt road. Beautiful. Picturesque. But full of a secret past.

Growing up on a Midwestern farm, Penny hadn't escaped fast enough to city life. Metropolitan bike paths and noisy, multilane highways were her thing now. The barn, with its lonely mystery of fading red paint and old, splintering fences, tapped into the girl who'd loved to explore wild, rolling hills and abandoned buildings. She'd long ago left that life—and the girl—behind.

Resuming her walk, she emerged from the trees and spotted a Colonial-style house that stood just as neglected as the barn, door and windows boarded up, just like the farmhouse of her childhood. After her mother sold the place, it had gone to disrepair. She hadn't understood how lonely her childhood had been until her senior year in high school. That realization had driven her away from Midwestern life.

Jax hadn't told her there were historic buildings on his property. Maybe half the source of her unwanted curiosity stemmed from that. Her boyfriend had said the only difference between his second home in this remote area of the Wasatch Mountains and his upscale apartment in Salt Lake City was the view. How wrong he'd been.

Reaching the double doors of the weathered barn, she lifted the heavy, awkward latch securing one of the doors and pushed.

Dust particles drifted through the newly disturbed air, sparkling in sunlight. The smell of old hay took her back in time. Old everything. Old wood. Old leather. Old hides. She used to love playing in hay, getting dirty all day and fighting her mother when told to take a shower.

A white pickup truck parked at the far end stopped her short. Partially hidden by stacked hay, it seemed so out of place. She walked to the clean, new vehicle and saw a dent in the driver's-side door. Peering through the window, she noticed nothing odd except newness and cleanliness. Immaculate cleanliness. She tried the door handle. Locked.

What was a nice truck doing in an old barn like this? Had the previous owner left it? That didn't seem likely. Why leave a vehicle that was worth something? Maybe the engine blew up. Walking to the front, she saw no plate. Nothing on the back, either. Someone had just dumped it here.

While that struck her as unusual, Penny supposed there must be an explanation. As she turned away, a tack room drew her back to her childhood again. She and her best friend had ridden horses almost every weekend. She fingered an old bridle and then brushed off the dirt that transferred to her skin. Some tools and a few other pieces of tack, all worn with age, kept her in the past until she caught sight of the truck again.

Who were the previous owners? Why had they sold? Had the homestead gone to shambles after the sale or had something happened to force them to leave? She didn't know how long Jax had owned the place.

Penny walked outside, seeing just a portion of the truck before latching the door. She looked toward the boarded-up house and let another wave of lonely nostalgia sweep her before hiking back up the hill.

Her mother had sold their farm when Penny started college and she moved to an old house in town. Cheboygan. Thinking of her mom only intensified the loneliness that pressed into her.

When had she last seen her mother? Christmas? They hadn't talked in a while. Penny had gotten so busy with her job, she'd even ignored her mother's calls. She missed her, of course she missed her. She loved the difference between her life here and her mother's back in that sleepy northern Michigan town.

At the top of the hill, she followed the dirt road along a white fence, feeling better now that she was out in the open with swaying wildflowers keeping her company. Still, the ties of her past tugged. Birds chirped and a mosquito buzzed in front of her face. She swatted that away, her trip to childhood vanishing. Time to go back to the city.

Reaching the end of the dirt road, she turned onto Jax's paved driveway. His house came into view and she saw him standing on the porch, holding a cup of coffee. He looked much different in jeans and a flannel shirt than the pricey suits she usually saw him in at work. His close-cropped dark hair fit the businessman more than the mountain man. In fact, he didn't strike her as a mountain man at all. His log home was modern, not rugged. His polish and sophistication and social appetite had attracted her when she'd first met him.

She smiled as she neared. "What a beautiful place."

He didn't return her smile. In fact, his reaction seemed off.

"Where have you been?" he asked with forced amenability.

She stepped up onto the porch, wary of his stiff demeanor, the affront in his keen brown eyes. Did he feel she'd taken liberties by exploring without him inviting her? How ridiculous. Why would he mind?

"I walk every morning," she said.

"Why'd you go that way?" he asked, pointing in irritation. "There's a path through the woods out back for hiking."

"Oh." She hadn't noticed. "I saw the dirt road that skirts the edge of your property." She turned to indicate the direction of the road. "You didn't give me a tour, so… I hope you don't mind."

He smiled in a way that was more calculated than genuine. "My bad."

Did that mean he *did* mind? Uncomfortable, she went inside. Walking through the mudroom, she went into the living room, catching sight of a digital photo frame cycling through thousands of pictures he had of him and his son. One passed of them in the mountains at a cabin, different than this one, which suggested they'd gone somewhere on a trip. It gave her something to look at other than him.

Jax followed her into the kitchen. "What did you find on your walk?"

Why was he so tense? And what did he think she'd find? That truck? She began to feel a need to get away from here, and then chided herself for overreacting.

Taking out a bottle of water, she let the refrigerator door close. "An old barn."

He moved toward her, stopping a couple of feet from her. "Did you go inside? That building is pretty old. It isn't safe."

"No," she lied, twisting the cap off the plastic bottle and taking a drink. "I saw the house boarded up and decided it'd be better to have company to go exploring." She felt him assess her.

"I had it boarded up when I bought the property," he said, seeming to relax a little. "The house needs too many repairs."

"Is that why you built this one? How long ago was that?" she asked.

"A little over a year."

The truck didn't look as though it had been in the barn that long. Had Jax parked it there?

"I was going to make you breakfast in bed," she said, trying to keep things light. "How about we have it out on your back patio instead?"

After several seconds, he murmured, "Sure. Next time you feel like exploring, take me with you, okay?" His dark eyes warned rather than showed concern. "It's dangerous out there alone."

Dangerous in what way? "I'm not a kid," she said with a fake smile.

"I'm talking about the wildlife. And an abandoned house invites other predators."

What did he mean by *other predators*? Him? Was he delivering a subtle threat? Maybe he didn't trust that she hadn't at least peeked into the barn. She began to feel as though she should make an excuse and leave. She'd never seen this side of him and, frankly, didn't like it.

Not a woman to give in to fear, however, she met his

calculating gaze without looking away. He was the first to break the tense moment. Grinning like the Jax she'd first met in a meeting at work, he pecked a kiss on her mouth.

"Breakfast in bed would have been nice," he said softly. "I'm sorry I missed it."

He seemed like himself again, but his reaction to her exploration lingered. She watched him go to the table and sit before his computer. When he lifted the top, she went about preparing a simple breakfast.

The television went to a news program just as the bacon was ready and the eggs were in a pan. Jax must have turned the TV on when he woke, something he did every morning to catch the weather segment. Right now he typed away on his laptop, working and oblivious to what was being said.

Not Penny.

"Police are asking for anyone to come forward with any information in Sara Wolfe's murder investigation. The eleven-year-old girl disappeared last month on her way home from school. Her body was found last week along the banks of a remote area of Cottonwood Creek," the female anchorwoman said sadly.

While the woman went on to recap all that the police knew of the kidnapping, Penny went cold and still as she listened to the reporter say that a witness claimed to have seen a white pickup truck around the time school had been let out and the girl would have been walking home. The driver had stopped along the side of the road to talk to a young girl who fit Sara's description. The witness hadn't seen the girl's abduction, but had noticed a dent on the driver's-side door.

White truck.

Dent on the side.

Was it possible?

She jumped as Jax appeared next to her.

Just as she smelled something burning, he said, "The eggs."

She faced the stove and pushed the smoking eggs off the burner. They were ruined.

"Something wrong?" Jax asked.

Maybe. Is that truck in the barn yours?

She glanced over at him. "That girl. The missing girl in the news?" She watched him perk up—in a suspicious way. "What happened to her is disturbing."

"You've been following that story?"

She hoped he couldn't see her pulse throbbing through the artery in her neck. Already she had to steady her breathing. He frightened her. No, her intuition frightened her. She could stand up to fear when it didn't involve murder.

"Yes. Haven't you?"

"No, not really."

Penny furrowed her brow in confusion. Jax watched the news every morning. Hadn't the story of a young girl's disappearance and murder touched him? What kind of person wouldn't be affected by such a tragedy?

"What do you say we go into town for breakfast?" he suggested.

"All right." And then she'd head home. He really did scare her right now. His aloofness. His insensitivity to the Sara Wolfe murder. His odd demeanor.

He slipped his arms loosely around her waist. "Then we can come back and do some more exploring."

Would he take her to the barn and the boarded up house? She highly doubted that, given his suspicious behavior.

Hoping to pull off an act, she patted his chest. "Actually this morning I remembered something I need to do for another project that's due Monday. I need to get home and work on it."

Back came his distrust. "You can do that tomorrow."

She shook her head. "I need tonight and tomorrow."

"Then you can work here. I'll leave you alone." He grinned. "Until tonight, that is. Quinten is going back home soon. You and I can have a romantic dinner together this evening."

They hadn't been dating all that long. Just a couple of weeks. She'd had reservations about going to his mountain house. Only his announcement that his son would join them had made her agree, that and his promise that she'd have her own room. Finding out Quinten would leave this morning sealed her decision to go home.

"Haven't I been a perfect gentleman?" he asked, seeing her hesitation.

"Yes." He had. But that no longer mattered.

"Then stay. I invited you here to meet my son and spend some time getting to know each other outside work."

That might have appealed to her prior to making the connection between the truck in the barn and the missing girl. Now she just needed to get away.

"Last night was lovely. Your home is lovely. But my boss has been breathing down my neck lately. I have to get this job done on time." She thought she sounded sincere.

"What's he going to do? Fire you?" He smiled crookedly, falling for her pretense. "You're his best ad executive. My brother will vouch for that."

As CEO of Ballard's Sporting Goods, Jax's brother, Dane, did have significant influence. Jax, too, as president. Penny had met her boyfriend when she pitched her idea for their ad campaign. Handsome and driven, he'd attracted her from the start. She, apparently, had caught his eye for the same reason. They had a lot in common.

He'd been the one to tell her Ballard's would hire Avenue One to do their advertising, a huge boost to her career.

Moving back, she eased out of his arms. "Ever since I delivered that Super Bowl ad, Dane's expectations have been grandiose."

"My brother counts on you, for good reason." He brushed his finger down her nose.

Disliking the affectionate touch, she stepped back.

"Sorry, I just love your nose with those big, sexy green eyes of yours." He chuckled. "I didn't mean to treat you like a kid."

A sick feeling plunged in her stomach. Why had he used the word *kid*?

Tucking her shoulder-length reddish-brown hair behind her ear, she said, "I'm going to go get ready." Penny turned to head for the stairs.

"I'll let you leave on one condition."

Let her leave? Putting her hand on the railing, she looked back and couldn't tell if he was joking.

"I get to come over Tuesday night and cook you dinner. Mondays are always a train wreck for me."

She nodded even though she didn't feel like it. "Deal."

That seemed to placate him, to put to rest any concern that whatever Penny had discovered hadn't spooked her away.

Going up the stairs, she ran into Quinten on the first landing, Jax's six-foot tall, eighteen-year-old son. Quinten's mother, only a teenager herself when he was born, had left him with Jax when she was fifteen. Jax had devoted his life to the boy and it showed. Quinten had grown into a well-mannered young man with aspirations to go far in college. She'd loved their conversation at dinner.

"Morning, Penny," Quinten said with a sleepy smile

livening his hazel eyes. He looked a lot like his father, except younger, of course, and with wilder hair.

She smiled back at him. "Morning."

"My dad down here giving you a hard time?"

She laughed. "Not any more than I give him."

He passed her on the way down. "He likes you."

Not responding to that with anything more than an amicable look, she climbed the rest of the way up the stairs. She felt a bit of a kinship to the boy, growing up in a single-parent household like him. When she'd asked if he wanted to find his mother, he said no. She'd seen the love Jax had for him and it reminded her of how her mother loved her.

Would a man who'd raised a son like Quinten be capable of harming young girls? It didn't seem likely. There had to be some explanation.

Breakfast passed without incident, with Jax being his old self and not that weird, suspicious man who'd confronted her after her walk. But the time had passed painfully slowly and she couldn't be happier to be— finally—home. Dumping her purse on the table in the wide, wood-floored entry, she sighed, feeling tension leave her shoulders. Her airy apartment with views from every room welcomed her. She took in the sunny city scene through the big windows along the far wall of her living room, metal and glass sparkling.

After removing her shoes, she passed stainless-steel appliances and gray schist granite countertops of her kitchen and padded down the hall to her office. Bright green, white and gold accents made this her favorite room. She was her most creative here. But creativity wasn't on the agenda for today. Truth was, she had no other work project going on as she'd led Jax to believe. Sitting down at her white desk, she started up the computer and began her research.

Reading about the eleven-year-old girl disturbed her. An adorable, blue-eyed, blond-haired angel, Sara Wolfe had a big smile, and innocence radiated off her in the photos Penny found. Active in sports, she played the piano and had joined theater. She came from average parents who lived in a clean suburban home in the Sugar House area, a normal little girl who had a lot going for her until she'd been robbed of her bright, promising future.

Penny had never aspired to be a mother, but she didn't have to wonder what they must have gone through—were still going through. The police had only one lead, the one they'd received from a witness who'd seen the white pickup truck. The killer had so far gotten away with his horrible crime.

Tipping her head back, Penny closed her eyes as she contemplated what to do. Tell the police. Yes, she wasn't trying to talk herself out of going to the cops. That had to be done. She had to do the right thing. But could she find a diplomatic way of going about this? Could she find a quiet way of finding out if the truck belonged to Jax and whether he'd used it to abduct an eleven-year-old girl? He was her boyfriend, after all. She liked him—except for this morning after her walk. Before she accused him of such a horrendous crime, she had to be more certain. What if he hadn't done it?

Lowering her head, she stared at the last article she'd read online. The parents had contacted a private detective to help them find their daughter's killer. The man had said he'd consider their request. Why had they asked this particular man?

Kadin Tandy.

She did a search on his name and found an article.

Will Renowned Victim Rights Activist Join Sara Wolfe's Murder Investigation?

Intrigue made her click on the link and peruse the article. Sara's parents had reached out to a man who'd gained noteworthiness after single-handedly solving his own daughter's kidnapping and murder case. After the sick pedophile had been thrown into prison, Kadin quit his impressive job with New York City's Cold Case Squad within the Fugitive Enforcement Division to start up his own private detective agency. As Penny read, she became certain the man was more of a vigilante than a law enforcement officer.

She found a photo of him half-sitting on the tailgate of a pickup truck parked at the threshold of a dark alley. In jeans and a short-sleeved dark blue T-shirt with a logo on the upper left side, he posed with one leg planted on the ground. A cowboy hat shaded his eyes, but the camera had captured their stunning and unflinching gray intensity. Unruly black hair stuck out under the rim of the hat. A boldly displayed shoulder harness held two guns, one on each side.

She sat transfixed by the picture, by the man. Powerful. Highly intelligent. Dangerous good looks. Those impressions and more drew her in.

Penny read on to learn that his wife had died of a drug overdose not long after their daughter's body was discovered. She'd apparently been unable to survive the loss of their little girl. A few months later, after Kadin had tracked down the killer, he'd opened Dark Alley Investigations in Rock Springs, Wyoming. His daughter had been kidnapped and killed in New York. Was the choice to move to Rock Springs because of that? To try and escape his unbearable pain? Kadin had lost his wife and child. His family. That kind of tragedy would forever change a man.

Did anyone ever recover from something so awful? Kadin had focused his energy on private investigations of violent crimes. Each case must be a battle to avenge his daughter.

She looked at the photo again, a sentinel in a dark alley. The imagery evoked a blatant declaration to go where most would never dare. And do whatever it took to bring perpetrators of violent crimes to justice. He needed no advertising. The media had done that for him.

He hadn't yet agreed to help with the Wolfe case, stating only that he'd look at the file. Kadin was probably a busy man with the reputation he had. Or would Sara Wolfe's case be his first since his little girl was killed? Penny could well imagine how difficult an investigation like that would be on a father who'd lost his daughter to a pedophile.

Still, she couldn't believe he'd turn his back on the Sara Wolfe case, not with his past. Maybe Penny could sway him. She could go to him before going to the police. He could help her find out more about the truck. But just a description of what she saw wouldn't be enough. She needed more. Proof.

Penny waited until later that night to drive back to Park City. The winding road leading to Jax's house was a lot eerier than the first time she'd been here. When she reached his long, dirt driveway, she turned off her headlights and drove straight onto the one-lane, rutted road with flowering weeds growing down the center. Making her way under moonlight, she reached a clearing and spotted the house and barn.

Stopping in front of the barn, she retrieved a small flashlight she always kept in her car and got out. Closing the door, she put on a pair of leather gloves and looked around. Moonlight cast shadows where the meadow met the thick line of trees. Anyone could lurk within the trunks. If Jax had seen her drive by, would he follow her here? She wasn't even sure he was still at the cabin. Most likely, he'd stayed in Salt Lake City for the workweek. She was being paranoid, and perhaps for good reason.

Her boots crunched over the dry gravel and she heard a stream running about a hundred yards down the hill. The white paint on the house was peeling, the trim warping and falling off. The boards over the door and windows gave it a haunting look. A big cottonwood tree shaded half of it from moonlight.

At the barn doors, she lifted the wood bar and pushed one side open. It creaked and gravity took it swinging against the side of the barn with a bang. Something scurried inside the barn and a bird squawked as though startled from sleep. She heard it fly away but didn't see it. Checking the road, seeing no headlights or hearing anything, Penny went inside the barn. It was pitch-black in there. She flipped on the flashlight.

The truck was still there.

Jax must have believed her when she'd said she hadn't gone inside. She berated herself for jumping to conclusions. He might not be guilty, after all.

Searching the barn, she spotted the tack and went there to find something to break a window out of the truck. She found a rusting metal rake and carried it over to the passenger's-side window. Swinging hard, she bashed in the glass, spraying the seat. She reached in and unlocked the door manually, and then opened the glove box. It was completely empty. Weird. She looked under seats and in the middle console. Nothing. It was as though someone had thoroughly cleaned it before stowing it here.

Getting out of the truck, she began taking pictures with her smartphone. She took several shots of the dent and made sure she got the serial number in the dash and then tucked her phone back into her front pocket. She hurried from the barn, looking around before she closed the door and hooked the latch. Turning, she searched the treeline and road. A flash of light caught her eye. Someone walked through the trees with a flashlight. She could make out his shadowy form coming to a stop at the edge of the clearing.

Walking briskly, she saw the flashlight go dark. Had Jax walked through the woods? Impossible. He hadn't returned. Or had he…? Maybe he'd anticipated she'd come here, or at least been suspicious. Or was it Jax at all?

Back in her car, she spun her car around and raced down the narrow dirt road. As she came to Jax's driveway, she saw no movement around the log house and only a few lights were on.

She made it to the highway and almost felt in the clear when she noticed a car behind her. Had whoever had the flashlight followed her? She sped up, passing a few cars and weaving back into the right lane. The car behind her did the same thing.

Penny slowed down. The car slowed down as well and allowed more distance to separate them.

All the way to Salt Lake City, Penny kept track of the other car, a dark Jeep Wrangler she didn't recognize. Rather than drive home and lead a potential killer to her residence, Penny headed to the Salt Lake City Police Department. When she parked in front, she watched the Jeep zip by, darkness and tinted windows preventing her from seeing the driver.

Chapter 2

The short, bubbly applicant had an exhausting, fast-talking, high-pitched voice. Kadin Tandy looked past her curly hair and heavily made up face, her voice drifting off into white noise as he looked through the window of his Rock Springs, Wyoming, office. He could see part of the street and some of the oldest buildings in town, red-and-tan brick trimmed in varying colors, rooflines square and some with signs that lit up at night. Heat waves rippled on the pavement and Rosa Romero unlocked the door of her Mexican restaurant, The Spicy Habanero. Her green chili was the best he'd ever had.

Having his office here made him feel at home—as at home as he could, anyway. He'd rented the upstairs apartment so that he could spend more time working. Dark Alley Investigations had been open a couple of months now and he'd accumulated enough cases to warrant some help. And then he'd received that call from Detective Austin Cohen, the lead in the Sara Wolfe case. He'd attempted to read the file before the applicant arrived but hadn't gotten past the first paragraph. The little girl might as well be his own.

Would he have this kind of trouble with every child case? He felt like a useless coward for reacting the way he did. He could help those parents. Why didn't he? Why *couldn't* he? Why did he even have to think about it?

Because he'd seen the file detectives had put together on his daughter's case.

Because he'd tortured himself with those images until he captured her killer.

Because the pain had not lessened in three years.

He still ached with loss, still yearned for the impossible, to see and hold his little girl again, to go back to the time before her abduction and be ready to miraculously save her. Daddy to the rescue.

Except it hadn't happened that way.

"Mr. Tandy?"

Kadin jerked his gaze from the window to the applicant. "Is there anything else you'd like to ask me?"

The woman had to know he'd wandered off somewhere far away from this interview. "No. Thank you for coming by." He stood, needing to get rid of her, to be alone so that he could get thoughts of Annabelle out of his head. "I'll call you if I need to talk to you again."

The woman looked disappointed. People knew when they were being rejected. "Oh. Okay." She stood up. "Thank you."

He walked the woman to the door and as he watched her go to her car, he spotted Lott Trumbauer getting out of his blue Jaguar. A trust-fund baby who was a fishing guide, Lott spent a lot of time on the banks of the Green River. That was how they'd met. Kadin had gone fishing and had run into Lott with a family, teaching them how to fish. They'd struck up a friendship. That was fifteen years ago.

"Great," he muttered. Just what he needed. More badgering. Lott had been talking to Kadin's mom about the shocking news of his resignation and move back to Rock Springs.

He went to his corner office next to the conference room where he'd just conducted the interview. He had a view of a side street from here. That was where he stood until he heard Lott enter. Then he turned as his friend's booted feet creaked over the old wood floor and he stopped at the office door with a smile.

"Nice," Lott said. A tall, charming jet-setter with bright blue eyes and dark brown hair cut short, he wasn't married but always had a girlfriend. They never lasted more than a few months. Kadin had attracted women like that before he married his one and only love. Maybe he still did now that he was single again and just didn't notice. Lack of interest did that. He had too much to do, anyway.

"What brings you to town?" Kadin asked.

His pal stepped into the office, checking out the barren walls. "How's business?"

The diversion tactic told him enough. Lott had come to talk unpleasant things. "I've got three cases."

"All cold?"

"Cold enough."

Lott stopped at his desk. "I saw a girl leave here in tears. Are you interviewing again?"

"She was crying?"

"You have a way of doing that. I can't figure out if all your murder investigations have desensitized you, or if you've just installed a switch to shut off your emotions."

He gestured with his hand toward the bare walls. "Are you *ever* going to decorate this place?"

Kadin grimaced. He cared about how he made people feel, and truly hadn't meant to hurt the girl. It was an interview, for God's sake, not the budding of a new romance. As for decorating, he'd only furnished one conference room and his office. "I haven't had time to do more."

"You could make time."

"Why are you here, Lott? Talking to my parents again?"

His friend grinned but not with genuine humor. He was caught. "Your mother is worried about you. She called again." Kadin blinked and turned toward the view. A man walked by in the afternoon, late-summer heat, a dry heat in this western town.

"I'll call her."

"She asked me to check in on you. I don't think they understand why you moved back here."

His parents had wanted him to stay out East. He'd grown up in Massachusetts.

"I lived here for ten years."

Lott nodded. "That's what I told her. She thinks you're obsessing over their deaths."

"And that by moving here I don't put it behind me?" Kadin looked back at his friend, who cocked his head in a yeah-I-know gesture. "There are some things I don't want to forget. And that's everything I had when we lived here. Them. Before…"

"I get it, Kadin. You should call your mom and tell her. Then maybe she'll stop using me as a messenger."

Lott was like a second son to his parents. They had been around a lot more than Lott's had. In some ways, Kadin thought his pal had learned how to live from them, and his healthy attitude about money was one indicator. He didn't take it for granted and he valued being productive.

"Sorry you had to come all this way," Kadin said.

Lott stared at him, somber. "It's okay to be different after what happened to you, Kadin. All the people close to you want is for you to heal. Start a new life. Not forget them, just…move on."

Kadin just nodded, waiting for him to stop.

After a bit, Lott grinned. "I didn't just come to give you another lecture. I'm going down to the Green River to do some fishing."

Lott had frequently come to visit him and his wife and daughter on that excuse. He hadn't just come to see them, he'd come to fish. But Kadin wasn't fooled. His mother wasn't the one who'd put him up to this visit. He'd been talking to his parents ever since Arielle had overdosed, checking in without Kadin knowing.

"Okay."

"So." Lott perched on the corner of his desk. "Business is good, huh? How is it that you already got some cases?"

Kadin moved to stand before him. "They called."

"You've gotten a lot of media coverage."

Kadin recognized the congratulations. His daughter's disappearance and murder had attracted a lot of attention. When news broke that he was venturing off on his own to fight similar crimes, the media had swarmed him. But that only masked what was really going on.

"I'm fine, Lott."

"Are you?"

He really hated talking about this. A thousand knife stabs might as well pierce his chest. Then that heavy weight came next, along with an overwhelming sense of helplessness. "Yes." Just thinking his wife's name brought that terrible day back. Finding her already dead. After enduring so much tragedy already. He'd nearly gone insane. The only thing that saved him was moving to Rock

Springs, Wyoming, a quiet, wildly beautiful place that asked nothing of him other than to breathe.

"I mean it, Kadin. You have to move on, not close yourself off to the world and immerse yourself in cold case murders."

"I am moving on." As much as he could. The only way he knew how.

"Shut off from everyone who cares about you. I don't mean to sound like a sap, but I miss my friend. He disappeared the day his daughter did."

Kadin didn't know how to say he'd never be the same man he once was. He just knew. And that man hadn't gone until the moment he learned Annabelle's body had been found.

Body...

Her twelve-year-old body. Not Annabelle. Her *body.* Such powerful, unfathomable grief had racked him, for days, for months, a slicing machete going to work on his insides. Trapped in his lost and desolate mind with no way out, he hadn't noticed how far Arielle had slipped into oblivion. Then the day had come when he'd found her. All of that emotion had imploded on him. He'd felt it bleed out of him until only empty darkness remained. Everything had become mechanical after that. Until he'd stumbled across some photographs of Annabelle when they'd lived in Wyoming.

"I was a cop before my daughter went missing," Kadin said. "I'm doing what I'm meant to do." His talent was being put to good use. And if he could use it to help others who were going through the same thing he had experienced, then that had to be good. That was his only joy. Every time he caught a murderer, he avenged his wife and daughter.

"You're alone here," Lott reminded him.

"No, I'm not. I know practically everyone in town. Besides, I'm hardly ever home. Not every cold case is in Sweetwater County."

"I'm afraid you're going to bury yourself in these investigations, Kadin. When is it going to be enough?"

Lott, like everyone else, didn't understand. Home and family had different meanings to him now. Warm and full of optimistic love before the tragedy, starkly realistic after. That was why he'd opened this agency. This agency was for the people who knew life's darkest reality. People like him.

"Look," Lott said in his silence. "I know you hate talking about this. I'm worried about you. Your parents worry about you. I stop in every once in a while to check on you. I've done my duty. Now, since I'm staying through the weekend, how about we camp and fish this Friday and Saturday?"

"You're staying that long?" Lott didn't usually stay longer than a day or two.

"Yeah, I met a girl the last time I was here. You might be seeing me more often."

Figured, a woman had drawn him here. Women drew him everywhere he went.

"Are you free this weekend?"

"Maybe."

"Maybe?" Lott angled his head, a quiet demand for more information.

"I might take on another case." He didn't feel like explaining the Sara Wolfe case.

The front door jingled. He'd left the old bells there so that he'd know when someone arrived. Whoever had entered couldn't have chosen better timing.

Kadin started toward his office door to go see who'd arrived.

"Don't forget you have other things in your life besides hunting down killers," Lott said as Kadin passed. And then as he followed, "Camping. This weekend. No talk about the past, I promise."

"Another reason I moved here. To get away from old friends." Lott would know he was kidding. Sort of.

"You couldn't go far enough to get away from me." Lott stopped beside Kadin in the lobby, where a woman stood looking around.

Lott whispered a whistle only Kadin could hear.

Few women caught Kadin's eye anymore, but this one sure did. He had to agree with Lott. On the tall side, pushing five-nine, she had a thick head of wavy auburn hair that would look great spread out on bed sheets, and wide, long-lashed sea-green eyes that would add to the moment.

"Hi. Which one of you is Kadin Tandy?" she asked.

She wore skinny, distressed jeans, with knee-high, spiky-heeled boots and a fancy top with flashy accessories. She wasn't afraid to be tall and stand out in a crowd. And she must have a creative streak.

"That would be him." Lott strode to the door. When he was behind the woman, he waved as though the heat were getting to him and mouthed, *She's hot!*

"I'll see you Friday," Kadin said gruffly.

Lott left, walking backward and pointing both fingers at the woman's butt and nodding with a mouthed *oh yeah*.

The woman glanced back and Lott shut his mouth and turned, heading for his Jaguar.

"Friend of yours?" the woman asked.

"One of the best." Minus the frat house sexual innuendos and constant meddling. "How can I help you?"

She surveyed his business space—the front entry and the vacant reception desk, the open conference room doors, his office and finally the walls. "Haven't been here long, huh?"

"You're the second person who said they didn't like my decorating."

She laughed good-naturedly. "What decorating?"

"I just moved in." Two months ago, but who was counting?

She walked farther into the office space. "This is a beautiful building. I wasn't expecting that."

What was she expecting? He'd never met her before. "I'm sorry. You know my name but I don't have the pleasure of knowing yours."

"Oh." She laughed again, another big smile. "Penny Darden." She walked over to him.

"Penny." He shook the hand she extended. "I assume there's a reason you came to see me?"

There it was, the grim circumstances that had led her here, dimming her beautiful eyes and sweeping away her cheery smile. A victim's family behaved that way. Or maybe this woman was a friend. Didn't matter. Murder never made people happy.

"Sara Wolfe's parents came to see you," she said at last, daring to look into his eyes.

He managed to cover up the jarring surprise that gave him. "They didn't come to see me. The lead detective in her case called me."

"Oh…of course. I'm sorry." She seemed nervous. What made her nervous? Him as a man or the Sara Wolfe case?

"Are you media?" he asked.

"No." She clasped her hands in front of her, a vulnerable action for such a dynamic woman. He felt her energy, could see her basic strength. He saw a lot about people he first met. Those first impressions carried weight.

"I drove here from Salt Lake City after I read about you."

She'd read about him? So her nervousness came from fascination, not the Wolfe case.

"First of all, I'm really sorry about what happened," she said softly. "About Annabelle. And your wife. It must not be easy. Losing them like that."

More dreaded talk. For the second time today, he felt sick to his stomach. He started to get angry. He couldn't stand sympathy. People offered it when they had no idea what kidnapping did to those who had to live through the torture.

"Just tell me why you're here," he bit out.

At the hard clip to his tone, she checked herself. "Right. Sure." She glanced down and then unclasped her hands and rubbed them on her jeans, shaking off awkwardness. "I actually came to talk to you about Sara Wolfe."

"Are you related?"

She shook her head. "I heard about her murder on the news."

"All right…"

She searched his eyes, hesitating but needing something. Without saying anything, she wandered across the small lobby, past a desk to the wall where nothing hung.

"Why don't we start with who you are?" She'd told him her name but nothing else. "What do you do?"

She faced him. "I'm vice president of Client Services at Avenue One. We're a big advertising agency, getting bigger each year."

"How do you know Sara Wolfe?" he asked.

"I—I don't, I just…read about her murder, and you, after…" She searched his eyes again.

"After what?" he said to help her out.

"One of our biggest clients is Ballard's Sporting Goods. Have you heard of them?"

"Big sporting goods chain. Yeah."

"Well, I've sort of been seeing the company's president," she said. "I met him when we landed the account and started working with him on their ad campaign. Jax Ballard. His older brother founded the company and they run it together."

"What do they have to do with the Sara Wolfe case?"

Her gaze turned hard and determined, the businesswoman in her coming out. "This is where I have to be very delicate, Mr. Tandy."

He didn't have to guess why. "You think Jax Ballard may have something to do with Sara Wolfe's murder?" No longer sensitive about the case, he felt his detective instincts kicking in. This woman could have a significant lead.

"I need to be sure before…"

"Just tell me what you know." A little girl had been killed. He'd offer no sympathy to her if she had information that could lead him to the killer.

"I accompanied him to his cabin last Friday night. I walk every day, so I left for one early Saturday morning, before he woke. I followed a dirt road on his property and came upon an abandoned house and barn. I went into the barn and saw a truck parked inside. A white truck with a dent on the driver's side."

All Kadin could do was stare at her after she stopped talking, her revelation—and what it could mean—tearing through him, bringing him back to those days and hours when he and the other investigators were closing in on the man who'd abducted and killed his precious little girl.

"I—I'm not saying it's the same truck. I—I just need to be sure before I go to the police."

"Did he know you found the truck?" he asked.

"I told him I saw the barn and that's it."

Kadin lifted his brow. "He believes you didn't see it?"

"I'm not sure."

She'd seen the truck parked—no, hidden—in an abandoned barn and had heard about Sara Wolfe. Then she had taken action. While he didn't approve of her not going to the police, he did commend her for coming to him.

"I went back." She began to rummage in her purse.

"Back to the barn?" Kadin stepped toward her as she pulled out a cell phone.

He waited while she navigated.

"I took these pictures."

He looked at them all and inwardly cheered when he saw the one with the VIN. As he lifted his head, his gaze collided with hers. "What made you decide to risk going back to get these?"

"Evidence," she said, as though he ought to know.

"You put yourself in danger."

"I was a little worried Jax might catch me, but what if he moved the truck? When I left the barn, I saw a man in the trees. He was carrying a flashlight. He could have been anyone."

"A man wandering the woods at night? Alone?"

"I thought it was strange, too. And then he followed me. At least I think he followed me."

"He followed you? For how long?"

"Until I parked in front of the police station."

So the suspect might think she went inside and told the police about the truck. That might compel the criminal to do something.

"Good thinking, getting these pictures," Kadin said. "I'll get the wheels moving to get a search warrant. We need to look for DNA or fiber evidence. And from the sound of it, we need to move fast."

"A search warrant?"

"There's no other way." Her boyfriend would know someone had told the police about the truck, and that someone was Penny.

She sighed. "How long will the search warrant take?"

"Hard to say. The location is remote and outside Park City. I'll have to coordinate with the county sheriff."

"Days?"

"Hopefully not more than two. Tomorrow or the next day. Will you have to work with Jax?"

"Yes, possibly."

She had a couple of days to prepare. "Just act like nothing happened."

"It's more than that. If I'm wrong about this, I could lose my job."

That seemed rather drastic to him. "How so? You're doing what has to be done by reporting what you saw."

"My boss will probably fire me." She folded her arms, her purse swinging at her side as she bent one slender knee, a picture of vexation. "He's been acting strange lately, putting a lot of unnecessary pressure on me ever since I landed a few big accounts."

"He's threatened by you?" Kadin took in her stance and felt the nervous energy bouncing off her. "There are laws he has to follow."

"He'll find some legal way of doing it."

"Would you let him get away with that?"

She huffed out a laugh and lowered her arms. "No."

He liked strong women like her. She had a heart but didn't waste much time on sympathy. He found people—women—like her easier to be with than those who expressed their feelings too much.

"Are you going to take the case?" she asked.

Solving murders of adults differed greatly from violent crimes against children. Kadin felt the encroachment of dark memories and didn't answer. Would he? How could he not? An innocent young girl had been killed. How could he stand back and let others work the case without helping?

Her clever green eyes took in his face, reading him well enough. "A man who doesn't easily commit." Then, as though on their own, her gaze lowered into a quick and flirty once-over. "We have that in common."

She offered a diversion and he took it. "You don't commit?" Biting down on her lush lower lip, she shrugged. Clearly neither of them was talking about Sara Wolfe's murder investigation. And his gut was telling him she liked to play too much to be the type of woman to commit easily. The man to win her heart would need to hit all the marks on her demanding score sheet.

"So…do I need to go to the police directly?" she asked, breaking the awkward silence.

"Jax Ballard will know he's a person of interest no matter who gets the warrant," he replied.

"I'll handle Jax Ballard."

He gave her a slight bow. "I have no doubt you will."

She smiled, the flirt in her popping out again. He found that rather irresistible, her lightness of heart, her lack of hesitation to engage with a man. Him.

"Do you have a card so I can call you?" he asked.

Those eyes blinked and that smiled continued to dazzle, until she realized he wasn't trying to hit on her. He only needed a way to contact her. After the search warrant was issued and a crime scene unit was sent to search the truck.

"Oh." Flustered, she dug into her purse.

Flirting with men must be almost a second nature to her. Easy. Natural. He remembered when he'd been the same way. Now there was no light left in him for that. He had no desire at all to pursue anyone. Although he had to admit, Penny was the first woman he'd encountered since his wife passed who stirred the hint of interest. Not enough to make him act.

She handed him a card, eyeing him guardedly.

He took it. "I'll be in touch."

She nodded, very businesslike. "Thank you."

"Have a nice day."

She looked at him as though checking to make sure he was serious, smile gone, a soundless *oh* on her lips.

He'd tried to sound casual and professional. Maybe he'd tried too hard. *Have a nice day? Jeez.*

"You as well, Mr. Tandy. I'll be waiting to hear from you." With that, she turned to go, sauntering out the door without looking back. A woman like her didn't need to. She carried confidence like a politician, except with her, it came naturally.

Kadin went to the window, drawn by the trail only a fascinating woman could leave in her wake. Her long, slender legs glided in the high-heeled boots, butt firm and fit, thick red locks bouncing. He watched her get into her white BMW Z4 convertible on the street in front of his office. His building was on a corner, and the only parking lot was in the back and shared with other businesses. As she drove away, another car pulled away from the curb across the intersecting street, a black Jeep Wrangler with darkly tinted windows that followed her departure.

The next morning, Penny got out of her car and walked through the parking garage beneath Avenue One. Her shoes clicked against the concrete on her way to the elevator. She rode to her floor and stepped out. People bustled around, talked on phones and typed away on their keyboards. Her boss was in a meeting inside a glass-front conference room. He saw her and scowled. She'd taken yesterday off and was late getting here this morning.

Heading for her office, she went inside and closed the door. All the way back to Salt Lake City and long into the night, she hadn't been able to shake thoughts of Kadin. The man in person didn't disappoint. He looked exactly like the photo she'd seen, minus the cowboy hat, his eyes brighter without the shade. Magnetizing. What had he meant when he said they didn't easily commit? After she'd had time to mull it over, she didn't think he meant going to the police. He'd meant *personally*. What had she done to make him say that?

That photo of him must have really messed with her head. So mysterious. Sexy, but in a dark, brooding way. She'd never been drawn to a man like that before. Her norm gravitated toward the executive type. The man who owned rugged but didn't walk rugged. Kadin walked rugged. He knocked her off her game. He'd flustered her. Those eyes. Nothing could have prepared her for the impact of them in person. A light, glowing gray, the intelligence in them had captivated her. Their lightness sparkled with life, but what beamed out to the world told a much more ominous story. Dark intelligence. The things those eyes had seen must be incredible.

On top of that distraction, she had to wait to hear when the search warrant went through, and then she'd have to brace herself for Jax's wrath, especially if she was wrong in her suspicions.

Looking around her office, down on her desk and then at her computer where several emails waited to be read, she lost hope of all productivity. Penny buried her face in her hands. It was going to be impossible to concentrate on work today.

A knock on her office door brought her head up. Her boss stood there.

She waved him in.

Mark Pershing walked into the office, shutting the door behind him. "Where have you been?"

"I had something personal come up."

He had his panicked look on right now, beady brown eyes wider than normal and side parted hair falling out of line from raking his fingers through it. Average in height, he wore a pale yellow dress shirt that washed out his face and was buttoned too tight over his slightly round belly. His anxiety seemed over-the-top. What was going on with him?

"This is a bad time to be taking time off, Penny. I need you here."

"The Ballard campaign is under control." She took in his overall disheveled appearance. "What's the matter?"

"I had your direct reports coming to me with questions all day yesterday. They fell behind schedule."

In one day? "Mark, nothing is wrong with our schedule. Are you all right?" Penny stood up and stepped around the desk to stand before him. "What's going on? Why are you so tense?"

He smoothed his hair in support of the side part. The hair fell where it was before. "I'm getting a lot of pressure from the board."

Why? The board couldn't have any complaints about her campaign with Ballard's. They were ecstatic over the account, and she stayed on top of every issue.

"Are we losing money somewhere else?" she asked.

He looked at her strangely for several seconds, his panic going behind a mask. "I need you here, Penny."

"I *am* here. Trust me, I want this as much as you do."

"I'm sorry." He shoved his fingers through his hair again. "What happened with you? Can you talk about it?"

"No...not yet. It's nothing dire." She caught what she'd just said. Well, not for her, anyway. "I just need to get through it." Maybe. That depended on when Kadin lined up the search and Jax confronted her.

When Mark continued to subject her to his thin-lipped doubt, she said, "We're in production for the first ad. They won't need me until next week. I've been meeting with Jax on the camping equipment ad. Stop worrying."

"But I do. Especially when you vanish so abruptly without an explanation. This is a big account, Penny. We're all counting on you." And then he added, "*I'm* counting on you."

Hearing the desperation in his tone, and certain he knew something she didn't, she tried to placate him. "I know." She put her hand in his upper arm. "Just trust me, all right?" If Avenue One was in trouble, then she'd do everything she could to save the company.

Reluctantly, his lips curved into a small smile and he nodded. Then he put his hand over hers on his arm, curling his fingers to hold hers. The touch made her withdraw her hand. He hadn't gotten over her rejection. Would he ever? And now he tried to hang the Ballard account over her head. For what reason? To cover a mistake he'd made? She wished he'd talk to her.

Up until now, she wouldn't have labeled her boss as weak, but he sure seemed that way now. She wouldn't be fooled. Mark was a smart businessman. A little egotistical, but smart. Decisive at times. Few, if anyone other than her, had seen him like this.

She began to realize that her job might be in more jeopardy than sending cops after Avenue One's number two client.

"Is there something you need to tell me?" she asked quietly.

Mark's usual impenetrable self returned. "No. Get to work." With that he left her office, closing the door behind him.

Her cell rang. Seeing the caller ID, she debated whether to answer. It was Jax.

She reluctantly picked up.

"Where are you?" he asked.

In a flash she remembered they had made plans to meet for a working breakfast today. "Oh, darn." She hadn't eaten yet. "I forgot all about it. I've been so busy."

"Your assistant said you were out all day yesterday."

"Something came up on another account. I'm sorry. It's that project I told you about." She really disliked lying, especially since she sounded good at it. "Where are you?"

"I'm on my way up," he said.

Here? He was coming to her office? Apprehension drained her face of color, and prickles chased through her arms. Lying about her job differed from pretending to still be interested in Jax.

"You were going to show me the mockups for the new ad," he reminded her.

"Yes." She gathered her aplomb. "Why don't you meet me in the conference room? The one off the lobby." There would be a lot of people passing the windowed wall.

"I'm just now getting off the elevator."

"Okay."

Penny took her laptop and went to the conference room. She was hooking her computer up to the overhead projector when Jax entered, a visitor badge hanging around his neck, silk suit flowing down his lean body.

She plastered a smile to her face.

"Hi," he said with a guarded grin.

Had he seen through her fake congeniality? Since they were at work, he didn't walk over to kiss her. Instead, he put his briefcase on the floor and simply took a seat.

She remained standing and began her presentation. "We were thinking about taking a *Parent Trap* theme for one of the commercials. Something with an air mattress floating on a lake." She clicked through a few slides with examples of lines and props.

"Maybe something a little more modern," Jax said.

"Already thought of that. We envisioned starting out in the past time and then flashed forward to modern time." She showed him an animated clip of what they'd turn into a real commercial.

When it ended, he nodded slowly. "I like it. But I'm not sure how many people will be familiar with a movie like that."

"We can explore other options."

"Let's do that."

Penny moved to his side and sat down, turning her laptop so he could see it. For the next hour and a half they researched other movies and came up with a few that might produce a few scenes they could mimic in the commercial. It was easy to fall into the work. Penny loved what she did. She'd always been a creative person, and Avenue One gave her busy, intellectual stimulation.

"This is good," Jax said when they finished for the day. "Good progress."

"Mark will be relieved you feel that way." Maybe he'd get off her back.

He angled his head. "Oh? He has concerns?"

Penny curbed her tongue. She wouldn't air corporate speculation. "He's always concerned. He wants you and your brother to be happy with these ads." And so did she, at least until he was arrested for kidnapping. *If* he'd be arrested…

"I have no doubt that we will." He smiled the way he always did, warm and affectionate.

She was glad to hear him say that.

He stood, checking his phone. "I've got meetings the rest of the day. Are we still on for tonight?" he finally asked.

She felt her stomach churn with fear, but she nodded with a congenial, "Of course. How about eight?"

"Eight it is. See you then." Jax looked down at her mouth as though wanting to kiss her. Thankfully they were in the office. Tonight would be another challenge.

Chapter 3

Kadin yawned for the umpteenth time as he followed Penny's BMW into the parking garage of her apartment building. He'd kept vigil outside Avenue One all day. So far, no sign of the black Jeep.

He'd had a rather boring day, except for the email arrival from an old friend who still worked at the Bureau. He'd sent detailed information on Penny's background. That had kept him engaged for a few hours. He didn't like admitting that she interested him more than her role in the Sara Wolfe investigation. While there was nothing in the pretty ad exec's background that gave any new leads, there had been other information that he'd tucked away for himself.

Not married. Never divorced. Penny was an only child raised by a single mom. Her dad skipped town before she was born. After a couple of calls and internet searches, Kadin had found him in North Dakota with a wife and three kids. He'd bet Penny didn't know that and wondered if she'd be upset if she did. He wasn't sure if or when he'd tell her. He should keep his association with her professional. And what if she didn't want to know anything about her father? That kind of personal meddling made him uncomfortable.

Or…any kind of personal meddling with her.

He'd reacted to her as he hadn't for any other women since Arielle. The way he felt reminded him of when he'd met his wife, only different. Arielle and Penny were as different as their names—Arielle much more fragile, looking to him with hero worship. He doubted if Penny had ever been fragile and she'd probably be insulted if he treated her too old-fashioned. She may have felt awkward coming to him at first, but the sharp business woman hadn't been far from the surface.

Her mother had apparently done a good job bringing her up on her own. Penny had gone to college at the University of Michigan and then moved to Salt Lake City after getting a job at Avenue One, where she'd worked her way up the executive ranks. No police record, but she had a rap sheet of speeding tickets. Right in line with his impression of her. Full of energy. A go-getter. Very independent. And a flirt… Parking near where Penny had parked, Kadin got out and waited for her to notice him.

Stopping short, she raked her eyes up and down his body, and then glanced beside him at his car, a modified five-hundred-horsepower, 1969 Charger.

He walked toward her. "Ms. Darden."

"What are you doing here?" she asked, recovering from her shock. "Did you get the search warrant?"

"The sheriff thinks he can get it signed by morning."

"Why are you here, then?"

He stopped before her on the sidewalk in front of the

elevators. "Someone followed you to my office. Didn't you see them?"

After another stunned moment, she shook her head. "No. All the way to Rock Springs?"

She hadn't expected anyone to follow her and so hadn't looked. "Mind if I come up?" He gestured toward the elevators.

Her head flinched backward slightly. "To my apartment? Uh… Jax is coming over to cook me dinner. He'll be here at eight."

Kadin checked his watch. "Plenty of time. Why don't you let me set up a listening device before he arrives?"

Her sea-green eyes blinked a few times, the pistol in her coming out. "Wait a minute." She held up a hand. "Is that really necessary? Why did you want to come up to my apartment?"

"Since someone followed you, that tells me you're in danger. And that person could have been Jax. He may reveal something and it will be easier for me to protect you if I can hear if something goes wrong."

She took a moment to think on that and then her gaze wandered down as it had when she'd come to see him in Rock Springs. When she looked up, the flirt in her returned. "Yes, I suppose that would be a good idea…" She glanced over at his car. "Is that yours?"

"Yes."

"Nice." After batting him a look, she walked to the elevator and pressed Up.

"You like cars?" he asked, playing along, but sensing she'd used charm to hide her nerves. She didn't like him coming up to her apartment. Why? Because it wasn't her idea? Did she prefer control with her men? It fit. The nervousness didn't.

"I've been known to go to a drag race or two."

She drag-raced? He got into the elevator with her.

"You're the German car type," he mused as she pressed her floor. "New. Expensive."

"I like older cars, too. My mom drove me to kindergarten in an orange GTO Judge."

He chuckled at the imagery as the elevator doors opened. She led him down the tiled hall. Inside the apartment, Kadin briefly noticed an open expanse of dark wood floors and big furniture on an enormous area rug. Clean. Tidy. Colorful. Like her...and her mom's GTO.

"The truck is registered to Jax Ballard," he said.

She sucked in a rush of air and stopped, pivoting to face him as she lowered her purse to an entry table. Not the news she'd hoped for, which was why he got it out of the way.

"Does that mean..."

"Jax is our kidnapper?" She needed some reassurance, but he wouldn't sugarcoat anything. "He's looking pretty guilty in my eyes. But without evidence, we have nothing. We need something from the truck." In every murder investigation, evidence ruled. A body might be found, but evidence linked the crime to the killer. The bodies were always the hardest to stomach.

While Penny walked farther into her apartment, he remembered the day he'd gotten a visit from his partner during his daughter's investigation.

"I'm sorry to have to tell you this," his partner's voice echoed in his head. *"Your daughter has been found."*

Sorry...

Found...

"What is it?" his wife had asked from behind him, panic and fear and desolation in her eyes.

He hadn't had to tell her. She could see it in him. All he'd said was, *"She's been found."*

Unspoken was, *but not alive.*

"I'm so sorry. She's been murdered. I'm so, so sorry." His partner had broken down into tears.

Arielle had started screaming, a wretched wail and repeated *"No!"* He'd taken her against him and silently, with his eyes, told his partner to excuse them. He'd shut the door and held his wife until she went into a kind of catatonic state.

"Kadin?" Penny stepped toward him.

He'd let the memory go on too long. Sometimes that happened. As much as he fought them, they seeped past his defenses.

He went to her kitchen and opened her refrigerator, taking out a soda. Snapping the can lid, he saw how Penny observed him. He gave her credit for not saying anything, for not confronting him or forcing him to talk.

Penny was anxious despite knowing Kadin was nearby, listening in case she needed him. Finding out Jax owned the truck disturbed her. It would disturb anyone. But she'd never been so close to a pedophile before—a *potential* pedophile. He sure looked guilty...but was he?

When he'd first arrived, she'd felt his tension. He was acting just as much as her, both of them pretending that nothing was amiss. She'd picked at the manicotti he'd prepared. Talk had been scarce and nothing of significance.

Now she cleaned up the mess, glad for something to do. He sat at the island, watching her.

"Did you hear anything new about that missing girl?" Jax asked.

Penny dropped the pan she was rinsing and looked at him. "What girl?"

"Sara Wolfe."

"Oh. No. Nothing new." She put the pan in the dishwasher. Why was he bringing this up?

"The only thing they have to go on is that white pickup truck."

"That's what the news said." She began wiping the counter.

"There's got to be a lot of white trucks that have a dent on the side."

Yes, but were they all hidden in an abandoned barn? She said no more and finished cleaning the kitchen. Now she had no choice other than to join him. She wished he'd just leave.

He stood up as she left the kitchen, stopping her with a hand on her elbow.

She faced him, not liking how close he was or the calculating look in his eyes.

"I would hope anyone who sees a truck like that is careful about whom they accuse," he said softly.

There could be no mistaking his meaning. He thought she'd seen the truck and wasn't telling him. Her pulse quickened, but she held on to her courage.

"I'm sure they'd gather evidence first."

One side of his mouth hitched up as though he found that mildly amusing. Her audacity.

"Why don't you join me this weekend at the cabin?" he murmured. "Last weekend was cut so short."

"I—"

"We can take a walk together," he said. "You can show me where you went."

Would he arrange some strange accident that would befall her? "I'll have to see what my schedule is like…"

"Right. That new project you have going on." He leaned down and pressed a kiss to her mouth before she could retreat.

Then he lifted his head and, with a clear threat in his eyes, said, "Be careful, Penny."

Or what? "It's getting late."

"I'm going now." He straightened and stepped back. "Will I see you again?"

"Of course. The ad campaign—"

"I couldn't care less about the ad campaign. I care about you."

She had no intelligible response to that.

"Do you believe me?"

Slowly, she nodded. He cared, but how did he care? In an obsessive way?

"Good. Then we don't have a problem."

Not yet…

After Jax left, Penny breathed deep in the silence of her apartment. Going into the kitchen, she was about to get a glass of milk when her doorbell rang. She went back to the entryway and saw Kadin through her peephole. She opened the door.

"That went well." He stepped inside.

"He knows."

As he turned to face her in her living room, He wasn't wearing a cowboy hat, but subtle bulges under his shirt told her he wore his guns.

"The search warrant went through," he said. "A team is headed to his cabin right now."

Walking toward him, she stopped and tipped her head back a little to look up at him. "Great."

"You want to go get a drink?" he asked.

Taken aback, she studied him to determine why he'd asked. Did he want to spend some casual time with her or did he need an escape? Sara's murder investigation must take its toll on him.

"Is that how you handle stress?" The teasing question came unbidden, attraction making her do what she did normally with men.

"Never. I just know I won't get to sleep anytime soon tonight. And you don't seem like you will, either." He hitched his head in the direction of the street outside the apartment building. "I saw a nice-looking pub down the street from here. Why not get away for a bit?"

So, even with his rocky past, he didn't turn to booze. He just wanted a change of atmosphere, to be surrounded by the sound of happy people and the smell of good food.

"I'd love that."

They walked out the door and then made their way outside, Penny ever aware of the man at her side. She couldn't recall if she'd ever felt such strong but intangible vibrations about a man before. In the elevator, seeing him look at her in her peripheral vision. Walking along the sidewalk, sneaking peaks at his long stride and proud carriage. Nothing could take this man down.

At the small, upscale pub, he opened the door for her.

He sat beside her at the bar and ordered a beer. She ordered a martini. Dirty.

He eyed her as though that kind of drink said something about her. "Most women like fruitier drinks."

"Too sweet."

"You like things spicy?" he asked, his steely gaze going down the front of her shirt.

Did he think she was spicy? "Yes."

His eyes met hers for an inscrutable assessment. "It suits you."

"How so?"

"You're successful. Single. Always on the go." And beautiful. The last he said with his eyes, a brief exposure of interest before he locked it down.

"How do you know I'm always on the go?" She sat back with her drink, unwinding and beginning to enjoy herself.

"Your apartment doesn't look like it's used a lot."

He'd noticed that? "I keep it clean." She sipped slowly.

"You're there a lot?"

"Well, no." She worked long hours sometimes. "I get bored by myself."

"Do you have lots of friends?"

Was that another thing he'd noticed about her or had he read something in his background check? She set down her drink. "Best friend from high school, except she still lives in Michigan. Coworkers. College friends. My neighbors are all nice. Except the crotchety old widow at the end of the hall. She likes to be left alone. I bring her things from the bakery down the street. I think I'm the only one she likes in the building."

He grinned, leaning back against his chair as she had, relaxing. "Are you from Michigan?"

She nodded, unable to keep from appreciating the broad slope of his chest and shoulders. "I grew up on a farm near Cheboygan. My mother moved to town when I went to college."

"You two are close?"

He already knew about her family, and his question was more of a coax to tell him more. Except she had to think about that one. "Yes, well, we used to be. She never married and I don't have any sisters or brothers. Just two divorced aunts. Our holidays are cozy."

She laughed because every time she thought of holidays with the Darden crew, there were always jokes and some kind of twist on tradition.

"No men, huh?"

"No." She didn't think that had been intentional. It had just happened that way. The single Darden women…

"Kind of explains why you're so independent," Kadin said.

Because she grew up without a father figure? Penny didn't see how that related.

"What made your holidays cozy?" he asked in her silence.

She fell easily back into fond memory. "My mother hangs jasmine instead of mistletoe. She thinks it attracts love and money. I sometimes tease her because jasmine oil is supposedly an aphrodisiac. For someone as disenchanted with men as my mother, it's an odd choice." There were some things about her childhood that hadn't been lonely. Her mother did have color. "She's über-political, too. We had a whole set of president ornaments, except the ones she didn't like. Pig roast instead of turkey for Thanksgiving, complete with a big, fat apple in its mouth. Once we all flew to the Caribbean and had Christmas in July that year."

"Your dad leaving must have hurt her quite a bit."

The fond memories shifted to darker ones. "She didn't talk about it much. She just said she was glad he left if he didn't love her. I never met my dad…he left before I was born. I never saw how it affected her, except for how picky she is about men." She blew out a breath. "And she often told me she was happy alone. That she hadn't yet met a man worthy of her trust."

"But she wishes she could find someone special," he murmured.

She found it peculiar that he'd picked that piece out of what she'd said. "Yes, but it isn't that important to her. She has me. And she's extremely stubborn. She's not what you'd call a traditional woman."

"How so?" he asked curiously.

"Well, not only is she distrustful, but she's very set in her ways. Most men don't like that. And, as I mentioned, she has definite political views. Loves history." Her tone softened and she sighed. "She took me all over the world when I was growing up. Her social nature made it easy for us to mingle with locals. Everyone in Cheboygan knows her. She's active in the community. A real prom queen in her sixties."

"You sound like you're trying to convince yourself of that."

She frowned, not understanding what he meant. "That she's a sixty-year-old prom queen?"

He chuckled. "No, that she isn't lonely."

Penny could only stare at him. She often did wonder if her mother was lonely.

"She sounds a lot like you."

"Should I be offended?" Penny sipped her martini.

"I meant no offense. Your mother made her own choices. Just be glad you have her."

"What about your family?" she asked, disliking the direction of this talk. "Where are you from?"

"Massachusetts. My parents and both sets of grandparents live there. I have a sister who's married and has three kids."

They all lived in Massachusetts? "How'd you end up in Rock Springs?"

"You know, you can always go work somewhere else if your boss fires you," he said.

Well, he had blatantly ignored her question. What about Rock Springs was such a touchy subject for him? His daughter had been taken in New York. A wild and remote place like Wyoming seemed like a haven to her.

Instead of asking him about that, however, she went with his new direction. "I love my job at Avenue One. I figure if anybody should go, it's him. I'd like a chance to make that company thrive again."

"You love having the fate of a company on your shoulders?" He drank from his bottle of beer.

"I would run it if the opportunity presented itself." She preferred calling the shots, not answering to anyone but herself.

"Ambitious."

Yes. She had always been that way. All the way through school, she'd been active in all kinds of activities. Never homecoming queen but she was class president once. Straight-A student. Surrounded by friends.

"You tutor for a girls' club. You coach a girls' soccer team. And you give occasional motivational seminars for teenagers. Where do you find the time when you're not striving to take your boss's job?"

She narrowed her eyes at him. "Boy, you don't miss a thing, do you?" That had all come up in his very thorough background check.

"Not often."

"Not very humble, either, are you?"

"Just honest."

He was good at what he did. Is that what he meant? He must attract cases that way. Families who lost loved ones whose killer still walked free needed to know they had someone capable on their side.

"What else do you know about me?" she asked.

He didn't respond right away and she wondered if he felt he had to choose his words carefully. Did he think she might accuse him of invading her privacy? Hadn't he already?

"That's pretty much it."

Good. She didn't feel like talking about her work anymore.

"Why did you leave your mother?" Kadin asked.

The question took her aback. Why did he ask? She didn't feel like talking about that, either.

"I didn't leave her. I got a job here."

"Did you want to get away from your mother?"

She felt insulted. Even more, defensive. How dare he ask that? And then she realized she *had* wanted to get away from her hometown. Her mother. Not because she didn't love her. She did. She just got tired of her preaching about how to pick the right men. Penny wanted to have fun right now. She didn't want to be tied down with anyone. Maybe she'd never want that. Having grown up with a mother who had control of her own destiny, Penny was the same way.

"No," she finally answered. "Not her. Maybe just the life there."

"What about your dad? Do you want to find him?"

"Not really. He left." She'd thought about it once in a while. Sometimes she got curious, where he lived, what he did for a profession…why he left—his version. She'd heard her mother's over and over. The scorned woman version. She'd loved him, but he hadn't loved her. Ya-de-ya-de-ya.

"Did you ever try to find him?"

She shook her head. "Why bother?" Her father hadn't cared enough to stay, so why subject herself to that?

"Why didn't she ever get remarried?" he asked.

Penny sipped more of her martini. "You know, this isn't fair." She set her glass down and pointed her finger at him with her free hand. "You know everything about me and I know next to nothing about you."

"You know everything about me."

Maybe to him she knew everything, everything that mattered. His daughter. His wife. Solving cold cases. One, two, three.

"I don't mean to sound harsh, but that's a pretty shallow life," she remarked.

He sat back against the stool, taking no offense and charming her because of that. Confident men were especially attractive to her. That was what had initially drawn her to Jax.

"Why do you live in Rock Springs?" she asked.

"You're going to make me talk about this, aren't you."

"It's only fair."

His grin turned wry. "I met Arielle there. Her father owns a ranch not far from the city. My daughter was born there."

Good memories.

"Do you see her father?"

He shook his head, no longer smiling as darker thoughts apparently pervaded. "I haven't been able to."

Penny couldn't say she'd do the same if she had gone through what he had. Was he hanging on to his wife and daughter? Who wouldn't? And what was wrong with doing that? Then it dawned on her. Carrying the heartbreak everywhere with him for the rest of his life wasn't healthy.

She'd never met a man like him before, one who was so far off-limits to her. And he was. His heart was so damaged she'd be a fool to invest too much of herself in him. Backing off from her interest in a man went against her nature, though. She loved men. She loved to flirt with them. There was no risk when it was all in fun. She'd always held the principle that when she fell in love, she'd know. She'd flirt as usual, and if it was meant to be, the flirtation would grow into more. Naturally.

Yet, with Kadin, even though she was powerfully attracted to him, she felt herself holding back. That was new to her. She never held back. She wasn't afraid of love. She wasn't afraid of relationships failing. Actually she didn't view the endings as failures. They were simply not the epitome of love. How could she call that a mistake?

"Do you see your family often?" she asked, sliding another look at his light gray eyes and the hard angles of his stubble-shadowed face.

"Often enough."

There it was again, that sign of a man who worked hard to bury tragedy. He wasn't open to talking about it at all. He bottled it up.

"What about friends?"

"You met one of them at my office. Lott is my closest friend. He stops by to annoy me regularly. We're supposed to go fishing this Friday."

Curiosity nipped her good. She had to know more. "You like to fish?"

"Ever since I was a kid."

And he still did, despite what he'd endured. He could still get away and relax catching a few fish. But fishing could be a solitary sport.

"Did you have a lot of friends in New York?" she asked.

"Yes."

"Do you keep in touch with them?"

He faced the bar, taking a drink of his beer. After he put the bottle down, he looked at her. "No. Lott is the only one, and that's only because he comes to see me."

That was so sad. He'd alienated himself from everyone he knew. They must all be constant reminders. Was he afraid they'd talk about his wife and daughter? Moving to Rock Springs probably gave him an out. He could push their deaths out of his mind and only let the happy memories in. And, she suspected, anyone who got in the way of that might risk being pushed out of his life.

"Good for him," she finally said, and that was all she'd say. The extent of his grief infused her soul. Nothing anyone said or did would change what he'd lost. There was no recovering from it. It would always be there, a deep, painful, permanent scar.

"He's a nosy jet-setter," Kadin said. "His dad is an oil man. He's the one who was checking out your butt when you came to my office."

"He *was* checking me out. I wondered."

"My advice to you? Stay away from him if it's a meaningful relationship you're ultimately after. He likes to mess around."

"Thanks for the warning." She nodded with a smile, hiding her disappointment. He seemed not to care if she was interested in his friend. She'd never had to discipline herself with men, but this one had an invisible no trespassing sign posted over his heart. Instinct reminded her not to flirt, that he wouldn't welcome any kind of female attention. But the independent spitfire in her rebelled. What would happen if she *did* come on to him?

"What about you?" she asked.

"Me?" He looked genuinely startled that she'd asked. He was that closed off to women. He behaved as though he were still married, making reference to his womanizing friend as though she'd been interested in him. It had obviously not crossed Kadin's mind that she might be interested in him.

"Should I stay away from you, too?" It felt good to be her brazen self. She flashed a smile, watching him look at her big white teeth and then into her eyes. She felt a spark of arousal as he seemed to fall into the same kind of awareness.

"Yes," he said at last.

Without saying so, he'd told her that he wasn't in the market for a woman. His suffering had made him jaded. Damaged. Too bad. She'd like to spend some time with him, intimate time. But that would be kind of pointless, wouldn't it?

"How old are you?" she asked, anyway.

"Thirty-seven."

"I'm thirty-four." Keeping her gaze locked with his, she sipped from her martini. This didn't have to be anything serious. She'd been with men in a casual way before, knowing they wouldn't last. Some men were nice and good-looking enough to give a try even though they weren't *the one*.

As the moment stretched on, she enjoyed his involuntary, heating attraction. The man in him recognized the look of an interested female. She didn't have to say anything to send out signals.

Satisfied that he hadn't completely turned her away, she leaned toward him, really close to his mouth. "Don't worry, Detective. You're safe with me." She watched him look from her mouth to her eyes and then added, "In case you didn't put it together by now, I'm not the settling-down type."

She stood, staying between the stools, seeing him look at her breasts. That was encouragement enough. Taking a chance, she put her hand on the side of his face as he tipped his head to gaze up at her. Then she leaned in and pressed her mouth to his, just a little, just enough to send desire curling to her toes. She loved how he responded, eyes startled but burning with desire. "I'm going home now."

With that, she left her drink half-finished, walking confidently toward the exit, breathing through her mouth to calm her excitement. Lord, he set her on fire! She hadn't expected it to be that potent.

Outside, he caught up to her. "What did you do that for?"

"I wanted to see what you'd do." As she walked, she

didn't look at him. She stayed strong, something she usually had no trouble doing, but he was unpredictable. She stood a good chance of being shot down. For some reason, that only made her want to tempt him more.

"Did I do what you expected?"

"You did what I hoped." She glanced at him, not having to explain that he'd melted into the kiss right along with her.

"What did you mean by what you said?"

That he didn't have to worry? That she wasn't the settling-down type? "Exactly what it sounded like."

"I wasn't hitting on you," he said.

Was he concerned he'd somehow encouraged her?

"No, silly, I hit on you, and it worked." She smiled.

"Penny... I don't want you to get the wrong idea."

So *professional*. She'd bet he hung on to that like a badge, his ready defense whenever a woman got too close.

"I don't have the wrong idea. You kissed me back." Oh God, was she really doing this? Flirting with fire? And this wasn't ordinary flirting. This was war. She stopped and made him face her. "Look, whatever happens, happens. There are no rules when you're with me." She didn't go by any rules, either. If the right man came along, she'd know it. If he wasn't right, he wasn't right. But this man...

A nagging inner voice said she'd better establish some rules.

"You..." He searched for the right words.

"If it's just sex," she said, shocking herself and then berating herself for worrying. "If it's more than that, then it's more. Whatever it is, it just *is*." Now, that felt natural, in line with her philosophy on romance.

He took in her whole body then. And finally his expression cooled and he repeated, "I wasn't hitting on you."

She turned and walked up the street. "Are you saying

you felt nothing when I kissed you? I won't believe you if you say no."

He chuckled huskily. "I'm not saying that. I felt something."

She tried to subdue the smile that wanted to burst free. "Thought so."

He grinned. "You're a daring woman, Penny Darden. I had you figured for a go-getter, but I wasn't expecting this."

"Don't expect anything when it comes to me. I'm in this for me, not you."

"In what?" he asked, chuckling again.

She doubted he'd had this much fun with a woman since before his daughter's kidnapping. "For now, sexual gratification."

"You want to have sex with me?"

She was so hot for him she almost said yes. Instead, she just sent him a teasing smile as she walked beside him.

They passed an alley. Shortly thereafter, Penny noticed Kadin glance back and then grew aware of footsteps behind them. She looked back. A man wearing a hoodie with his hands in his pocket had emerged from the alley.

She glanced at Kadin, who slipped his arm around her and guided her across the street. Almost to her apartment building, she looked back. The man was gone.

"Who was that?" Jax was taller and bigger. That man looked thin and under five-ten. And he had a gangster kind of swagger.

"Might have been no one related to Sara's murder."

"He was in the alley." How creepy.

He guided her ahead of him into the parking garage. His car was in here, and he'd probably escort her at least to the elevator. She was glad for that.

* * *

Kadin looked behind him once more before as he walked with Penny toward the elevator. No one was there. He wasn't sure he should leave her alone tonight. Or any other night until he found evidence pointing to Sara's killer.

"Will you be all right tonight?" he asked.

"Yes. The building is secure."

Still… He glanced back in the direction they'd come and then across the cars to where light from the street illuminated another entrance to the garage.

"You want to walk me up to my door, Detective?"

At her coy tone, he whipped his head back and saw the seductive curve of her lips, soft, glossy lips. She sure did like to flirt. What he didn't like was the response she got out of him.

"How many boyfriends do you go through in a year?"

"Depends on the men I meet." She stepped closer and ran her forefinger down his chest. He watched her do that, unable to prevent desire from gathering down low.

"I told you that you're safe with me," she said.

"Are you inviting me up to your bed?"

"No. Not yet. You have to show me you're worthy."

He grunted a half laugh. Was she serious? Part of her was teasing. But he'd bet if he tried, he could have her naked tonight. Strange, how that didn't drive him away. He might not notice most women who showed signs of attraction, but the few he noticed had were half as bold at Penny.

"How do I do that?"

"With you?" She met his eyes and her demeanor changed, becoming more serious. "I'm not sure."

A sound behind him made him turn. Someone stepped out from behind a cement column. Seeing a gun, Kadin acted fast. He pulled Penny down and behind a parked car just as gunfire exploded.

"Stay down," he commanded as he untucked his shirt.

Pulling out one of his pistols, he inched around the rear fender. He caught sight of the gunman an instant before a bullet hit the fender. Kadin ducked back and then moved to fire back. Hitting the concrete right by the gunman's hooded head, he stood and charged toward the man, firing his gun as he went. The man ran, crouching low to take cover between parked cars.

A car that had just entered the garage backed up with squealing tires.

Kadin chased after him, crouching the way the other man had done and zigzagging in and out as he took cover between cars. The other man darted behind an SUV. Kadin hurried there, searching for where he was. At the SUV, he flattened his back against the rear side and then peered around the back. No sign of the man.

Then he popped up with a raised gun. Kadin crouched as bullets shattered the windshield of the car where he'd taken shelter. He rose just enough to see over the hood of the car and fired three rapid shots, breaking a rearview mirror next to the gunman's head. The man ran.

Kadin fired until his clip was empty and then exchanged that gun for the other one in his holster. The man sprinted across the garage and disappeared in more parked cars. Kadin raced after him. The man fired once more at him before his gun emptied. Then he crouched.

Moving slowly, Kadin made his way toward the area where he'd last seen the gunman. Going one car away, he took cover at the rear and then swung his gun between the rows. The gunman was gone.

Kadin moved slowly through the parked cars, listening, searching. Sirens echoed against the concrete walls.

Seeing the man pop up and run for an exit, Kadin took off after him. Outside, he spotted the man running down the street and fired again. He dashed around the corner of the building across the street.

Kadin didn't go after him. Instead, he jogged back to Penny and the flashing lights of police cars and fire trucks.

Penny was dead tired by the time the police let them go. The sun was coming up and they'd been awake all night. The crowd of observers and emergency personnel had nearly dispersed when Kadin stood alone with her.

She faced him and was about to say her farewell.

"I should stay with you," he said.

That drew her head back. "What?"

"Someone shot at us. I'm not going to take any chances, at least not until after the search."

"My apartment building is secure."

"Yeah, but you're not when you leave it. And if Jax sent that gunman here, he did so before the search warrant went through. If he was threatened then, he'll be especially so now." He extended his arm toward the elevator.

She didn't move. Whereas before she wouldn't have hesitated, now she did. She might flirt with him but him in her apartment presented the real possibility that she'd follow through with her desire.

"Do you have a guestroom?" he asked.

"Yes." He relieved her by asking that.

In the elevator, she leaned against the opposite wall, eyeing him uncomfortably because she still wasn't sure him in her guest room would stop her from keeping her bedroom door open.

"Don't worry. You're safe with me." He repeated her own words to her.

The elevator came to a stop at her floor. The doors

opened and he waited for her to precede him. She did, walking down the hall.

Inside her apartment, she watched him register a modern and spacious layout with splashes of color and a warehouse-like open living and kitchen area.

Penny put down her purse and removed her cell phone. She was about to hook it up to the charger when she saw several calls had come in. She looked at her land line and the digital display indicated she had two messages there, too.

"Jax tried to call me." With all the excitement, she hadn't thought to check her phone.

Kadin walked over to her.

She played the first message on speaker.

"Penny, it's Jax. Call me back." The next one was more emotional. "Penny, I know about the search warrant. I've got cops swarming my cabin and the old barn. Call me." In the third he said, "You can't ignore me, Penny. Why did you call the cops? Do you think I actually kidnapped that girl?" He sighed audibly. "I didn't know the truck was in there. Call me or I'm coming over."

Penny looked at Kadin.

"He won't come here. He sent someone to kill you," he said.

"Or someone else did."

"Do you believe him?"

Penny turned and wandered over to her windows. The sun had risen. The view normally made her feel good, not alone, part of the city. Not this morning. She wasn't sure what to believe. Jax had sounded sincere.

"I don't know. What do I do if he comes to see me?" She'd have to interact with him at work. Unless he canceled the contract with Avenue One. She couldn't be sure what he'd do.

"Just go with whatever he says. Don't offer any information." He moved closer, brushing a few strands of her hair back from her face, the touch on her cheek causing an electric tingle. "In the meantime, we both need to get some sleep."

"Yes." With the mention of sleeping—both of them in her apartment—Penny grew awkward as she recalled her earlier flirtation. Being shot at had doused her play.

"I'll show you your room."

She led him across the living room and past the kitchen to a short hallway with four doors. Her office was across from the main bathroom and there were two master bedrooms at the end of the hall. There, she paused in her doorway. He stood in his.

In the quiet of her apartment, with adrenaline gone and lethargy weakening her defenses, she looked at him. His intense gray eyes, his manly, muscular form, proportioned by his height. She saw him the way he must have been before death had changed him, available and eager to explore a woman. Nothing holding him back. Had she really read that in his body language or was her own infatuated mind fooling her?

"Good night," she made herself say.

After a moment he said, "Good night."

His pause reinforced her intuition, that he was as physically drawn to her as she was to him. But she no longer felt as brazen as she had in the pub.

Penny pushed her bedroom door so it would close, turning her back and undressing mechanically. She was beyond tired. Punchy. Not herself. Kadin's presence alone made it difficult to stop thinking about him. That kiss…

What she'd meant as play had ended up being much more, something unexpected.

Down to her bra and underwear, she turned to retrieve

a nightgown and saw that her bedroom door had drifted open. She hadn't pushed it hard enough to latch.

Across the hall, Kadin stood at the door, shirt off, jeans still on, hand on the doorknob. He must have been in the process of closing his door when he'd seen her.

Now she could see his upper body without the curtain of clothes. He'd unfastened his gun harness but hadn't yet removed it. That along with the rippling muscles of his stomach tickled her desire.

She had never slept with a man this soon after meeting him, but she also wasn't afraid to explore. Did this qualify? Why not?

This feels different.

He had a lot of personal baggage. But did that matter? She wasn't looking for a future with him or any other man. Not right now. Still, his cut body tempted her. The longer she looked, the hotter he made her.

He didn't move in her direction. Would he take the initiative? With a past like his? Doubtful. On impulse, she decided to throw caution aside.

Facing him, she unclasped the front of her bra and let the garment fall to the floor.

He turned. Stepped forward. One. Two.

Chapter 4

Whispering passion against her mouth. The feel of her bare breasts against his chest. Removing her pants, sliding them down her long, slender legs inch by inch. Her fingers urgently unbuttoning his jeans. He couldn't get her out of his mind. He couldn't get their lovemaking out of his mind. Each touch, each sensation, kept him in a state of awe.

The more he'd kissed her and she kissed him back, the more he'd fallen into a swirl of smoky seduction. Time fell away now as it had last night. Everything faded away except her. The light of passion in her eyes, her beautiful body, all of her had aroused him beyond comprehension. All he'd wanted to do was run his hands over her. And he had. With her on the bed, he'd touched her everywhere, a slow caress over soft skin. Kissing her just as slowly. Over round lush breasts. The curve of her hips. Toned thighs and calves. Up the inside to the moist treasure between.

Her catching breath had drugged him further. Instead of

touching her with his hands, he'd used his mouth. Tongued her taut nipples. Her belly.

While he drowned in her, she'd done her share of touching and raking her fingers through his hair, kneading his butt, and then, when she couldn't wait any longer, took his hardness and urged him to enter her. He had. But he'd made her wait longer. Going torturously slow had spun him into another world where time stopped and no darkness existed. Sliding into her and pulling back with measured stimulation. Only her cries of uncontrolled ecstasy had driven him to thrust harder. And then both of them had erupted into incredible, star-bursting sensation.

Even when it was over, Kadin had floated in an otherworldly glow. He'd fallen asleep with her wrapped up in his arms. No words exchanged. Just utter peace. Peace he hadn't felt in years.

And that was what disturbed him now.

Kadin leaned with his hands on the edge of the kitchen table, head bowed. What had happened last night? He'd not been with a woman since his wife died. He'd not been tempted. And now Penny came along and he'd been swept straight to her bed.

How? Why her? Why so suddenly?

Mass confusion consumed him. He struggled to hang on to logic. Order. Routine. All of that seemed shaken this morning. He'd felt something similar after he found Arielle lying on the bathroom floor, dead from too many painkillers. He'd held her stiffening body. Kissed her blue lips. And cried. The doctors had said she'd likely lost track of how many pills she'd taken, and the last few had been too much.

On the way home, he'd considered driving himself into the abutment of an overpass. The next day, he'd considered using his pistol to join Arielle in her peace. Indeed, he'd thought of every way possible to end his life. End the suffering. Nothing about living had enchanted him. Every breath came with a price, a constant, terrible fight to survive.

He'd learned that peace was an illusion and happiness a complacent kind of equilibrium, forces of nature tricking the mind into a false sense of balance. Offset that balance and bad things happened. Children were kidnapped and tortured and killed. Mothers died trying to numb their agony. And fathers…fathers contemplated suicide until the thirst for revenge emancipated them.

Making love with Penny had given him a glimpse of what he'd had before the physics of his breathing life had thrown him into merciless, execrable chaos. But now that he was back in hell, he wished he hadn't been reminded. Over the past three years, he'd learned to live with demons. Control them. Make them behave on his terms.

Penny, with all her open, courageous zest for playful love had upset his artificial balance. Her ambition to have him…she'd faltered some tonight, but seeing him across the hall had rejuvenated her. Something about that had inexplicably pulled him in. She made it easy to go to her, to let go—if for just the night—and feel the love of a woman again.

He couldn't allow her to do that again. Last night was a onetime experience. She didn't matter in the context of love because she *couldn't* matter. She had to be a vessel. Thinking of her as anything more would tear down his cracked foundation, the order he'd managed to create, the very thing that had kept him from taking his own life.

Kadin straightened, took several long, deep breaths. He needed to decide how he was going to handle this. He hadn't had to think about it until now. Getting involved with a woman had been the furthest thing from his mind.

He hadn't even contemplated the possibility. Moving on without his wife and daughter had consumed him. Still consumed him.

He didn't want to hurt Penny, but he didn't think he was ready for a relationship. He didn't even know what she expected out of this.

You're safe with me...

Did she mean she wasn't looking for a relationship? While he hoped that was the case, he made up his mind. He'd talk to her. He'd tell her he wasn't interested in long-term. Marriage. Family. Hell, just the thought of that gave him the chills.

He'd communicate with her. As long as he was up-front, no one would get hurt.

By the time he heard Penny emerge from the bedroom, he'd restored his equilibrium. Illusion or not, it was what kept him sane.

He'd showered and dressed already and saw that she had, too, when she rushed into the kitchen.

"Why didn't you wake me?" She clanked and clattered around, getting a thermos from the dishwasher.

"It's only seven."

"I'm going to be late to work."

Is that all she cared about? "Sorry." Here he'd been lamenting over sleeping with her, and her only concern was getting to work on time. "I'll drive you," he offered.

"You don't have to."

"I want to."

She carried her thermos and stopped before him. Lifting herself up on her toes, she pecked a kiss on his mouth. "Last night was fun."

Her sparkling eyes held no worry, only truth in her declaration.

"Yes. Fun." He eyed her as she moved past him to the

ottoman in the living room and bent over her purse to search for something.

He walked to her, perplexed and uncertain as to how to proceed.

After seeing her car keys on the side table, she snatched them and put them in her purse. Then she straightened and faced him with an unabashed once-over.

"You're pretty good, you know," she said.

Good? Was she playing with him? Acting as though last night didn't matter when in fact it had?

"We should talk about that." Realizing how that came across, he said, "I mean about having sex…and…what each of us expects going forward."

She waved her hand in dismissal. "Don't be one of those guys. So we had a little horizontal refreshment. Big deal."

"You really feel that way?" She seemed as though she did.

"Yeah. Well, it *was* really, *really* hot. Whoo." She flapped her hand to air her face and then smiled as she patted his chest. "I'd like more of the same if you're up to it, maybe a lot more." She sobered, but her light didn't dim. "I know you've been through a lot, Kadin. If one night's all you can handle, that's okay with me. I'll have a fond memory."

She was overly exuberant. Bubbly, even. More so than usual. "That's it? You just…sleep with a guy and don't expect him to stick around?" Never mind his having *been through* a lot.

"I don't sleep with just any guy. And it's even rarer that I sleep with someone I haven't known a week, but, hey, something clicked between us, right? We had great sex together. Who can complain about that?" She laughed lightly. When he didn't share her flippancy, she put her hand on his cheek. "It'll be what it'll be, Kadin. Stop over-analyzing. Let's just…*be*, okay?"

He looked into her lively green eyes and glossed lips that he'd like to devour right now and then finally found his voice. "Okay."

Penny wore a mask of carefree abandon until Kadin dropped her off in front of Avenue One and she entered the building. Then the pretense ended. In the elevator, her shoulders fell as the tension eased and she leaned her head back against the back wall, looking up at the dusty fluorescent light. Dear God, what had she been thinking when she'd taken off her bra, letting her boobs do the inviting?

Not thinking.

The elevator stopped and she stepped out into the office area. Mark wasn't in his office or any of the conference rooms. Small blessing, that.

"Good morning, Penny," her assistant said.

"Good morning, Jordan. Where's Mark?"

"He's running late."

"Good."

Paula laughed. "Jax Ballard called. I scheduled him for an hour at ten."

Penny had thirty minutes before he arrived. "Thanks." Jordan was only doing her job. She didn't know their client was a possible murder suspect.

She went into her office and shut the door. She needed to switch gears from waking to Kadin gone from her bed to professional executive. When she'd opened her eyes this morning, she realized she was going to be late to work. Then she realized she'd slept with Kadin and he wasn't in the room.

Clear recollection had followed. Her toes curled just remembering.

She was glad he'd left the room. That way he didn't see her despair. She didn't expect to start seeing him like other normal couples. She really didn't. He was an exception. He had to deal with his emotions on his own, at his own pace. She didn't want to corner him. But she also couldn't forget herself. She couldn't compromise her needs to suit his. Ordinarily she wouldn't put so much importance on a man so early in the relationship, but this felt different. Maybe his expert touch had warped her. Ruined her.

Why had he made love to her so intimately? She'd never forget him. Touching her everywhere. Kissing her from head to toe. And then pushing into her, sinking into her heat. Moving. So slow. So…right there.

She had her chin in her hand, staring off into space, when her assistant opened her office door.

Penny dropped her hand and sat straighter, startled out of her steamy daydream.

"You okay?" Jordan asked.

"Yeah." She nodded. *Peachy.*

"Jax is here early."

Double peachy. Might as well get this over with.

"Send him in," she said.

Jax entered and shut the door with a slight bang. "What are you doing?"

She watched him storm toward her, seeing both emotional betrayal and anger. He'd genuinely liked her. She'd liked him, too. And now this.

"A search warrant?" He walked over to her desk and leaned over. "I thought you didn't go into the barn."

Stay diplomatic. "Jax—"

"Why didn't you tell me you saw a truck?"

"I—"

"You should have told me." He straightened and paced across her office, pushing the lapels of his suit jacket back to put his hands on his hips, facing the window. And then, finally, pivoting back toward her with a hard sigh, looking disappointed, frustrated, anxious.

She said nothing, just waited for him to say his piece.

Finally he said, "Penny, I didn't put my truck in the barn. I reported it stolen last week."

He had? That would be easy enough to check. "Jax." She rose from her chair and moved around her desk to stand before him. "Your truck was parked in an abandoned barn on your property. Why would anyone steal it only to put it there?"

"You'd have to ask the thief that."

He expected her to believe that it had been someone random? She supposed the kidnapper could have discovered the barn and planned to hide it there. It would take suspicion off him, especially when the truck was traced back to Jax.

"What would you have done in my position?" she asked.

"I'd have asked you about it."

Would he have? "I was afraid."

"Of me?" He stepped closer, something she didn't like much.

Raising her hand in resignation, she sighed as he had earlier. "I didn't know what to do. I wasn't sure. I needed answers."

"Which you could have gotten from me, had you asked."

Would he have told the truth? Was he now? She didn't trust him.

Studying her face, he rubbed a hand down his face and turned back to the window. "The cops asked me a lot of questions. They think I kidnapped that girl." He faced her again. "Do you know what that felt like? Being accused of kidnapping and murdering an eleven-year-old girl?"

No, and she never would. But he seemed honestly shaken by the experience.

"Her name is Sara Wolfe," she said. "Did you do it?"

He smirked in irritation. "No. I did not."

"Then we don't have a problem." She switched on her diplomatic hat. Even though she wasn't convinced he was innocent, she wasn't entirely convinced he was guilty, either. She needed time to secure her job, with or without the Ballard account.

"Actually we do. I don't think I can work with you anymore, much less see you."

Did he think she still wanted to see him? "I can still do your ad campaign."

"My brother is talking to Mark right now."

His brother came with him today? "Dane is here?"

"I asked him to talk to Mark about reassigning the account."

Not canceling it? There were contractual requirements. Maybe Jax and Dane were trying to figure out a way to back out.

Jordan opened the door again. Penny had told her she needn't ever knock.

"Sorry to interrupt. Mark is asking for you. He's in his office with Dane Ballard."

"Thank you." Then to Jax, she said, "I assume that means you, too."

He let her go before him, controlled loathing in his look. That and devious scheming. Did he have secret plans for her? Like continuing to try and kill her?

She reached Mark's office and stood to the side as Jax entered behind her. Mark invited them all to the seating area in his office.

"Mr. Ballard was just telling me he has some concerns about his account with us," Mark began.

Penny looked at Dane and then at Mark, uncertain how much she should say about her relationship with Jax. Her trip to Park City had been personal.

"The police searched Jax's property for a truck that could have been involved in Sara Wolfe's kidnapping." She didn't mention that the child had been murdered. She didn't have to. Mark blanched with the revelation and Dane had no reaction, since his brother had already told him.

"Penny told them I had a white truck."

"With a dent on the driver's side," she clarified. "What makes you think I told the police anything?"

The hard lines of Jax's face deepened. "You're going to try and tell me you didn't?" He turned to her boss. "She stayed at my house near Park City and went for a hike without me."

"I saw a truck in an abandoned barn that matched the description in the news," Penny explained.

"You stayed in his house?" Mark asked.

Dane remained shrewdly silent, but he watched Penny closely.

"We can discuss that later," she said. "I did see a truck. But I didn't report it to the police." She hadn't; she'd reported it to Kadin. He was no longer a cop. He was an independent investigator.

"My brother's truck was stolen prior to the girl's disappearance," Dane said. "And the barn caught on fire last night. It burned to the ground."

Penny couldn't stop her jaw from dropping. She turned a look to Jax, who wore that eerie calculating expression.

"There was a truck inside," Dane continued. "And it is Jax's, but he didn't put it there."

"I didn't start the fire, either," Jax said.

Guilty people were always innocent, weren't they? He

didn't park his truck in his own abandoned barn and he didn't start the fire after suspecting she had seen it. *Yeah, right.* Sighing, she pinched the bridge of her nose, fighting frustration. If the barn had burned down with the truck inside, police would have a real difficult time finding evidence.

"Do you own a black Jeep?" she asked Jax.

"No, why?"

"Well, then. Why are we having this meeting?" Penny said. "He's *innocent.*"

"I am innocent," Jax insisted.

Dane held up his hand and patted the air a few times, telling them both to stop. "My brother has expressed concern over working with you." He looked pointedly at Penny. "I wanted to come here and see for myself what we're dealing with."

"Penny is my top operations executive," Mark said.

"I'm sure she is."

"Her reputation is known across the industry. She'll see to it that her team delivers a competitive product."

"Yes. I've done some reading about her." Dane turned to Jax. "Let's continue as we have been."

"Dane, you said—"

Dane cut him off. "I said I'd talk to Mark."

Jax's jaw tightened and she sensed a rift between the siblings. Dane ran the company. Jax worked for him. Clearly her ex didn't have the final say.

"She turned me in to the police for something I didn't do," Jax finally said in outrage.

"She didn't call the police," Dane answered calmly.

"Then who did?" his brother asked.

Didn't he already know? Was he acting?

Penny didn't say a thing.

"You didn't kidnap anyone," Dane said. Then he turned

to Penny. "The police will get nothing from the barn or the truck. As I said, Jax's truck was stolen. We don't know why the thief put it in his barn."

"Who set the barn on fire?" Penny asked, earning a warning look from Mark that she readily disregarded. Did he not care that a young girl had been murdered?

"The police will find the thief," Dane said. "In the meantime, I need these ads to stay on schedule." He stood. "This meeting is over. Jax, you'll continue to work with Penny as usual." He nodded once to Mark. "This has been an unfortunate misunderstanding."

Her boss smiled and stood with him, shaking his hand with a desperate sounding, "Thank you, Dane."

Jax glared at Penny.

She met his wrath indifferently, when inside she was a tight bundle of nerves. She did not want to work with him any more than he wanted to work with her. And Dane…

An unfortunate misunderstanding…? Was he protecting Jax? Who's side was he on? He'd just done what Mark wished, catered to his concern over the account. But something definitely felt off.

Kadin waited in the reception area of Penny's office. Jordan told him she was in a meeting. He'd followed Jax here, and now he just needed to make sure she was all right. Then he'd tell her about his conversation with Detective Cohen.

Penny appeared ahead of Jax, who said something heated close to her ear. He was furious. Kadin stepped forward so they'd both notice him.

Penny stopped short and Jax followed her surprised gaze.

"Is everything all right?" Kadin asked.

Ballard looked from her to him and back. "Who the hell is this?"

"Kadin Tandy." He stuck out his hand. He figured there was no point in hiding the truth now that Jax's barn had burned to the ground before the search could be conducted. He'd gotten suspicious of how much Penny knew and had taken precautions.

Jax didn't take his hand. He looked at Penny expectantly.

She offered no explanation.

"You must be Jax," Kadin said, lowering his hand.

"Should I know you?"

"Sara Wolfe's parents have asked that I help them find their daughter's killer."

As Ballard absorbed that, he slowly turned to Penny in accusation. She hadn't told the police, but she'd told this man.

"He's a private detective," Penny said.

"Clever, aren't you?" Jax moved toward her. "You didn't tell the police what you saw. *He* did. Do you think that makes this any better?"

Penny moved back from his angry face as he leaned closer and closer as he spoke.

"I knew you went snooping where you shouldn't have," he ground out.

That almost sounded like an admission of guilt. Kadin stepped forward, putting his hand on Jax's chest and pushing him back. The two faced each other in a standoff, Jax letting emotion storm his face, Kadin a rock wall of certainty. He would not allow Ballard anywhere near Penny right now.

"It's probably best if you keep some distance from her until this is all resolved," Kadin said, taking one side of his jacket and opening it enough for Jax to see he was armed. "Unless you can calm down."

Jax noticed and then studied Kadin with new curiosity. Then he asked Penny, "How did you meet him?"

Didn't he know that already? Hadn't he been the one who followed her?

"I read about him and then went to see him," Penny answered.

"Read about him?" Jax eyed Kadin and then her. "Are you sure there isn't more going on? I saw the way he looked at you."

How had he looked at Penny? Kadin moved closer to her, putting his hand protectively on her lower back. "Maybe it's best if you leave now."

Jax took in the personal touch, and his ire renewed. "I've heard some things about you, Penny. I didn't believe them, but apparently they're true."

Kadin had to stop himself from asking what things. She didn't succumb to his goading, but she did seem taken aback.

"You're not looking for commitment. You're just looking for your own gratification."

Was he referring to sex? While Kadin was at odds with what had happened last night, he had no issue with women who had sex without needing commitment. He never understood why it was it okay for men to sleep around and not women, and he didn't think of Penny as the type to sleep around with just anyone, but that was what Jax insinuated. Out of anger. Resentment.

"Has she slept with you yet?" Jax asked Kadin.

He didn't answer. Not only did he feel it was none of his business; it was an inappropriate question.

"Jax, stop," Penny said in a quiet voice. "You're upset. I understand, but there's no need to be rude."

His disdainful smirk eased. "I really liked you."

She said nothing.

Kadin understood the man's disappointment, but even a pedophile could feel that way when a normal-appearing relationship ended.

"I'll have my assistant call yours to arrange our next meeting," Jax said, and then he turned and walked away.

Penny lowered her arms with a sigh. "Come on, let's go into my office." She led Kadin there. "What brings you by?"

He finished checking out her office. Like her house, it was modern and clean and tidy, except her desk had lots of papers on it. Her phone rang. On the second ring, it stopped. Jordan must have answered.

"Detective Cohen called," he explained.

Penny nodded as though she knew what the detective had said. "The search was done. Barn burned to the ground. Jax told me. That's why he and his brother were here."

"He suspects arson."

"So do I." She folded her arms in front of her. "Is he any good? This detective?"

Cohen was more of a small-town sheriff with little to no big-city crime experience, which Kadin considered all child abduction cases to be. He categorized them as such, even if they did occur in small towns.

"He's a little abstemious. I hear his parents made him go to law school and he stumbled into his career." The morbid nature of the job might have dulled him over the years. "But he's detail-oriented. He'll follow the law and get a conviction. He just needs a good analyst."

"Which is where you come in." Penny smiled fondly.

"They're going to ask Jax to go in for questioning,"

Kadin said, instead of responding. "Cohen is waiting back at Ballard's corporate office to talk to him."

"Fantastic. Jax's brother still wants him to work with me."

"You can handle it." He grinned, knowing she could. She was no shrinking violet. And then he wondered why his brother didn't back up his request to sever ties. "Is Dane that sure Jax is innocent?"

Penny shrugged. "Must be. He also wants the ad campaign done on schedule."

That was the business reason. "Do they get along?"

Her forehead creased with that question. "As far as I know. Jax never said otherwise. They run the company together." Her brow smoothed and lifted. "But Dane is the CEO. Jax reports to him."

Kadin nodded once. "We'll have to wait for the crime scene evidence on Sara Wolfe's case."

"You think Dane might have something to do with this?" Penny asked, evidently not ready to stop talking about the brothers.

"Not at all. But if they don't get along, that might work in our favor." If Dane didn't like his brother, he'd be more inclined to talk to the police. Or him.

"Detective Cohen invited us to be present for the questioning," Kadin said.

"Us?" She unfolded her arms to point from him to herself.

"I'd like you to stay close until this is resolved."

She lowered her arms and smiled. "You going to protect me, Detective?"

There she went again, flirting, getting more confident with it, too. He didn't think he should like that anymore. He didn't respond.

"Is now a good time to leave?" he asked instead, ignoring her fleeting but stunned reaction to the subtle rejection.

Penny entered the room on the other side of the interrogation room, and Kadin came to stand beside her. His aloofness after she'd tried teasing him had her out of sorts. Maybe treating this casually was the wrong approach. She'd come across as shamelessly throwing herself at him when he wasn't all that in to her. Or was he? He'd sure been into her last night, in more than a physical sense. She didn't think she'd imagined how his passion had matched hers. If she pushed, would he finally crack and she'd have a new and exciting man in her life? But what if that never happened and she ended up longing for more than he could ever give?

"I thought Kadin Tandy was in charge of this investigation," Penny heard Jax say through a speaker connected to the room on the other side of the glass. He took a seat, smoothing his tie and jacket.

"He's agreed to assist us in the investigation." Detective Cohen sat down, putting a recorder on the table with a querying look to Jax. "Would you mind answering a few questions?"

Jax opened his hands from where they were clasped on the table. "Whatever you need."

The detective started the recorder.

"Is he legitimate?" Jax asked. "Kadin Tandy?"

The detective looked at Jax, putting his hands on the table, unassuming and methodical. "As in…law enforcement?"

"He seems to have taken the law into his own hands. Opening that agency. Dark Alley Investigations? Did Penny do his ad? He looks like an underwear model."

Detective Cohen's grin curved in humor. The detective rarely smiled.

Penny looked at Kadin, unable to suppress her own appreciation. Kadin didn't react to the comment or her look, only watched the interrogation room.

"I can assure you he's no underwear model," Cohen said, his humor short-lived. "He was one of New York City's top homicide detectives. Solved every one of his cases, including his own daughter's. Damn near killed her murderer. Took half a dozen officers to pull him off the man."

This time when Penny looked over at Kadin, she felt no amusement. His jaw had tensed and the muscles in his arms seemed harder than before as he must have been recalling that day, the day he'd captured his daughter's killer. She had new respect for him, for his expertise and for his aversion to discussing his great loss.

When she turned back to the interrogation room, she saw how Jax's ridicule had vanished into disconcertion. Having the likes of Kadin Tandy on the case made him uneasy, a homicide detective with plenty of motive to be good at what he did. Catching killers.

Did he regret agreeing to come talk to the detective? He should.

"Why do criminals talk to police when they don't have to?" she asked Kadin, keeping her voice low even though she didn't have to.

"That's always amazed me, too," he said, also in a low tone.

"Will you please state your name for the record?" Detective Cohen asked, matter-of-fact.

"Jax Ballard. I already talked to the police."

"This is more of a formal statement." Detective Cohen leaned back against the chair. "Why don't we start with the day Sara Wolfe was kidnapped? Where were you that afternoon? Were you at work?"

Logically, that would be where he ought to have been. But Jax said, "No. I had taken the afternoon off to be with my son, Quinten."

"What time was that?"

"I left work at about one."

The detective nodded. "One. All right. Then what?"

"I went home to change and pack and then picked up my son and we drove to my house in Park City. We went to a movie."

"A movie? What time was that?"

Jax reached into his jacket pocket for his wallet. Opening that, he pulled out a receipt and handed it to the detective. "It was a five o'clock show." He pointed to the receipt. "See the time and date? And the amount is for two."

Penny found it odd that he'd come so prepared. She glanced up at Kadin, who kept his attention on the room through the glass.

"Thank you." The detective picked up the receipt. "May I?"

"Yes. I made a copy."

"Good." Detective Cohen kept everything friendly, deceptively so. "Take me through the whole day. When did you notice your truck missing?"

"At about seven in the morning. I saw it in the parking garage the night before and it was gone when I left for work the next morning. I called to report it missing on my way to work."

"When you left work, did you stop anywhere?"

"No," Jax answered.

"Did you drive by Miller Elementary School?"

"No. I wasn't anywhere near there."

"What time did you get to your apartment?" Cohen maintained a friendly demeanor and tone.

"No later than one-thirty. And I left by about two."

"What did you drive to Park City?"

"My Mercedes."

"You drove with your son?" Cohen asked.

"No, he was already up there."

The detective studied Jax a moment. He had plenty of time to go by the elementary school, and had no alibi for the entire afternoon.

"Did you park your truck in the barn on your property?" Cohen asked.

"No," Jax said with conviction.

"Then how did it get in there?" The clever question came unassuming and subtle.

"I don't know. I didn't put it there. Like I said, it was stolen."

The police had a record of the report.

"Mr. Ballard, is there anyone who might have something against you?" Detective Cohen asked, a well-placed shocker he must have planned. "Someone who'd burn down your barn?"

Was the detective trying to throw off Jax? Shake him up? Catch him in a lie? Penny glanced at Kadin again, who continued to focus intently on the interview.

"Not that I know of," Jax replied, and then after thinking in a way that suggested he'd dreamed up a lie, he added, "Sometimes you have disgruntled employees. Why? Do you think someone is after me?"

"I'm trying to establish motive. It could be your motive or someone else you know, such as a disgruntled employee?" He explained this as though he were talking to a young boy.

Jax had to know why he'd been asked to come here and

answer a few questions. Jax took a few moments before he responded. "I fired a man a few weeks back. He did construction on the side. I paid him to do a small remodeling job at my house in Park City."

"What's his name?"

Jax provided the name.

Detective Cohen looked across the table for several seconds, a picture of study. "Is there anything else you'd like to add to your statement?"

Jax shook his head.

"All right." Detective Cohen stood. "That's all I need for the moment. Would you be willing to provide a DNA sample and complete a lie detector test for us?" When Jax hesitated, the detective said, "It's standard procedure. Just so we can clear you as a suspect."

After a beat, Jax nodded. "Sure." And then he asked, "Are there any other suspects?"

"So far we only have persons of interest." The detective seemed genuine and reassuring, but he had to be practiced in making criminals comfortable. "Thank you for coming down today."

Jax stood. "I hope you catch whoever killed that girl."

Detective Cohen said nothing as Jax was allowed to leave.

"He sure tried hard to present an alibi," Penny said to Kadin.

"If you can call it that. Sara's school got out at three-thirty the day she was taken. He had plenty of time to abduct her and drive to Park City for the movie with his son."

Chapter 5

The only reprieve that Penny had from Kadin was work. Although he hovered outside or at a nearby coffee shop when he wasn't meeting with the lead detective in the Sara Wolfe case, she didn't have to look at him. It pained her to look at him. Now two weeks later, they were still waiting on news from the forensics team and Kadin had camped out in her guestroom. He seemed to try to avoid one-on-one time as she did. He woke before her and stayed busy on his other cases in the evening.

She'd grown to like listening to his deep voice and the intelligent way he spoke with other law enforcement types. There was one man he spoke with on a regular basis, an FBI agent who helped him process clues by accessing databases Kadin didn't have the authority to access. He seemed to have a lot of contacts like that, colleagues from his days as a detective in New York, men in the military. His reach appeared endless. And while she couldn't hear the other side of the conversations, she could tell everyone respected him and held him in high esteem.

She stepped into Avenue One an hour earlier than usual. The more time she spent with Kadin, the more she liked him. She struggled to contain her urge to let loose her desire. But doing so might make do something she'd regret later.

The catch of his gaze. The sinewy movement of his biceps. The way he walked toward her. Whatever he was doing at the moment, she saw him. He captured all her attention. Stirred her. Heated her. It didn't help that she knew what it felt like to kiss him. And more. She tried not to go there.

Recalling their night together presented a major distraction.

Lost in thought, she didn't notice Mark until she reached her office door, which was open. She stopped in the doorway, seeing him sitting at her desk, her laptop docked and her desk monitor lit. What was he doing?

He looked up and saw her. "Penny."

She watched him click the mouse and close the screens he'd had open.

"You're in early." He stood up, doing a bad job of trying to appear innocent.

"What are you doing on my computer?"

"Company computer. I was looking for a file."

"What file?" she asked, stepping into her office.

"The presentation we gave to propose the Super Bowl ad." He moved out from behind her desk as she reached him, allowing her to sit in her chair.

"You could have asked me to send it to you."

"Didn't want to bother you, since it's so early..." He headed for the door.

"Does this have anything to do with why you're so worried about Avenue One?" she asked.

"What?" Turning to look back at her over his shoulder, he laughed in a nerdy, awkward way that gave away his guilt. "No. Of course not. It's just a file."

"I sent that to you before we proposed the account," she said.

"Yeah, but I couldn't find it. Must have deleted it." He shrugged. "Sorry. I'll wait for you to get in next time." He patted the door frame once and started to leave again.

"Did you find it?" she asked.

He stopped and turned. "Find what?"

He'd forgotten so quickly? "The file."

"Oh." He smiled. "No."

"I'll send it to you."

"Thanks."

After he left, Penny stared at the office door, certain she hadn't imagined his purpose in coming into her office had been secret and suspect. And he hadn't been looking for the proposal on the Super Bowl ad.

She looked at her computer. He'd closed all the screens he'd had open. She checked the recent files and there were none that had been opened since she logged on yesterday.

Navigating to the folder where she kept the proposal, she opened that file and scanned all the slides. There was nothing unusual. Nothing that would reveal anything sinister. Nothing they wouldn't have wanted the client to see.

She searched through a few other files but couldn't find anything suspicious. She had a lot of files. Status reports. Deliverables to the customer. Video files. Much more. What had he been looking for?

A knock on her door brought her head up. Kadin stood there, sexy as hell in jeans and an Under Armour shirt. He entered.

"Detective Cohen is on his way up," he said.

Still busy drooling over his hard, muscular physique, she barely heard him. He must not be wearing his guns. Running her gaze down his body, she saw a slight bulge at his ankle and surmised he at least had one gun on him.

"He called when I pulled into the parking garage."

"Oh." Penny snapped out of her trance. "He must have news."

"Yes." Kadin stepped toward her desk, stopped and then walked to the door. After glancing toward the elevators, he turned and came back.

He was anxious.

And she understood why. Getting up from her desk, Penny went to him as he was about to take another walk to the door. She put her hand on his arm.

He stopped and looked down at her, the tension around his eyes and mouth conveying all of his torment. This must be like reliving his daughter all over again.

"I wish there was something I could do," she said softly.

Instead of comforting him, this increased his tension.

"Don't," he said.

Don't talk about it. "Kadin…" She wasn't sure why she felt compelled to try to break his hard shell.

"Penny?" Jordan said. She must have just arrived to work. "There's a Detective Cohen here to see you."

Penny stepped back from Kadin. "Send him in, please."

Kadin faced the doorway with her as the detective entered, looking very Sherlock Holmesy in his suit jacket and hat, giving personality to his otherwise deadpan demeanor.

"Ms. Darden." He nodded. "Kadin."

"Please, call me Penny." She was honored that the two of them included her on this meeting. Although Kadin had been on his way here when the detective had called, so she couldn't be sure he'd include her otherwise.

"Jax Ballard's alibi for the evening Sara Wolfe was kidnapped checks out. He did go to the movie with his son," the detective said to Kadin. "We also traced cell phone calls the night of the fire. He was here in Salt Lake City when he made the calls. The last one was around eight and was to his house in the mountains. Video surveillance at his apartment showed him leaving shortly thereafter."

Just as they'd thought, Jax had plenty of time to get to his log house and burn down the barn.

"Why was he calling his house?" Kadin asked.

"Maybe to get a hold of his son," the detective replied.

"Or to make sure he wasn't there?" Penny countered, voicing her own opinion.

"He made calls to Quinten's cell phone, as well. In fact, that was his last call. They spoke for three minutes."

Long enough to make sure Jax's son wouldn't be around to witness him setting the barn on fire.

"Are you going to bring him in for more questioning?" Penny asked.

"Not yet. I don't want him to know we're onto him any more than we are until we have solid evidence."

Kadin nodded a couple of times, nonchalant and giving nothing away as to how this effected him.

"About the main reason I'm here…" the detective said. "We found some trace evidence from Sara's crime scene. A fiber. Forensics is running tests to determine what type it is."

"That's good, isn't it?" Penny asked, turning from Detective Cohen's flatlined face to Kadin's hard but intelligent indifference.

"It might be," Detective Cohen said. "We have DNA, but no match against anything in our database."

That meant whoever had killed Sara hadn't been arrested for any other crimes.

"What about Jax's DNA sample?" Penny knew his DNA could match and not be present in the database. He had no criminal record, but he could still have killed Sara Wolfe.

"Still being processed," Detective Cohen said.

"All we can do is wait," Kadin added with a note of frustration.

Detective Cohen studied his reaction. "I know how difficult this must be for you."

Penny watched the tension rise in Kadin, his ever-ready wall of numbness. "But you should know that your expertise is invaluable to us. Sara's parents included, and any other parent of a child you might help in the future."

Kadin's jaw worked beneath his Batman outer casing. Next to nothing could get past that protective layer.

"Focus on that while you assist with this investigation." It sounded like fatherly advice, but it was advice from one seasoned detective to another.

"Call me as soon as the tests are processed," Kadin said.

Summarily dismissed, Cohen tipped his head at Penny and then met Kadin's hard gaze once more before putting back on his hat and leaving.

Deciding not to corner him about his trouble with child murder cases—who wouldn't have trouble? His was just much more severe—she went to close her office door.

"I caught Mark looking through my computer this morning," she said.

Kadin frowned. "What was he looking for?"

"He said a proposal, but I don't think it was that. I think he may have accidentally sent me a file with information in it he doesn't want me to see."

"What kind of information?"

"You mean you didn't hear?" He'd bugged her office, after all.

"You ran out of the apartment early this morning. I

didn't have time to listen in. I had to make sure you were all right."

"Well, in answer to your question, I don't know what kind of information. I have a lot of files on my computer." She ran down a list of types.

"Show me the financial files."

"I don't want to take you away from the Sara Wolfe investigation. Dane and Mark seemed awfully chummy when I met them in Mark's office. That's the main reason I'd like to look into it." That and her boss could be doing something illegal.

"Okay. His association with the Ballards might lead to something," Kadin said.

And his embezzling could lead to information? Penny didn't see how, but she went to her computer and sat. Kadin came to stand behind her. When he leaned one hand on the desk, his sinewy arm caught her off guard. Warm awareness seeped through her. She glanced up at him, seeing him look down at with the same reaction. This was the way it had been between them ever since they slept together. Smoky looks. Sizzling heat. She had a hard time concentrating.

Shaking herself back to reality, she began to search for files.

"I don't see the detailed financials," she informed him. "Only summaries that Mark reports to the board."

"Maybe there's something in one of those that he didn't clean up before sending it to you."

Penny opened the folder where she stored the monthly status reports that one of her program managers created for her. She accessed the most recent Excel file and she and Kadin looked through the data. Finding nothing that stood out there, she opened the next file. The first thing she noticed was the extra tab.

Kadin saw it, too. He pointed as she went to click there. Columns of numbers appeared. Penny saw the total for the month and then went to the main tab where he'd generated a summary.

"The totals don't match," she said.

"Could mean something." Kadin reached for the mouse and ended up covering his hand over hers. An instant flash of arousal circled down low. She slipped her hand away from the mouse and let him navigate to the extra tab. "This looks like a working spreadsheet. He must have generated the summary from these."

"But the totals should match."

"Can you do some research on these?" he asked.

"Yes."

He tilted his head. "How hard would it be to get other files from Mark?"

Still leaning down, his face close to hers, his pleasant, manly deodorant wafted into her senses.

She almost forgot to answer. "Hard. I'd have to get on his computer."

Could Mark have been the one to go after them in the parking garage? He didn't seem the type. To her, he was a nerdy executive. But he faced prison time if he was caught stealing money from Avenue One.

"Why is he so worried about Avenue One if he's siphoning money?" she asked, biting her lip. "He's been on me to get the Ballard ads done."

Penny turned and found herself face-to-face with him. He didn't respond right away, but his eyes flamed awareness of their nearness and stirred her own smoldering attraction.

"Maybe he's only worried about getting caught. And as long as Avenue One is making money, he can keep taking."

"Yeah, but why single me out? He doesn't give anyone else a hard time."

"Maybe he's offended that you rejected him. Some men are weak that way."

"You're not." She smiled up at him to let him know she was teasing.

"No, and you've done a fine job of rejecting me."

She drew back a bit. "I have?"

"Yes."

Did he want her to go after him? No. He hadn't encouraged her. Not in the least. He'd only noticed her withdrawal. She'd kept her distance and he saw that as rejection. Somehow she suspected he'd voiced something he wished he hadn't. He wanted her, but something held him back. Past hurt. A giant past hurt.

His gaze roamed her face, spending long seconds reaching deep into her eyes, and then he stared longingly at her mouth. He might as well physically touch her. More and more, it seemed, they were losing the battle of wills.

For two weeks she'd kept her desire for him under wraps. Now that resolve crumbled. Undeniable chemistry they generated intensified. She looked at his mouth, drawn there by temptation. He brought his mouth closer. Almost there. She tingled with anticipation.

"I can't stop thinking about that night." His warm breath bathed her skin.

"I can't, either."

What are we going to do about that? she wanted to ask.

In that instant, her office door opened and Jordan appeared. Penny jerked back and Kadin straightened abruptly, both of them caught in an intimate pose.

"Oh," Jordan said awkwardly. "Sorry. Jax is on the line. This is his third call."

Penny hoped her face wasn't as flushed as it felt.

Kadin cleared his throat and had difficulty looking at her. "I'll pick you up at five."

She watched him walk to the door. Jordan moved out of the way, watching with Penny as his long strides took him to the elevators—and an escape.

Jordan turned back to her. "Is he okay?"

"Just a little girl-shy." Penny smiled to lighten the moment.

"He doesn't look girl-shy. He's cute." Jordan had never said anything personal to her before. That she was relaxed enough to do so now struck Penny as peculiar. And she'd hardly call Kadin cute. Hot. Sexy. Manly. But not cute.

"Sorry," Jordan said. "It's just that I've never seen you that way with a man before."

She'd noticed her with men? "Oh…really?" What way? Penny didn't ask but the answer was obvious. *Hot. On fire. Deeply, thoroughly attracted.* Had any other man made her feel that way? Maybe a little…but definitely not so intensely.

"Most men know they don't have a chance with you," Jordan went on to say. "You're a hard catch."

A hard catch? She'd always told herself that when the right man came along, she'd know and that all the others before him wouldn't matter, regardless of how the relationships ended. Why was Kadin so different? She was suddenly afraid to analyze that.

"You're an inspiration." Jordan put her hand on the knob of the door, daring to go on. "More women should be as sure as you and not give in to what men want. You seem to know what you want and you don't accept anything less. It's made me take a closer look at my relationship with my boyfriend. He wants to move in together, but I don't think I'm going to. Because if I did, I'd be doing it for him, not me."

Penny smiled, this time genuinely. "Thank you." She meant that. Not many people shared their thoughts with her like this, not at work or anywhere else in a professional setting.

"Anytime. I had to say something. I hope you don't mind. That private investigator has it bad for you. And I don't see you turning him away." She wiggled her eyebrows. "Maybe he's the one."

Penny couldn't control the electric jolt of alarm that sent prickles of apprehension across her skull and down her arms. "I'm not sure that's such a good thing. Not with him."

"Why not?"

She debated over how much longer she'd allow this chatter to continue. And then decided, what was the harm?

"His daughter was murdered three years ago and his wife overdosed as a result of her grief."

Jordan's face fell with sympathy. "Oh. How terrible."

"Yes. So Kadin is obviously not ready for a new relationship." Usually men fell at her feet and she called the shots. Not with Kadin. With him, there were potentially insurmountable uncertainties.

Penny shifted to a more professional tone. "Thanks, Jordan. Send Jax's call through, would you?"

Jordan smiled as she headed back out to her desk. "Right away."

A moment later, Penny's phone lit up and she answered, "Hello, Jax."

"What are you doing for dinner later?"

"Wh—" She stopped herself. "You want to have dinner...with *me*?"

"Your courier sent over your team's latest mockup, but I had questions and no one was there to answer them. Then

I started thinking about the other— Meet me for dinner, Penny. We can talk about everything then."

He sounded put off but not as angry as he had been two weeks ago. "Are you sure you want to meet me in person? Should I send someone else?" Even with Kadin nearby, she didn't feel safe being alone with him.

"No. I want to talk to you about us, too."

Them? Did he still have feelings for her? "Oh." What could she say? If she could get him to slip up, maybe he'd give her a clue. "All right."

"I'll make reservations for six at Teddy Merlot's."

Kadin was picking her up at five. He'd probably already heard this conversation anyway, with the listening device he'd placed in her office.

"Okay. I'll meet you there."

At five, Penny left the building. She had made it three steps off the elevator when Kadin stepped out from between two cars. She let out a shriek.

"God, you scared me half to death!"

"Sorry." He stood before her. "Dinner?"

She took in the hard planes of his face and realized jealousy had put him on edge. "With Jax, yes. It's a business dinner. We used to do that all the time, and he isn't the first man I've met for dinner for a business purpose. It's not unusual."

"He wants to talk about you and him."

Penny sighed. "He's a child molester. Hardly attractive to me."

That put him in check. His edginess receded to a mask of calm. "Suspected child molester."

"This might lead to something. *If* I can get him to talk…"

"Yeah, yeah. I know." The edginess came out in his tone now.

"What are you so worried about? You won't be far away." She patted her purse. "And I've got your handy little gadget right here." He'd put a tiny transmitter in her purse.

He lifted his hand, palm up, to reveal another device. "Clip this to your bra."

She took the thing. "Jeez. You're a real Longmire. Younger, though."

His brow lifted. "Who?"

"Never mind." The association was still lost on him, she saw from his face.

"Is that supposed to be a compliment?" he asked.

Should she dare to let her spitfire personality shine? He wasn't familiar with the sexy Longmire. "Sharp homicide detective like you are? Yes, I'd say it's a compliment."

She looked up as she clipped the device to her bra and saw him watching her with riveted interest.

"If you need me to interrupt your dinner, the code is 'it's salty.'"

"So…" His deliberate lack of acknowledgment of her detective comment made her tease him. "Are you hoping I use the code?"

A flicker of a smile came and went on his lips before he reached for her. His hand glided along her face until his fingers combed through her hair. Then he tipped her head back and brought his face hovering over hers. She was so startled she didn't move. Not before he kissed her. Chaste at first, and then the mysterious fire that had brought them together before roared. Penny sought more of him and he gave her more.

And then he abruptly drew back.

When she regained some coherency, he said, "That should take your mind off Jax tonight."

Chapter 6

Kissing Penny dispensed a potion that Kadin hadn't anticipated. Instead of taking her mind off Jax, he'd sabotaged his. She'd only turned up the heat when she emerged from her bedroom in a black, body-con mini dress with cutouts above her cleavage and on her shoulders. All the way to the restaurant, he'd glanced over at her, the creamy skin of her cleavage and slender, smooth thighs stirring his desire.

"Did you have to wear that?" he'd asked her.

She'd looked over at him, well aware of the effect she had on him dressed like that. "Wishing you were the one having dinner with me tonight, Detective?"

Damn, she was such a flirt. He'd almost pulled over and shown her how much more than dinner he wanted. Instead, iron will drove his Charger to a secluded parking spot, and then he'd had to watch her butt in that formfitting dress as she made her way under outdoor lighting to the front door.

Kadin spotted Jax standing there. In an expensive suit, he completed them as a couple. Sharp dresser, connoisseur of fine things, he fit well in his top-executive role. He'd also chosen a nice steak and seafood restaurant. He held the door open for her, and Kadin could no longer see her.

A hostess led them to a table. Hearing Penny breathing through his equipment, he imagined sliding that short hem up to find her without underwear. Yes, he'd damn well like to be the one across from her tonight. Her breathing quieted as they looked over the menu.

After ordering wine, Penny laughed at a not-very-funny joke Jax had made about the search warrant. He made light of the incident, which only raised Kadin's suspicion more. Then Ballard started in on the business purpose of their meeting. He didn't seem angry anymore. Did he have a reason for his change of heart? Yeah. Penny. Plus, no evidence pinned him with any crime. *Yet.* So why not try to reclaim her? What man wouldn't want her?

The waiter came with their wine and took their orders. Did Penny have to wear such a statement of a dress? Imagining Jax enjoying the delectable view as he sat across a table from her, Kadin clenched his jaw. He did *not* like her with another man. As soon as he realized that, he wondered why. What about Penny drove him to such a heated state? Her energy. Her beauty. Her fun, flirty demeanor.

You're safe with me...

Was he? Did he need to be? As long as they didn't become a family, he didn't see a problem. He had devoted his life to catching killers. The threat of something getting in the way of that mission balled up his insides, made his palms sweat.

"I caught Mark in my office this morning," Penny said, snapping Kadin to attention. Why had she brought this up with Jax? To see if he knew of any reason why his brother had supported Mark so unconditionally?

"Caught him?" Jax asked after a beat. Maybe he wondered why she'd told him, too.

"Yes, looking for something on my computer. He said he needed a proposal from another project, but I don't think that's true."

"What do you think he was after?"

"I don't know, but did you notice anything unusual about him and your brother when we met in his office?"

"About Mark?"

"Yes."

Jax didn't respond right away. Penny referred to the meeting about the search warrant. Jax had been angry then.

"Unusual…how?" he finally said.

"I can't put my finger on it. Anxious. Intimidated, even."

"Like Mark would do anything to keep Dane happy?"

"Yeah," Penny replied as though Jax had nailed what she'd tried to say. "He's desperate to keep the account, but…he just seems…"

"Overly motivated to please?" Jax helped her out again.

"Yes." Kadin pictured Penny's beautiful, oval face tilted in interest. Jax had noticed something about Mark…

"Your boss and Dane have known each other for years," Jax said. "Hasn't Mark told you that?"

"No. He never mentioned it."

Dane and Mark were friends? Did Mark's embezzling have anything to do with that friendship?

"They met in high school. Mark was always jealous of Dane." Jax grunted a derisive laugh. "Who isn't jealous of my brother? He's smart. Successful. Ambitious."

"Mark's not exactly failing," Penny reminded him. "He runs Avenue One."

"You really don't think Mark is failing?"

Kadin heard Penny take a breath and then exhale as though deciding not to say what she'd almost said.

"Dane gave him our ad account to help Mark," Jax continued. "I fought the decision, but as usual, Dane had to have his way."

He said the last with a notable tone of disdain. Jax didn't like playing second fiddle to Dane. He didn't like taking orders. He wanted to be in control.

"You wouldn't have chosen Avenue One?" Penny asked curiously.

"I wouldn't have." Jax paused and Kadin imagined he might be sending Penny a warm look. "But I can't say I regret my brother's choice."

Even now? Even after she had turned him over to the police?

"Avenue One is one of the leading agencies in the country," Penny said.

"Yeah, but Mark is in trouble. He's not the businessman Dane is, even though he tries awfully hard to be. Dane uses that to his advantage at times. You see, when it comes to business, my brother can be a ruthless son of a bitch."

Dane used his friendship with Mark to further his own agenda? How? By threatening to take away the account? He didn't sound like much of a friend to Kadin.

"Why do you say Mark is in trouble?" Penny pushed for more.

Good girl. Exactly as he'd hoped, Mark's trouble was leading to a connection to the Ballard brothers.

"Why do you think he puts so much pressure on you?" Jax asked. "You delivered that Super Bowl ad and now you're his superhero."

"But…"

"Oh, come on, Penny, you can't tell me you didn't know Mark is driving that agency into the ground."

"No. I mean, he's made comments alluding to that, but I had no idea we were in that much trouble."

Their food arrived and for several long moments only the sound of other diners and silverware against plates could be heard.

"How did you find out Mark isn't doing well at the agency? Did Dane tell you?"

After a notable pause, Jax said, "Dane hasn't told me anything."

Whatever he'd learned, he'd done so on his own, without Mark or Dane's knowledge.

"What is Mark doing to jeopardize the business?" she pressed.

"Find whatever Mark was looking for on your computer and maybe you'll have your answer. Do you have any idea?"

Penny didn't respond and when Kadin heard her glass gently touch the table, he wondered if Jax could recognize her tactical hesitation.

"I'm guessing something financial he may have accidentally sent me. I've looked, but I haven't found anything definitive."

Jax's lengthy silence wasn't tactical. "Why are you telling me all this?"

Why indeed? To gain his trust. To fish for information. But did Jax see that? Hopefully her stunning beauty blinded him. Kadin had firsthand experience with that.

"You asked me out to dinner." Kadin could see her flirtatious smile and felt the urge to go in there and drag her away from Jax.

"I did." He sounded equally teasing. "To talk business."

"We are talking business."

Jax chuckled. "I confess I did that more for me than business."

"Oh?"

"Yes. I didn't kill that girl, Penny. I'd hate something that ugly to ruin us. I understand why you did what you did. If I'd been the one to find that truck like that, I'd probably have done what you did, maybe go straight to the police. Point is, I don't blame you. I was angry at first, and I'm sorry for that."

"Jax—"

"I'm not saying we should pick up where we left off. I just…want to see you on occasion."

Would Jax have said that if Penny hadn't revealed her suspicion of Mark? Kadin didn't think so. She'd gotten back in his favor again, or had begun to. While Kadin admired her for that, he didn't relish the prospect of her spending more time with an ex-boyfriend, one she'd likely still be seeing if she hadn't stumbled upon the truck.

Penny left the restaurant satisfied that she'd won Jax's trust again. Hopefully his motives weren't to stay close to the investigation so that he could take preemptive measures.

"Where did you park?" Jax asked.

She'd driven with Kadin and he was in the Charger. "Way in the back."

"I'll walk you."

"No. I'm fine. The lot is well lit." Several people were visible, too.

"A single woman shouldn't be out at night alone."

She breathed a laugh. "I've been taking care of myself since I was eighteen. I don't need a man."

Jax chuckled, half sincere. "You are independent. Something I admire about you."

She rose onto her tiptoes and kissed his cheek. "Good night, Jax. I enjoyed the evening. Most of all, thank you for your understanding."

She waved and walked toward the far end of the lot, spotting Kadin in the driver's seat and wondering how he'd fared through the dinner, hoping he'd suffered at least a little.

Movement to her left made her turn. A man wearing a hoodie pushed off the side of a car where he'd stood in the shadows, out of the range of the nearest lamppost.

Maybe having Kadin so close gave her courage. She stopped.

The man threw down a cigarette and turned, walking away.

Penny followed.

"Penny! No!" she heard Kadin shout.

She kept on the man's tail, running to the edge of the parking lot and into a stand of trees.

"Stop!" she shouted.

The man glanced back and took up a jog. He didn't seem worried about her following him.

"Wait! Who are you?"

He kept going.

After eight, the sun would set soon. Meager light filtered through the canopy. On the other side of this group of trees, a park stretched to a neighborhood. She reached the edge of the trees and searched the deserted area.

Behind her, a twig snapped. Penny whirled and scanned the darkness but saw no one. Following the sound, she walked quietly. Another sound came, this more like boots scraping dry dirt as someone walked away, in the direction of the restaurant.

She caught sight of a form moving ahead. The hoodie man headed straight down the stand of trees. They bordered the park all the way around, but she recalled a parking area for park-goers near enough to the restaurant that the hoodie man could have used. Listening for sounds and watching for movement, she made her way through the trees.

Then, suddenly, the man appeared. He strolled leisurely along, unaware of her behind him.

Penny took note of his appearance. The dark gray hoodie still covered his head. It fell to just below his waist and he wore dark blue jeans. One or two inches shy of six feet, his lean frame moved with ease through the forest.

"Hey!" she shouted again. "Stop!"

The man did stop this time. Abruptly. She'd surprised him. He turned.

"What's your name?" she asked.

He looked back and all around and then to her.

"Are you following me?" she demanded.

Apprehension zapped her then. What was she doing? He'd obviously been spying on her and had tried to get away. Now she'd caught him heading for the park parking lot. Kadin was probably looking for her, but he wasn't here. Only she was here, alone.

Thirty or forty feet from her, the forest cast the man in shadows. She couldn't make out his facial features. He was no one familiar to her, though.

"What do you want from me?" she asked.

He drew a gun, a good enough answer for her.

Shocked and then berating herself for being so stupid, Penny ducked behind a tree. A bullet hit the tree next to where she'd taken cover. Before going after him, she should have considered the possibility that the man would turn on her.

Hearing him running toward her, Penny dashed away from the tree, glancing back and seeing him aiming. Tree trunks whizzed past her. She zigzagged to keep them at her back and a barrier if he fired again.

Looking forward, she nearly ran into another tree. Dodging that, she ran into something warmer but not much softer.

"Oomph."

Strong arms wrapped around her. "Shh. Don't say a word." She stared up at Kadin's face as he moved behind the tree, his back pressed to the bark.

Penny quieted her breathing so she could listen for the hoodie man. The forest was silent.

After a few minutes, she peeked around the trunk.

"He's gone," Kadin said.

She stepped back from him. "How do you know?"

"I saw him when you barreled into me. He turned and ran the other way."

One look at Kadin and he'd raced off. Kadin did have an imposing presence.

"What the hell were you thinking, going after him like that?" he demanded.

Penny swallowed hard. Chasing after the hoodie man had been impulsive on her part. Her only goal had been to find out his identity. But, in hindsight, she realized it hadn't been the smartest move.

"I'm sorry."

"You could have gotten yourself killed."

"I wanted to know who he was."

"And you thought he'd tell you if you asked?"

She lowered her head. "I know... I shouldn't have risked that. I wasn't thinking." Put her in an office and she dared anything. Outside, she never shied from adventure. But this was no adventure. This was real. Someone had tried to kill her. Again.

"From now on you do what I tell you. No more chasing after strangers without me. Understood?"

"Yes."

With his dark brow shading his eyes, he took her hand and led her in the direction the hoodie man had gone. A few minutes later, they reached the parking area. There were three cars there, all of them empty. Hoodie Man had gotten away.

Kadin brooded all the way back to Penny's apartment and she suspected the cause had nothing to do with her running after a stranger. He'd listened to every word of her conversation with Jax.

"Everything all right?" Maybe she could ease him into talking.

"Fine," came his terse response.

"You don't sound fine."

"I didn't anticipate having to save you from a killer. Again." He put down his keys and removed his T-shirt.

For a moment, all she could do was stare. All that smooth, bronze skin molded to hard muscle captivated her senses. He caught her noticing him that way and Penny faltered, flustered over whether to continue probing or turn and leave the room.

"I'm going to take a shower." He turned instead.

"Now?" She followed him down the hall to the bathroom, going back to what he'd said earlier. "My going after the man in the hoodie isn't why you're acting like this," she accused.

He stopped and faced her in the doorway.

Startled, she stepped back before nearly bumping into him. She leaned against the opposite wall, his naked chest interfering with her purpose. And what was her purpose, to make him admit he was jealous? Why did she want to do that?

"Are you taking a shower with me?" he asked gruffly.

He felt something for her. He had to. Otherwise, why the kiss before she went to have dinner with another man, and why the brooding afterward—after hearing Jax say he still wanted her?

"I should say yes." The return of her brazen personality felt good. Because she *did* want to take a shower with him. Because she wanted to do a lot more than that with him.

As her desire lit into a simmer, on its way to a searing boil, she checked herself. She might be a fool to test her heart with this man. Any other, she wouldn't hesitate. But Kadin? He presented new challenges. Once again, instinct reared up and warned not to discard caution. And once again, the idea of holding back struck her as foreign. Inconceivable. She had never had to deny herself like this before, never felt the need to until Kadin came along.

"Why don't you?" He angled his head as though coaxing.

Did he *want* her to take a shower with him? Was he daring her? Did he intend to carry on this affair? And then what?

Penny feared the *and then what* would be to her disadvantage. She was on unfamiliar ground, facing a big unknown. While the unknown had never intimidated her before, she took heed now. *Big* unknown changed the playing field.

"You *were* jealous tonight," she said, not caring if she sounded defensive.

His seductive look turned more shrewd. "I thought we were talking about a shower."

"I didn't start out talking about a shower." She wanted him to admit the truth.

"I'm not jealous."

Pushing off the wall, feeling more in control, she moved closer. "Then what would you call it?"

"Concern for your safety."

She scoffed at that excuse, amused and frustrated at the same time. "You were jealous."

"Of what? *Jax?*"

Her ex was still attracted to her. He must have picked that up from his side of the dinner conversation. "Of any man who desires me."

"Are you still interested in Jax?" he asked more as a test. His tone indicated as much, as did the challenge in the way he regarded her, that slightly lifted brow and faint upward curve of his lips.

"Not anymore."

He leaned his forearm on the door frame, biceps flexing, hip cocking in a sexy pose. "Then there you have it. Nothing to be jealous of."

Damn, he just refused to bend! He would not admit her dinner with an ex-boyfriend had bothered him. Why? Did he fear a budding relationship? No. Penny doubted much, if anything, scared this man. He'd made the decision to avoid serious relationships.

She faltered as his big, powerful arm distracted her, following the firm outline of muscle under golden skin from his shoulders to his chest and abdomen. When she began to grow too warm, she met his eyes again. He'd noticed her admiration and had partaken in a sampling of his own. Now warming passion hummed from him, making her hum in response.

Bizarre, how he took her on roller-coaster rides of passionate highs and cautious lows.

"Can I ask you something personal?" she asked.

"Why stop now?"

She liked that he could still let humor through his dark shield. "Do you ever see yourself falling in love again?"

He observed her through hooded eyes, trying to read why she'd asked. For herself. Out of curiosity.

"No," he finally answered. "I don't want to fall in love. And I don't want to have any more children. Nothing can replace the family I had."

Disconcerting, how sure he sounded. And he didn't even consider starting over with a new family. He didn't have to *replace* the one he'd had.

"Not even, like, ten years from now? Never?" she asked, unable to believe he'd actually go the rest of his life without finding someone to love. He might not think he would now, but maybe after more time passed, he'd change his mind.

"Once was enough for me. In ten years I'll be forty-seven. Too old for me to be a father."

"That's debatable," she said, stuffing her hands into her pockets. "Men can father children later in life."

"Yes, but not all of them want that."

Penny recalled the way he'd been after they had sex. The same as her. Troubled by how good they were together. Troubled even more over the unknown lurking in the future. Where this affair would lead. Withdrawing from the possibility. Protecting their hearts. A ride of highs and lows.

Penny had never felt the need to protect herself from any man. She liked herself better when she let her inhibitions go. Her instinct and desires had never failed her before, never led her into scandal or heartbreak. As long as she accepted that this might not lead to anything permanent, she'd be fine. Since when did she want to permanently attach herself to any man, anyway? She didn't, not yet, maybe not ever.

Why, then, did she keep having these internal deliberations? Did she need convincing to go after Kadin the way she went after any other man? Or did she need convincing *not* to?

"What about you?" he asked. "You don't seem to want to get married, either."

Boy, he'd nailed her thoughts down, hadn't he?

"My philosophy is not to force it to happen. The time and the man, if there is one, have to be right. In perfect harmony spiritually and for both involved."

"What if the time or the man is never right?"

Did he believe he'd had his one true love and no more would follow?

"What if the time and a woman you meet *are* right for you?" she countered. "Why not look for happiness again? I mean, maybe not now, but someday. I can't imagine why anyone would stop trying to find love."

"Maybe because they've already had it and that's enough."

"Is it?" she challenged. "Is it really enough? Or is living without love a sentence you don't deserve? No one should live with grief the rest of their lives." Isn't that what he'd done? Chosen to live with grief rather than love?

Dropping his arm, he stepped toward her. "You're doing the same thing. You push men away or keep them at a distance. Why is that?"

She backed up against the wall, taking her hands out of her pockets and resting them on her thighs. "I haven't found love yet."

But she could with him. The thought snuck into her head and shocked her.

"Why do people have to find happiness in marriage? There are other sources of happiness."

"Like what? Solving crimes? Isn't that what you were doing before your daughter was killed?" She doubted he'd talked this much about his loss with anyone before now. Before her. Maybe this was the first time anyone had made him examine his choices.

"Yes, but as a homicide detective, I saw my cases much differently after Annabelle was murdered. It became a different job."

His job had become more of a mission. He no longer caught killers of strangers. He caught killers like the one who'd taken his daughter.

"I had purpose before, but now that purpose is much deeper," he said, confirming what she'd thought. "I help others who are going through what I did. I fight the evil that did that to them."

While commendable, catching murderers didn't seem like a very healthy source of happiness. "What else?"

He searched her face before remembering her original question. "I find happiness in fishing. Friends. Any hobbies or social interaction."

Social interaction that didn't involve women and love. "Social interaction with what? A dog?"

He breathed a single laugh, soft and sardonic. "Sure, a dog. If I didn't travel so much."

She took pleasure in seeing his amusement, the easing of strain the idea of a dog brought out in him. He needed to feel like that more often, to be shown that life could throw devastation at people, but love made everything bearable. Life didn't have to be about doom and gloom all the time. Maybe he understood that. Maybe he avoided heartbreak by totally shunning the possibility of another wife and child. Maybe the reminders a new family would bring were just too painful to attempt.

"So, how about that shower?" he asked.

Was he kidding? If he believed he was safe with her...

Stepping toward him, she flattened her hands on his bare chest. "You think you can take a shower with me and come out of it unscathed?"

A lopsided grin hitched up his mouth. "Unscathed?"

Running her finger down his bare chest, she was melting inside by the time she reached his abdomen. So hard. Rippling. God...had he always been this hot? His wife had been a lucky lady.

She felt so much. This passion. This heated desire. She tipped her head back and he kissed her. Another night like the last and she'd be on her way to losing herself in him.

Don't risk it.

But that went against her nature. Risk? What risk? How would she know if he was the one if she *didn't* take a risk?

His mouth grazed over hers, his warm breath mixing with hers, sweet and healthy. She kissed him with all she felt inside and heard him groan.

This desire spiraled to the outreaches of her control, beyond any realm she'd experienced with any other man. She needed control.

"Am I the first woman you had sex with since your wife passed?" she breathed against his mouth.

Kadin stopped kissing her, his passion still roaring, setting his face with dark intensity.

"Am I?"

"Yes," he rasped, and then stepped back.

Her hands slipped off his torso and she stumbled backward, once again against the wall. So she was his first? Penny wasn't sure how she felt about that.

As long as she didn't expect anything from him, she'd

go on as she normally did. Building her career, no time for a serious relationship. Innocent flirting and really good sex. Did it get any better than that? No, not unless she *did* start expecting something from him.

Leaning her head back, she closed her eyes and ran her hands down her body, on fire for him. Desire all but crawled out of her skin.

"Don't do that," he growled.

A glimmer of hope opened her eyes. He watched her touching herself, her desire so palpable that he must feel it, feel how her body yearned for him. Having tasted his quenching of her before, the temptation only grew stronger.

"Why not?" she asked, not stopping her hands, moving them over her breasts and then back down to just above her crotch.

He didn't respond.

Emboldened, Penny left the wall and went to him, sliding her hands over his shoulders and pressing her body to his. Then, with one hand curved around the back of his head, she rose onto her toes and kissed him.

"You should think twice about this," he said against her seeking lips.

"Yeah?" She raked her teeth over his lower lip for a gentle nip. "Maybe *you* should."

"I have." He took her mouth for a harder kiss. "Do you mind being the rebound girl?"

She jerked back and searched his eyes. He meant what he'd said. She'd be the rebound girl, the first woman he'd been with since his wife died. Did she want that? Of course not. Maybe she already was his rebound girl. After all, they'd already slept together once before. But if she cooled things now, she could blame it on one night of stupidity, not a broken heart she could have easily spared herself.

She eased away, burning for him, near to giving in and taking the risk just to feel him moving back and forth inside her, hard steel stroking soft, hot flesh to shivering pleasure. What was it about him that turned her on so much? His mystery? The challenge?

Did she want what she couldn't have?

Stepping back some more, she studied him, needing to find the answer. Physically he turned her on more than any other man she could recall. His masculine body, so tall and strong. Shaggy hair. Piercing eyes. Rugged face. He had it all.

But more lurked in the silvery shadows of his eyes. Behind them. In the tragedy-stricken gleam of them. In the strength of them. This man would not lie down easily. Loss had not beaten him.

Penny suspected he still engaged in that battle. Maybe that was what intrigued her. How a man like him could fight so hard to avenge the deaths of his loved ones. Many would simply accept the loss. But Kadin had not accepted his. Would he ever? Did anyone who lost what he had? No, Kadin was a changed man.

Who was he before his wife and daughter died? And who was he now?

Homicide detective and family man before. Vigilante after.

She realized then that his bold, relentless spirit was what drew her. She'd met and been with fearless and smart men before, but none had the gritty edge this one possessed. It was what magnetized her, the very thing that should make her run. For that gritty edge was what would ultimately drive him away from her.

Even after three long years, Kadin was nowhere near ready for love.

Chapter 7

While Penny hosted a two-hour meeting that included Jax, Kadin sat in a nearby café searching through the files Detective Cohen had given him. At his request, Cohen had gathered up all the missing persons reports for the past five years in Utah. Kadin had just finished narrowing them down to two young girls whose disappearance bore similarities to Sara Wolfe's. One girl had been found murdered and the other was still missing. After organizing their files into a folder on his laptop, he checked his phone for the time.

Penny would be finishing up soon.

"Can I get you some more coffee?"

He looked up to see the smiling, twentysomething waitress. Her blinding-white teeth and sky-blue eyes hinted to interest that went beyond cajoling for a good tip. Her long blond hair was up in a ponytail. Left down, he'd bet, it would be thick and shiny. Two things struck him. One, she was a little young for him, and two, this had to be the first time he'd noticed a woman sending him signals since his wife died.

Did Penny have something to do with that?

"No, thanks, I'm finished."

"What are you working on?" she asked.

Kadin wasn't sure how to answer that. He didn't really want to get into an explanation. Neither did he think discussing the case with a stranger wise.

"Is it that girl's murder case?"

He turned a surprised look at her. "Excuse me?"

"I recognize you from the news. They said you were going to help catch her killer."

"Yes. I am. Can I get my ticket, please?" He began to put away his laptop.

"I just love your ad," the waitress said, obviously not getting the hint. "For your new agency? *Dark Alley Investigations.*" She wrinkled her nose and narrowed her eyes as though silently growling her kitty-like, desirous fascination.

"That wasn't an ad. A reporter interviewed me and asked me to sit like that." He closed his laptop case with a weary sigh.

"Well, it might as well be an ad." She pulled out a folded piece of paper from her apron pocket. "In case you feel like rescuing me sometime..."

Rescuing her? Kadin slowly took the paper. She actually gave him her number?

Next, she put his ticket on the table. "There aren't enough people like you in the world."

"Thanks." He smiled politely and she smiled back with a mouthed, *Call me.*

He watched her walk away, dumbfounded by her forwardness. Did he appear open to women's advances now or something? He didn't know whether to thank Penny or blame her.

Paying for his coffee, he left the shop and crossed the street. A short walk down the block, he reached the front entry of Avenue One. Up the elevator, he stepped out and entered the double glass doors of the ad agency.

"Mr. Tandy," the receptionist greeted with a smile. "I'll tell Penny's assistant that you're here."

He waited for her to make a quick call to announce his arrival. When she hungup the phone, she said, "Jordan will be right here."

"Thanks." He stepped away from the desk and looked toward the offices. Seconds later, a woman approached.

"You can come on back, Mr. Tandy," she said.

Penny's assistant led him toward the offices. "Penny told me about your daughter," she said as they walked through a maze of cubicles. "I'm so sorry. That's so tragic."

As always, Kadin felt like biting a bullet to control his annoyance. What were people sorry for? How could anyone feel regret or offer an apology for something that hadn't happened to them? *Sorry I didn't save your daughter, Mr. Tandy. Sorry you had to lose your little girl.* Sorry? Better if they just came out and said, *I don't know what that's like and I never want to find out.* Now that he'd understand and even respect.

"It's great what you're doing, though," the woman said when he didn't respond. "With your agency."

"Yeah," he replied tersely.

"Are you making any progress on your investigation?" she asked.

"No."

"Is Penny helping you?"

"Yes."

Hearing people approaching behind him, he turned and

saw Penny and Jax. She smiled over at the suave busi-nessman and he smiled back. Kadin didn't like the way he looked at her. Her beauty and sunny, confident aura seemed to be working its magic on her smitten ex. And whatever they'd just chatted about *clearly* hadn't been business.

"Well, if it isn't the famous PI," Jax said.

"Mr. Ballard," he greeted, shifting his glance back to Penny. She'd put her auburn hair up today and a few wavy strands hung down along her face. Green eyes fringed with mascara and nothing more looked back at him. Her plump lips were glossed a soft color. The white blouse beneath her dark gray skirt suit came to the start of her cleavage. He stopped his wandering right there.

"Penny."

"You turn up at the damnedest times," Jax groused. "Are you staked out somewhere nearby?"

Penny put her hand on his right biceps, attempting to placate him, to minimize his threatened ego. "I'll meet you at your log house tomorrow afternoon. I'll call you when I leave."

What? Kadin didn't try to hide his frown. She couldn't possibly mean that she'd go away with him again, some-where remote.

"I'll look forward to that." Jax grinned wickedly at Kadin.

When he strode away, Kadin turned to Penny expec-tantly. "Let's talk in my office."

Following her there, he couldn't help admiring her long, slender legs. Legs that had wrapped around him. Legs that were made to wrap around a man. That last thought only frustrated him for his lack of control over his thoughts, and instincts.

"You're not going to his house in the mountains," he bit out as he closed the door.

"He invited me. I couldn't say no." She dropped her notepad onto her desk and sat on her chair.

Kadin moved between the two chairs before the desk and leaned over from the opposite side. "Yes, you could have. All you had to do was say this, *No*."

She tipped her head to one side and eyed him defiantly.

"It's too dangerous," he said.

"You'll be there."

"Oh, I will? In the house with you?"

"Or outside." She waved her hands in circles above her desk to help illustrate what she meant to say. "With whatever gadgets you have."

He straightened from the desk. "Gadgets don't help if somebody has a weapon."

"Jax wouldn't try to kill me." She scoffed. "In his own home?" She picked up a pen and tapped it on a thick document.

"He parked a white pickup truck in his barn."

She put down the pen. "Allegedly."

He sent her a derisive look. She couldn't afford to be careless.

"He trusts me," she argued.

"He might be *pretending* to trust you."

"Okay. But he still might talk." She stood, hands on her desk.

Kadin sighed and went to the other end of her office. She could be walking right into a trap. But if he did go with her and camped outside…

While she slept *where*?

"I'll sleep in his guest room. That's where I slept last time." She stepped around her desk and approached, a teasing gleam in her eyes. Stopping in front of him, she said, "And you say you aren't jealous." Slipping her hands onto his shoulders, she leaned against him.

The roar of desire flamed through him. He put his hands on her rear for a brief caress…and then left his hands there. Her soft, moist lips called to him. So did the way her smile faded and smoky, sultry passion left her mouth parted and eyes dreamy. Without even trying she lured him.

Leaning down, he kissed her. The warm touch seared his senses. He kissed her harder. She answered the insistent request, melding to his mouth, fueling the fire hotter.

He pulled away, incredulous that she made him feel this way so easily. He stepped back. He'd lose control with her if this continued. Did he need control? Why did he feel he did?

Arielle.

And Annabelle, of course.

Penny had roused his passions so fast he hadn't had time to analyze how he felt about her—or any woman—getting this close to him. He should have prepared himself for this, for not being ready for commitment. Because that was what it felt like, the beginning of a serious relationship.

Everything in him resisted. "Do me a favor and stop telling everyone about my daughter."

"What? I didn't tell anyone."

"You told your assistant," he snapped.

"All I told her was that you lost your wife and daughter."

"Yeah, and she said she was sorry."

She stared at him for a long time, several seconds. He could hear her thoughts. His extreme reaction didn't match the offense. So her assistant said she was sorry. He should be able to handle that. Maybe he should even appreciate the sympathy.

"I don't like talking about it," he said.

"I'll ask her not to bring it up again."

"Forget about it. Are you ready to go? I am."

She stared at him for several seconds again, calling him on his behavior without words. "Sure. I just need a moment to gather my things. I'll have to work from home tonight."

"I'll wait for you in the parking garage."

Jax had a lunch ready when Penny arrived at his mountain home. His son, Quinten, was here again. At least she wouldn't be alone with him.

Closing the car door, she faced the house and opened her purse and said into it, "You'll be happy to know Quinten is here." Kadin's listening device was somewhere in there. "There'll be no mad, passionate lovemaking happening tonight. Guess I'll have to wait until you build up your courage again."

Leaving her purse open, she laughed quietly and headed for the front door.

When Jax let her in, she leaned in for a brief hug. Quinten was in the kitchen, taking plates out.

"I brought takeout from a good Chinese place in town."

"Fabulous." She put her purse down on the kitchen table and sat. The teenager handed her a plate and sat next to her, his dad across from him. She dished out some broccoli and beef.

"You starting college this fall, Quinten?" she asked.

He finished chewing a mouthful, fork in hand and hovering over the plate, lanky form hunched a little. "Yes."

"What are you studying?"

"Chemistry." He scooped more food into his mouth, a young person who could eat whatever, however much he wanted.

"He was always really good at math," Jax said. "He wants to be a pharmacist."

"Oh."

"I like mixing chemicals," Quinten said in his growing-into-a-man voice, a big smile spreading over his face as he chewed another bite.

"You can imagine all the explosions I had to deal with when he was in high school."

Penny laughed and ate a small bite of beef and broccoli. The strong smell of broccoli suddenly stood out from all the other aromas. A few seconds later, her stomach churned. She put her fork down. What was that all about? She put her hand on her stomach. She felt nauseated. Why did she feel nauseated?

"Have you ever thought about having kids?" Jax asked.

Penny slid a glance toward her purse. Kadin was out in his car listening.

She forgot about her upset stomach. "Not really."

"Career woman, huh?" Jax grinned. "A damn good one, too." He sipped from a bottle of water. "Seriously, though. Do you want kids someday?"

Penny pushed her food around, not liking having to think about that and not having an appetite, anyway. "I'm already in my thirties. I suppose if I'm going to, I should be working hard to find a man."

Jax grinned. "I'd like to have more kids."

"Dad," Quinten complained. "I'll be decades older than a kid brother or sister."

"What's wrong with that?" he asked.

Quinten shrugged, chewing and swallowing. "It's weird."

"Not if it's with the right woman."

Penny didn't like how certain Jax sounded, and the unmistakable suggestion that she'd be the one having kids with him.

Quinten sipped his water. "Yeah, if you get busy right now having one." He glanced at Penny with a playful grin.

She set her bottle of water down and said nothing.

Jax reached over and put his hand on hers with a squeeze. "You never know what can happen."

Quinten laughed while he shoveled more food into his mouth. "I don't know, Dad, she doesn't look too enthused."

"I don't think I want kids," she said. Not with him, anyway.

"Phew." Quinten wiped his forehead as though wiping off sweat. "I'm saved."

A quick glance at Jax and Penny didn't doubt he didn't like her statement. "You seriously want more kids?"

"I love kids." He looked fondly across the table at Quinten. "Raising him was one of the most satisfying things I've ever done in my life."

"Aw, shucks," Quinten teased. And then he turned to Penny. "He's a really great dad."

She smiled. "I can tell."

The young man got up, taking his empty plate to the kitchen. "I'll leave you two alone so my dad can get to work changing your mind, Penny."

"Hey. I thought I saved you."

He chuckled and came back to the table, going around to his dad's side. He leaned down and hugged him. "I'm driving back to the city this afternoon."

Jax gave him a pat on his shoulder. "Okay. I figured you would." He looked at Penny. "He brought a girl up here last night." He winked.

"Ah." She put her fork down and leaned back. This all felt so normal. Jax was a good dad and his son loved him. Maybe he had told the truth about his truck, after all.

When Quinten left, Penny got up and began to clear the table, a little disappointed that Quinten had gone.

Jax stood and came into the kitchen with her, leaning a hip on the counter by the sink. "Did you find anything else on Mark?"

She debated over how much to tell him. And then decided not being totally honest would get her nowhere. "Not really." She rinsed her plate and put it in the sink. "He sent me a file with an extra tab that had some different numbers than the ones we report to the board. I think he's doing something with the books."

"Embezzling?"

Penny finished rinsing Jax's plate and turned off the water. After drying her hands, she faced him. "I have no real proof of that, but yes, that's what I think he's doing, hiding it by sending the board wrong numbers in his reports, the ones I see."

Jax looked all over her face and finally said, "Dane and Mark robbed a convenience store in college."

"What?" That came as a total shock. "Mark?"

"He and Mark did a lot of things they should both be in prison for. Things off the record that your detective wouldn't know."

Penny decided to ignore that comment.

"They've always watched out for each other. Like that day my brother did what Mark wanted and forced me to keep working with you on the ads."

And Jax knew both their secrets. Why hadn't he gone to the police? Because Dane was his brother? Maybe that was why he was at odds with Dane.

"How do you know all this?"

"I grew up with Dane. We've always been close."

"You don't seem very close anymore."

He wandered over to the kitchen window and sighed.

"There's only so much I can take of my brother. I don't agree with some of the things he's done with the business. I think he's getting reckless, and keeping secrets from me." He turned to look at her when she came to stand closer. "I heard him and Mark talking one day. Mark said the board at Avenue One had begun to ask questions. He was in a panic. Dane reassured him that one of the board members was a friend of his. Just before Mark was about to leave his office, Dane saw me standing in the door opening."

"He knows you know about Mark?"

Jax nodded.

That was motive for Dane to protect either his friend or himself for his involvement.

"Why are you telling me all this?" she asked.

He didn't reply right away. "Why do you think?"

He wanted her to believe that he was innocent, that Dane might be a person of interest, too.

Kadin listened to Penny talk about nothing in particular with Jax. The weather. Something political on the news. They had an easy way together. After hearing Jax tell her all about his brother's shady past, Kadin began to wonder if he'd told the truth about his truck. He also began to wonder if he should take a closer look at Dane.

Penny's declaration that she would never have kids relieved him. While he didn't think he'd ever fall in love and marry again, he could do that more than he could have another child. All the emotion that went into having one, the overwhelming, incomprehensible love, the responsibility and care, haunted him. He could not risk feeling that way again. He could do without the torturous comparisons, too, always wondering if Annabelle would have done what the new child did, or be hit with bittersweet sorrow at milestones like proms and weddings.

His cell phone rang. Kadin answered, leaving the earpiece in his other ear in case something happened with Penny.

"Detective." Kadin sat straighter on the seat. He must have some news.

"Hope I haven't caught you at a bad time?"

"No, not at all." Jax was boring Penny with talk about Quinten when he was a young boy now. Did he hope to win her over to have kids?

"I received some test results back from the forensics lab."

Kadin gripped his phone tighter, remembering these calls after his daughter's body had been found. He struggled to stay focused and to listen carefully to what Cohen said.

"We have nothing from the truck, but we expected that. The lab analysis came back and we've identified the fiber found on Sara Wolfe as some kind of rope fiber."

"What kind of rope?" Ballard's Sporting Goods probably sold rope.

"The lab is still narrowing that down. They ran into some problems during testing and had to start over with a clean sample. Once that's complete we can start tracing where it might have come from."

The detective thought what Kadin did. He'd try to match it to something Ballard's sold. If Jax was their suspect, then he wouldn't have had to purchase any rope.

"I'm still waiting on DNA analysis on Jax."

"Good." Penny's ex seemed confident he wouldn't be a match. "Does he know you have DNA from Sara's body?"

"We didn't tell him."

Some criminals got overconfident when trying to convince others they were innocent. If Jax didn't know, he

probably felt sure they had no evidence and didn't anticipate them finding any.

"I've reviewed the files I asked you for," Kadin said, referring to the missing persons cases. "I picked out two that
resemble Sara Wolfe's case, but I'd like some more time to
analyze them." He went on to explain about the two girls.

"All right, let's stay in touch," Detective Cohen said.

"Will do." Then he remembered something. "Detective?"

"Yes?"

"What have you got on Dane Ballard? Penny told me
he has a suspicious friendship with her boss, Mark Pershing. I'm not trying to bust anyone for embezzlement, but
Dane is Jax's brother."

"I'll check him out."

They disconnected and Kadin used his phone to look up
the highway that passed Sara Wolfe's crime scene. Highway 190 connected to another highway that led to Park
City, a back way to Jax's mountain home, where his truck
had been found in an abandoned barn that had mysteri-
ously burned down.

Cohen had a rope fiber. Ballard's manufactured sporting equipment. If he could get inside Jax's cabin, he could
search. And he'd be closer to Penny in case Jax had lured
her here for some nefarious purpose. Why try to kill
Penny, though? She couldn't prove anything more than
the police already knew. Unless Jax didn't know they'd
recovered the VIN and she had pictures. If he thought she
could testify...

The man in the hoodie had only watched her. Now
that the police were involved, would he or Jax or whoever stand back and watch? And when they got too close,
strike again?

What better way to keep an eye on Penny than to earn her trust?

Kadin got out of his vehicle and trekked through the woods toward Ballard's house. He wouldn't be able to hear Penny but they'd still been in the kitchen. In daylight, he'd be easily spotted, but he only had Jax to worry about. At the clearing where the driveway widened, he stayed in the trees and walked the perimeter until he reached the side of the cabin. He couldn't see through the windows. Jax could be looking through one of them.

Seeing a woodland garden with native plants and boulders, he crouched and sprinted there, taking refuge behind a big boulder. Peering around the edge, he moved to the next boulder and then ran to a pine tree. From there, he took cover among some aspen trees and then made it to the back corner of the house.

Angling his head for a quick glimpse of the back and finding it clear, he ducked below the frame of one window and stopped at the edge of a floor-to-ceiling window. With his back against the house, he rolled to look inside. A large living room transitioned to a more formal one. Adjacent to that, Kadin caught some movement. Penny pointed at a digital picture frame and Jax came to stand beside her, talking. Probably telling her stories about each photo. She seemed interested.

Kadin crossed the patio to a sturdy trellis that rose to the bottom of a balcony. He jumped up and grabbed a horizontal, vine-entangled beam and pulled himself up. He climbed to the balcony and hauled himself over the railing. At the door, he tried his luck and gave it a tug.

It opened.

Finding himself in a bedroom, he checked the closet. The room must be for guests, but not Penny. Her things weren't here. Leaving that room, he went into the hallway.

An open railing a few feet from where he stood carried the sound of voices.

"Quentin used to love camping," Jax said.

"He doesn't anymore?" Penny asked.

"He goes with friends. Going with his dad isn't cool anymore."

Kadin quickly searched the next bedroom, a master suite with an overnight bag that must be Penny's. Across the hall, another master bedroom matched Penny's. She was going to sleep right across the hall from him?

Clamping down on the rebellion that stirred, Kadin went through Jax's drawers and looked under the bed and in the closet. He kept everything tidy, but that must be a housekeeper's accolade. Finding nothing upstairs, he made his way to the open railing.

Penny and Jax had moved to another area of the house, their voices fainter now. Kadin descended the stairs, pinpointing Penny to be around the wall from the stairs in the living room.

"That's beautiful," she murmured.

Kadin didn't like how genuine she sounded.

"We took a long trip to Banff. That was in the Selkirk Mountains," Jax said.

"That's Canada, right?"

"Yeah. They have bear crossing signs." Jax laughed once.

Weren't they getting *cozy*? Gritting his teeth, Kadin reminded himself to stay focused on the task at hand. He found an office on the other side of the wall from the living room. Began riffling through drawers.

"You don't strike me as the camping type," Penny said.

Jax didn't strike Kadin as that type, either. Narcissistic business executive who liked fine things and would love his brother out of the way. He'd rather lead, even though he probably wasn't the leader his brother was.

"Let's go camping, then," Jax said.

Penny laughed. "I'm a city girl."

"I have an RV. You wouldn't rough it."

"Ah," Penny said. "That's more like you."

Kadin stopped navigating through Jax's computer, straightening and going to the door to listen. Penny sounded so enchanted, enjoying the play. Did she play the same way with him, loving the game, the attention of a man? He should be glad. Sometimes the thought of starting over with someone new made him physically ill. What about Penny changed that?

She posed no threat. He didn't have to worry about any expectations of commitment.

Sometimes he thought she hadn't meant that all that about being safe with her. When she reacted to him, when he felt their chemistry heat up, he didn't feel safe. Did she still think they could just *be* and not worry about the future? Maybe she'd never truly believed that they could treat this attraction so casually.

He resumed his search of Jax's computer, not finding anything incriminating, distracted by Penny giggling over a fishing tale with Quentin that Jax recounted.

"Where is that?" she asked.

Then they must have finished going through the pictures because Jax said, "Why don't we go for a walk? It's a beautiful day."

Kadin put the computer back to sleep and walked to the door. She wasn't going to agree to that, was she?

"All right."

He cursed under his breath. Apparently she'd concluded the same about Jax, that perhaps he'd told the truth. He wished she wouldn't be so trusting.

"Great. I'll get us some water."

"I need to use the bathroom."

"Okay. Meet you by the front door."

Kadin peeked into the hall and saw Penny come around the corner, ducking when Jax appeared, looking at her rear. When Kadin peeked again, Jax had his back to him on his way to the kitchen and Penny's steps faltered when she spotted Kadin.

He stepped across the hall and into the bathroom.

She glanced back to check on Jax and then entered after him. "What are you *doing*?"

Kadin shut the bathroom door and faced her. "You're not going on a walk with him."

"It's just a walk." She put her hand on the two-sink marble counter. "It's the middle of the afternoon."

"It's also remote." He took in her slim hips in distressed, ripped jeans and then roved over her tight white T-shirt.

"You won't be far away." She smiled, having noticed his wandering gaze.

"Penny…"

She stepped forward and flattened her hands on his chest, rubbing provocatively, and then slid her palms up to his shoulders. "Yes?"

Her breathy response deterred him from his purpose. Standing in the bathroom of a potential murder suspect's vacation home, in the middle of an unauthorized search, he put himself in a vulnerable situation.

"What am I supposed to do? Hide in the trees?"

That smile remained, tempting, enticing. "Just knowing you'll be there will be enough." She rubbed her hands down his chest again.

"He's going to miss you."

She rose and pressed her mouth to his.

Fire furled in his core. He kissed her back and doubted

even she'd expected their chemistry to erupt this way, at this moment, with Jax in the other room. Somehow that enflamed him more, made him feel as though he were stamping his claim on her.

She made a soft sound low in her throat, parting her lips farther as her small, delicate fingers laced into his hair at the base of his neck. He gave her what she asked, capturing her tongue for a long, deep caress. She raised her thigh along the side of his, escalading this out of control. He lifted her, planting her butt between the two sinks, just on the edge so that he could press close to the apex of her legs.

"Are you all right in there?" Jax said from the other side of the door.

Kadin broke apart from Penny, staring at her while the two of them quietly caught their breaths.

She hopped down with a hand over her mouth. "Uh… yeah. Be right out."

"What are you doing?"

"I…I just got a little nauseated. I'm okay. I'll be out in a minute."

After a few seconds, Jax said, "Okay."

"Don't go on a walk with him," Kadin whispered.

"There's a hiking trail in the back," Penny said in an equally hushed tone. "The road at the end of the driveway goes to the barn and boarded-up house."

The burned-down barn.

"Don't go that way."

"Jax isn't going to hurt me." She shooed him away as she went to the door.

Kadin grabbed her hand and hauled her back against him. With one last kiss, he let her go, swatting her rear as she reached for the bathroom doorknob. She glanced back at him in reprimand.

Grinning, Kadin climbed into the shower, a tiled half wall with frosted glass on top concealing him from view. When Penny left the bathroom, he got out of the shower and stopped at the door. He didn't hear Jax until she reached the living room.

"Are you feeling all right?"

"Yes. Fine." She gave a self-conscious laugh. "Must have been something I ate."

Kadin almost chuckled as he finished searching the lower level, keeping an eye on Penny. They were slow to leave, Jax offering her a glass of soda to calm her stomach first. That gave him more time.

In one of two bedrooms on the main level, Kadin found sporting goods stored in the closet. Snowshoes, skis, a golf set...*climbing gear.* He went still for a second when he saw that. A rope bag drew his attention most. Crouching, he unzipped it and removed a small kit from his pocket. He'd custom-made this kit for uses such as this. Right down to the tiny sample bags. Using a scissors, he clipped some samples from each and used a mini-tweezers to place them in a small plastic bag, tucking that with the kit into his back pocket.

Leaving the closet, he paused at the side window, where he had a partial view of the back. He didn't see Penny. Not hearing her voice, he went into the hallway, easing away from the concealment of the wall as he entered the main room. They must have left through the front.

Going there, he peered out one of the big windows and spotted her walking beside Jax, hands moving as she talked, a bundle of energy. He left the house, hiding behind some aspen trees to make sure Jax hadn't looked back. Then he jogged to the thick stand of trees, where he kept up the pace to catch up to them. At the end of the driveway, he watched them head down the dirt road he'd warned her not to take.

Cursing softly, he crossed the driveway and stayed in the woods. He'd seen pictures and maps of this area from Cohen's investigation. Jax planned to take her to the burned barn and boarded-up house. Why?

Chapter 8

Penny focused outwardly on the beautiful day and the idle talk between her and Jax, when inside she worried why he took her in this direction and whether his easy way with her was staged. Killers were practiced at deception. She didn't give herself away by searching around for Kadin. She'd played coy with him when she said he'd be nearby, but not knowing his location disconcerted her.

They reached the clearing at the barn and house and Penny stopped short with the sight of the destroyed barn.

"Yeah, quite a mess, huh?" Jax said.

Black charred wood lay in piles of rubble. Nothing was left of the structure. One hot, blazing fire had done that. The police had taken the shell of the truck for analysis.

Jax took her hand and propelled her forward. She eased her hand free as they walked, looking toward the house and getting a strange feeling.

"Do you want to go inside?" He turned an expectant

look her way. "You went into the barn. You must have an adventurous spirit. Either that or old buildings intrigue you."

Why had he brought up her snooping in the barn? She kept her face neutral. "Both. I grew up on a farm."

Jax angled his head in curiosity, seeming genuine, harmless. "You did?"

"I was a real Midwestern girl."

He smiled slightly. "Come on, let's go see what's inside."

"You mean you haven't been in there since you bought the property?" She walked with him toward the old boarded-up house, unable to stop a glance behind and around her. No sign of Kadin. But he'd be near. Wouldn't he?

"No reason to," Jax replied, looking back as though wondering why she had.

"Were you planning to do something with the buildings?" *Besides burn the barn down?*

"No."

"You could fix the place up and rent it out."

"Yes, I could."

He just didn't want to. If she owned an abode this old and potentially charming, she'd turn it into a bed-and-breakfast or something. Or live in it.

Did she really just have that thought?

Penny stopped and really looked at the house. The square architecture featured rows of symmetrical windows on the first and second floors, one directly above the centered entry. A brick chimney stuck out from the middle of the medium-pitched roof. The wild growth of indigenous plants had long ago begun to engulf the first floor. The brick stoop covered by a rickety two-column portico led to a faded red door. Chipped and broken black shutters hung askance or had fallen off.

Then she noticed something different. "The windows and doors were boarded before."

"Police removed them when they searched inside."

A plausible explanation, she supposed.

The sound of the long, shrill call of cicadas added to Penny's growing apprehension as Jax climbed the steps to the door. He produced a key and unlocked the door with an antique click. The door creaked as he pushed it open.

She waited for him to precede her.

He looked back at her with a grin, personifying the tall, lean executive who'd attracted her initially, his short-cropped hair neat and void of gray. "Scared?"

She didn't answer. Just stepped inside. Straight ahead, stairs rose to the second level. Only dust and fallen material furnished the rooms to the left and right, one a dining area off a disheveled kitchen, the other a living room with a wood-burning fireplace.

"After the fire, I looked into who owned this place before I bought the property," Jax said, stopping in the living room and tipping his head back at the detailed crown molding that bordered the ceiling. "This place was passed down from generation to generation since the homestead was built in 1910."

She walked toward the back, where an arched doorway led to a family room with an entrance to the kitchen. "It stayed in the same family?"

"Yes." Jax followed her.

She admired the French windows taking up most of the back and imagined a few decades ago there must have been a wonderful view of the forest. Right now the only view they offered were sections of plywood. Going to the back door, she unlocked and opened it to let in some light.

There had once been some green grass grown in the yard, and the remnants of a treehouse hung precariously from a big, tall tree.

She turned to face Jax. "Do you know what happened?"

"The owners were about to foreclose but were fighting the bank. I made them an offer they couldn't refuse."

"You paid them more than market value?"

"I paid them a fair value. I hope it was enough to settle their debts. They had more than a hundred thousand above what they owed. They were just a couple with grown kids who'd run into hard times. I thought I helped them."

"When instead you drove them out of their family home."

"Unintentionally."

Had he really done something so noble? Paid more than the asking price because the previous owners faced foreclosure? Or was he only trying to make himself appear like a good guy?

Jax moved over to a window and fingered a loose nail. "The husband came to see me a few months after I finished building my house."

Penny wondered if he'd hesitated telling her that. He sounded tentative and yet compelled to share in an almost casual way.

"Why?"

He looked back at her. "He wanted to know what I was going to do with this house and the barn. I don't think he liked it when I said nothing. I think my words were something along the lines of *I'm going to let it be part of nature*. That didn't seem to satisfy him. He explained how much the land meant to him, and that he'd grown up there and didn't know any other way of living. He seemed lost. Sad." Sincerity shone in his brown eyes. "His last words were *Take care of my house*."

Well, that sounded kind of creepy.

Jax walked to the open back door, pushing it wider and keeping his hand on the edge. "And then, the day after you took that walk and found the barn, I saw a man in the woods."

Penny's breath came harder and she stopped herself from interrupting.

"He just stood there, watching my house." He gazed out toward the edge of the woods in back of the house.

Penny moved so that she could see his profile. "What did he look like?"

"I don't know. He wore a sweatshirt with the hood up."

How could Jax have known that unless he'd actually seen the man? The same man she had...

"Have you told the police?" she asked.

"I didn't think it was significant until now."

Hadn't he? Someone had been sneaking around on his property and he hadn't thought that relevant?

"He looked like he was hiking," Jax said.

Penny didn't know whether to believe him or not. She decided not to reveal the times she'd seen the stranger.

"Is there something going on between you and Tandy?"

"What do you mean?" she stalled. Why had he asked that? To change the subject? Maybe, but he also wanted to know about her and Kadin.

"He's hanging around a lot." Jax stepped closer, a man on a quest to unveil any secrets his woman might be keeping.

Ordinarily she'd tell a man who got too possessive that she belonged to no one, but these were extenuating circumstances. "Someone has been trying to kill me. He's protecting me."

"Yeah, but he seems— I don't know...maybe he's using that as an excuse."

To be close to her? "His only goal is to catch Sara Wolfe's killer." She could go on with a lengthy explanation on the truth of that statement. But doing so might reveal her own insecurities. And she didn't have a reputation for being insecure. Come to think of it, neither did Jax.

"You seem interested in him," he said.

She studied his now quite impassive face. Why was he asking about Kadin? Maybe she had this all wrong. Maybe he suspected she and Kadin were setting him up—or trying to. Maybe he had his own hand to play.

She relied on her diplomatic nature to formulate a response. "He's good-looking and interesting, but he's not available."

"He's not married." Jax moved toward the entrance of the kitchen.

"No, but he lost his wife and daughter."

He stopped and faced her again. "Three years ago."

Hearing his argumentative tone, Penny decided to expand a little. "Imagine if someone kidnapped and murdered Quinten when he was a young boy. If you were in love with his mother and she ended up overdosing, how would you feel?"

Jax blinked once and then sighed. "Yeah. I see your point."

"It would devastate you."

He nodded a few times. "I love my son. If anything were to happen to him, I'd feel like dying myself. He's my world."

She believed that. He'd raised his son as a single parent. Their bond must be close, closer than she'd already guessed just by seeing them together.

Jax smiled slightly and then moved his gaze from her to the family room walls, drywall breaking apart in places. "What would you do to this place if it was yours?"

Penny looked over the disrepair. "Bed-and-breakfast."

"You'd run it?"

She laughed a little. "Are you kidding? I can't cook. Okay, I'd fix it up and then sell it."

"I like my isolation."

That comment seemed odd coming from such a dynamic and successful businessman. He interacted with many people on a daily basis, engaged in big projects. Did his competitiveness with his brother have something to do with what he had become? Or did he hide a darker side of himself?

"Then I'd fix it up and use it as a guesthouse. Maybe hire some help to take care of some horses."

"Good idea. I might do that. Except there's really no one I'd have over as guests. I get enough interaction at the office."

She smiled. "Quinten, then. Someday he'll get married. It would make a great place for kids. Growing up on a farm was for me."

"Yeah, he might like it here." He looked into the living room and then followed the intricate trim. "There are some nice touches."

"Yes. Fixed up, this could be a real gem."

Jax walked into the kitchen, skirting the edge of an old, dirty red mosaic rug, the only adornment in the house. White cabinets with silver handles had seen shinier days, as did the laminate countertops. Meager light streamed in from the open back door. She saw a footprint on the floor, and then spotted more.

Looking behind her, she saw there were others mingled with the ones they'd just made.

"Police," Jax said when he saw where she looked. "Search warrant."

"Right." She smiled back. Doing her best to look apologetic.

Stepping forward, she walked over the rug toward him. On her second step, the floor made a snapping noise and then opened under her feet. Penny had a split second to process what happened, reaching for Jax, or something—anything—to get her to safety, even as the thought flashed that he might have led her in here for this reason. He'd skirted the rug. She'd walked right onto it. She tried to grab the edge, a surprisingly clean edge, as though it had been cut. The rug engulfed her and she fell with a scream.

"Penny!" Jax yelled.

She hit the basement floor with a loud crash and billow of dirt and dust, her head banging against something hard. In an instant, she went unconscious.

Kadin heard Penny scream and ran for the old house, furious with her for agreeing to go with Jax and tortured with fear for her safety. What happened? He had about twenty yards to go when gunfire erupted.

He dove for the ground and heard a bullet strike the side of the house. As he crawled across the ground, another bullet hit the dirt in front of him. Making it to the stoop, he kept his head low as more bullets struck the brick. Raising his head, he had to duck again as he saw a man firing from the trees.

Someone was going to great lengths to kill Penny—and him, since he'd involved himself in this investigation. Would stopping them divert suspicion away from whomever shot at him? Maybe the shooter wasn't threatened by Detective Cohen.

Adrenaline spiking, Kadin looked to the end of the house. The simple Colonial style offered little protection. If he ran to the side of the house to get in from the back, he'd risk getting shot. If he crawled up the stairs, the same risk applied.

Removing one of his pistols, he readied it to fire. When the bullets stopped, he figured the gunman was reloading. Rising up, he started firing and ran up the stairs and then into the house, shutting the door.

"Help! In here!" Jax shouted.

Jax knelt by an open door in the floor.

"Penny's fallen. She's not moving!"

Not hearing any bullets hitting the house, Kadin rushed there, sick with the time it had taken him to get into the house and afraid the gunman would come after them. Seeing Penny lying unconscious on a pile of rubble sent him into urgent mode.

"She fell through. The door…" Jax looked with him at the still-swinging door, as though wondering along with him why such a thing had been installed in the dining room of this old house.

Putting his gun away, Kadin sat with his legs hanging into the hole. Then he gripped the floor and lowered himself down far enough to jump to the floor below, careful not to land on Penny. She still hadn't stirred.

The sting of ripe apprehension chilled him and nearly interfered with what needed to be done. He crouched beside her.

"Penny." He touched her face, not moving her at all.

He began to check her body.

"Is she all right?" Jax called from above.

Kadin looked up at him. "Why didn't you come down here and help her?"

The fear in his eyes cleared as Kadin's meaning penetrated. "You don't think that I—"

He felt Penny's head and found the edge of a bump

where she'd struck the ground. He looked up again. "Someone shot at me outside. Any idea who that is?"

"What? No. I thought I heard shots." He stood up and looked toward the front door.

"You *thought*?" Kadin touched Penny's face again. "Penny."

Her eyes began to flutter open. She groaned.

"Lie still." Then to Jax, "Are you just going to watch or are you going to call 911?"

"Right." He swore. "I was afraid for Penny. I'll run home and call."

"Don't get shot on the way," Kadin said, "but something tells me you won't."

"I didn't plan for this."

"Get out of my sight."

Jax left the house and Kadin wondered if he'd actually call for help.

"Kadin?"

"I'm here, my darling. You're safe." For now. He looked up at the square hole. Enough light from the upper level revealed that some new hardware had been installed with some kind of weight-triggering device. The cut edge of the floor looked fresh.

Penny got up onto her elbows.

"Don't move." He touched her shoulder.

"I'm all right. I can move everything. I just hit my head."

He looked around him at the dark basement. Low ceilings and a stemwall offered no escape. Near a concrete support pier, he spotted an open-plank stairway. Standing, he took Penny's hand and gently helped her to her feet.

She winced and rubbed her side and then her elbow and then her head, lowering her hand to look for blood. A small amount transferred to her finger.

He put his arm around her. "We have to get out of here."

She swayed and put her hand on his chest. "Dizzy. What happened?"

As she looked up at the square hole, he lifted her into his arms and carried her to the stairs. Checking each one for sturdiness, he stopped at the top.

Penny turned the handle. "It's locked."

Kadin set her to her feet. "Hold on to the wall and step down a few steps."

She did, unsteadily.

He kicked the door down, drawing his gun soon after. With his back to the wall, he swung his aim as he searched the house. Jax had left the front door open.

Turning back to Penny, seeing she'd climbed the stairs on her own, he went to her and slipped his arm around her.

"I'm better now. Not as dizzy."

At the door, Kadin looked for the shooter. Only the cicadas and a gentle breeze broke the clear day.

He faced her and handed her the gun. She took it and he lifted her again.

"What are you doing?" she asked as he began to walk to the road.

"Carrying you. You keep guard."

She flipped on the safety and rested it on her stomach one-handed, having slid her other arm over his shoulders.

"It's a long way back to Jax's."

He looked down at her pretty face. "You don't weigh that much. And in case you haven't noticed, I'm a big guy."

"You are."

"And we aren't going back to Jax's. In fact, you aren't going to be with him alone ever again." By the time the police and paramedics arrived, they'd be gone and the message to Jax would be clear. Kadin had rescued Penny and he wouldn't allow her near the bastard again.

"I can't even accuse you of being jealous," Penny said with a sigh of mock dejection.

That made him smile. "Not today."

Penny reclined on her sofa in the glow of Kadin's attention. She told herself not to get used to this, his pampering, his man-protecting-his-damsel-in-distress role. Her accident had scared him, although he'd never admit that. Or maybe scared wasn't the right emotion. Angry, simmering anger that danger had gotten so close to her.

He brought her a steaming cup of tea, putting it down on the coffee table within reach. He'd taken her to the hospital himself, and she'd been released with a slight concussion and instructions to rest for the next week or two.

"How do you feel?" he asked.

"Good." She kept her smile to herself.

"No nausea?"

"None."

"Do you need anything else? Another pillow?"

She shook her head.

"Are you warm enough?" He adjusted her blanket.

"I'm comfortable. Really, I'm fine, Kadin. Thank you."

He met her eyes, somber and intense. "I'm taking you to Rock Springs to rest."

"I can't be away from work that long. Mark is already freaking out that I called in sick today."

"I spoke with him an hour ago."

Penny sat up a little more against her throne of pillows. "You did what?"

"He understands that you have to be away from work now. I explained his options. He understands."

In other words, he'd threatened her boss.

"You'll have your job when all of this is over," Kadin promised, adjusting her blanket again and then brushing back some hair that she'd disturbed when she'd sat up straighter.

"What exactly did you say to him?"

"Just trust me. And by the way, Detective Cohen is on his way here. He's got some questions for you."

"Way to try and distract me. What did you say to my boss, Kadin?"

"Basically I told him that if he gave you any trouble or tried to fire you, that he'd be hearing from me."

She searched his face, especially his clever, light gray eyes that held so much darkness. "What *really* happened?"

"I not only let him know that I could physically convince him to do what I want, but also hinted to my knowledge of his financial activities."

That must have really gotten his attention.

"I'm not taking a no, Penny. You're coming with me and we'll stay at my place until the forensics results come in and we have more leads. I need you safe while you heal."

Her enamored glow dimmed. His feelings for her might drive him, but his quest for justice drove him even more. Her apartment concierge called, signifying Cohen's arrival. She listened to him welcome the detective and then heard their approach. Penny sat up straighter, Kadin leaning in to move her pillows so they supported her better.

"Penny. Kadin told me what happened," the detective said by way of greeting.

"Trapdoor. Yes. Isn't that fantastic?"

He sat down on a chair across from her. Kadin remained standing.

"He said you saw a man the night you took pictures of the truck in the barn," Cohen added.

"Yes, but it was dark. He may have been the same man I saw in the restaurant parking lot, but I can't be sure."

"It's likely that whoever is doing all this is the same

man who hid the truck in the barn. Kadin thinks the killer feels certain that if he eliminates the two of you, he'll escape the law." Cohen looked up at Kadin without any indication that he felt injured the killer didn't consider him a threat, too.

"Kadin does have a reputation," she said.

Kadin stopped pacing. Penny only then noticed he had been.

"And you went snooping around and are close to Jax," he said.

That piece confused her. "I don't think it's Jax."

"No, but let's not forget Mark's suspected of embezzling," Kadin reminded her, resuming his pacing.

Yes, the embezzling that implicated Dane as a not-so-honorable man. She met his gaze as he confirmed her unspoken thought.

"Dane's background checks out," Cohen said. "But I plan to talk to his associates."

There were so many ways this could go. Penny rested her head back against the pillows and closed her eyes. Her head had begun to throb. Jax seemed as potentially guilty as innocent. Then something her ex said popped into her mind.

"We can talk later," Kadin said to the detective. "When you have more from Forensics."

Penny opened her eyes. Kadin had stopped pacing.

"I'll let you rest," Cohen murmured to her.

"Jax mentioned he saw a man in a hoodie," she said in a rush. "He described the same man I saw. And he told me about the previous owner of his property. The man came to see him after he built his new house and said something cryptic to him. *Take care of my house.* He didn't want to give up the property."

Kadin looked down at her as the implication of that

settled. If Jax had seen a strange man, could that person be the previous owner of his property?

Penny thought of the trapdoor and Jax leading her inside and the gunman outside. Had they been working together? If Kadin hadn't been so near, would Jax have locked her in that basement? The plan could have been to kill Kadin and lock her up—to what, kill her later? Jax could have just been pretending to try to help get her out. Or had the previous owner intended the trapdoor for Jax? But why go to all that trouble…and how would the previous owner know Jax would go into the house? Jax working with the hoodie man seemed more plausible. Lure her inside. Trap her. Kill Kadin if he interfered. But what if Jax told the truth? What if he *was* innocent?

Chapter 9

Penny had to convince Kadin to allow her a few extra days to wrap some things up at work before leaving for Rock Springs. She'd met with her skittish boss, who'd kept eyeing Kadin warily. Kadin refused to allow her to go anywhere without him now. It was a huge imposition. And then…not. She smiled over the many exchanges they'd had, most of them silent yearning to find a bed.

She'd assured Mark that she'd work remotely and now, packed and ready to spend some time in Wyoming, she stared out the window of Kadin's Charger as they sped down Interstate 80 toward the Wyoming border. She hadn't felt good all morning. The breakfast Kadin had prepared had made her sick to her stomach. She'd tried to swallow a few bites and then had gone running to the refrigerator for a carbonated soda.

"Are you all right?" he asked from the driver's seat.

"I feel like I'm going to throw up." Had the strike to

her head done that? She put her hand to her head. "Will you stop so that I can get something for my stomach?"

"Sure."

The exit for Coalville came up a few minutes later. By then, Penny had to keep swallowing and taking deep breaths. She was really going to be sick.

Kadin parked in front of a small gas station and she got out and walked quickly inside. Rushing to the back, she found the bathroom. Inside the stall, she barely made it over the toilet before she lost what little she had in her. When she finished, she sat against the stall partition, trembling, pale and weak.

"What the hell?" she asked herself.

Flashes of Kadin sliding into her wet, eager flesh inundated her senses. She, arching as she came, an incredible explosion of pleasure while he continued to move inside her.

She hadn't had her period yet.

Penny sat forward, staring at the opposite wall in shock. How late was she? A week. No…two weeks.

"Oh, baby Jesus."

Baby.

No. She couldn't be pregnant.

Her? She wasn't going to have any kids. She didn't want any kids. She wasn't ready for a kid.

But neither she nor Kadin had taken any precautions. Penny usually made sure either she or the man used protection.

She recalled how she'd felt sick at Jax's house and covered her mouth with her hand. *No. No. No.* She could *not* be pregnant.

Penny cupped her breasts. They'd been a little sore. She'd thought that was her period approaching. Yeah, but she'd never thrown up before a period. First time for that.

Penny climbed to her feet, picturing Kadin sitting out in his car, completely oblivious to her realization. He'd had a daughter. Still mourned his daughter. He'd had a wife. Still mourned his wife. He wasn't ready for this any more than her. No, he was even less ready than her. He'd freak out if she told him.

Wasn't she freaking out right now? Penny stopped from opening the bathroom door. She had to get a hold of herself before she faced him. *Daddy.*

"Oh, sweet Lord." She thumped her head against the door.

Her career fast-forwarded through her mind. She'd have to fit day care in with her work schedule. When would she find time for a baby? She'd never advance to CEO if she couldn't invest the time. She'd become a mom.

Penny moaned her despair, rolling her head back and forth on the door. Maybe she wasn't pregnant.

Swinging the door open, she left the bathroom and began searching for a pregnancy test, feeling like a wild, crazed animal fighting for air.

Finding the aisle, she stopped before the family planning items.

No planning involved in this...

Reaching for one of the tests, she caught sight of someone approaching. Tall, big, imposing, Kadin walked toward her in the aisle. She jerked her hand back and turned as though looking for stomach remedies.

"Are you okay?" he asked as he stopped next to her.

"I can't find the nausea medicine," she said.

"It's down there." He pointed down the aisle.

"Oh." She waved her hand as though scattered. "I walked right past it." She went there and began selecting which one.

Would any of them be safe to take if she was pregnant?

"Here." Kadin picked up a pink box and handed it to her.

She didn't take it. "You know what? I feel better now." She actually did, other than being stunned over her possible condition. "I threw up. Let's go."

She walked to the front of the restaurant and out the door, waiting at the passenger door of his Mustang. Kadin paused on the other side, looking at her over the hood.

"I just need to lie down," she said.

Lie down and wrap her brain around her future as a mother. *Without a husband.* How would Kadin react?

He unlocked the doors and she sat inside, resting her head back and closing her eyes to avoid his speculative glances. At least she could blame her concussion for her nausea. Didn't everything happen for a reason?

Late that afternoon, Kadin sat at his square bistro table with his head submerged in the files of the girls that Detective Cohen had copied and given to him. Jessica and Vanessa were twelve and fourteen. He studied their backgrounds until he felt as though he knew them. Two young girls he'd never met who could have been his own daughter, their youth robbed from them, their future erased. He'd studied their files before. Each time he absorbed more, instinct and experience combing to give him an investigative strategy.

Hearing Penny, he looked up and saw her coming down the stairs against the redbrick wall, her hand gliding over the decorative bronze railing. Light streamed in from the three tall, arched narrow windows and as she stepped into the rays, she looked angelic.

"You're up early," she said.

As she came closer, he thought she looked a little green.

"It's after seven. How's your head?" he asked, opening the file on Jessica.

She went into the kitchen behind him and he listened to her open the refrigerator. "Okay."

"Still feeling sick?"

"A little." She poured something into a glass and then came over to the table, standing beside him, looking down at his piles of scattered papers. "What's that?"

"Files on two other girls. Cold cases."

She drank some of the orange juice she held. "Related to Sara's case?"

"Possibly." Rather than let his interest in her silky cream-colored PJs veer out of control, he returned his attention to the file on Jessica. Her abduction had occurred prior to Vanessa.

Penny sat down adjacent to him and slid Jessica's file so that they could both see it. He watched her stare at the picture of the long-brown-haired, hazel-eyed girl. It looked like her school picture. Kadin had given the police a photo of Annabelle when they went to the zoo. Head tipped up at him as he took the snapshot, she smiled big in the sunlight, some strands of reddish-brown hair flying in a slight breeze.

"It's hard to look at them," Penny said with a sad face. "They're just kids."

Kadin didn't respond. What could he say? To him, no worse crime existed.

"What do you know about her?"

He turned his gaze down to the file, already knowing everything the pages contained. He fell into his role as investigator. It was what spared him extreme grief, looking at each case as a piece of a puzzle, with the grand prize being the capture of a dangerous and demented individual, a person who had severe mental issues and had to be separated from society.

Sometimes he had trouble accepting that mental imbalance had a lot to do with why people killed children. He still wanted to tear each one of their throats out. Slowly. He wanted to make them suffer the way each of their victims suffered. He wanted them to feel every second of the pain and horror they inflicted on each girl. And then rationale returned and he understood that justice had a process and the best he could hope for was a death penalty.

But that didn't mean he couldn't inflict at least a little of his own brand of justice before turning them over to the police.

And really, the best part of capturing killers was the satisfaction of knowing he'd been instrumental in stopping them from hurting anyone else. *Stopping* them. Taking their demented pleasure away from them.

"Jessica was walking home from a friend's house after a sleepover. She took a shortcut through a field. Her friend is the last one to have seen her alive. She watched her from her bedroom window until she disappeared beyond some trees and over a hill. Her backpack was found a short distance from that point."

"How long ago was she murdered?" Penny asked.

"Three years."

She looked up at him, as though seeing if the time frame had affected him. It had. And like his daughter's, this young girl's body had been found.

"They've got DNA," he said.

Penny didn't ask how. She could read the details in the file. They were too gruesome to voice.

Penny picked up the file on Vanessa.

"Vanessa is a little different." He showed her the notes.

"She went to bed and was never seen again," Penny said. "She could still be alive."

"If she is, I'm going to find her." He felt his whole body light up with that prospect, of finding a girl alive and returning her to her parents. The other missing girls resembled Jessica's case, so he didn't hold much hope of finding them alive.

She looked down at the files. "How did you isolate these girls?"

"By area. Timing. The way they disappeared. Their ages."

She looked thoughtful as she took in his face. "You really are good at what you do."

He grinned at the compliment. "Yeah, but I like to think I was good before my daughter died."

She smiled back, hers more genuine than his. He didn't find anything redeeming about getting good at what he did because he'd lost his daughter.

"You probably were."

He enjoyed her soft, sea-green eyes awhile, and her smooth lips revealing a sliver of pearly teeth. She had olive skin he could reach out and caress right now, and a petite nose that made her eyes stand out with those long, black lashes.

Instead of torturing himself with that vision, he focused on Vanessa's file. He'd already read through the information once, but sometimes the second pass revealed something meaningful.

Penny leaned in to read with him. "She talked to a boy the night she disappeared?"

"After school." Kadin flipped that page over so that Penny could read on. "He went missing the next day, after he stopped at a convenience store. That's where he was last seen."

"The two have to be related."

"That's what I thought." He tapped to a line farther down in the report. "The boy was found in Dallas, Texas, a few weeks later. Returned to his parents and ran away again. He comes from a broken home where the mother has been in and out of jail for DUIs. He himself has been arrested a handful of times for theft and once for hitting a girl. He denied ever seeing Vanessa or knowing her whereabouts. Her family seems pretty normal, but her sister claims Vanessa didn't get along with her mother."

"What teenager does?"

He waited while Penny read the rest of the report.

When she looked up, he said, "The boy was last seen in Houston three months ago, but the police there have been unable to locate him."

"Or Vanessa. She's been gone what…?"

"Almost a year." He felt sure the girl had run away and also sure that she wouldn't have if not for the boy. She'd listened to the wrong person.

Penny reached into him with her eyes. "What are you going to do?"

"Well." He turned the page and showed her the last paragraph. "I was just about to call the lead detective and ask him why he hasn't talked to anyone at the tattoo parlor where the boy was seen."

"He hasn't?"

"Nope. The detective said a girl reported seeing him after she realized he was reported missing. She asked him about a tattoo." Kadin pointed to the paragraph.

According to the girl, the missing boy had gotten the tattoo the week before.

"I'm going to fly down there as soon as we have time."

Penny fell into thoughtful silence and then reached to put her hand over his. "You're a good man, Kadin Tandy."

Needing a dose of humor, he said, "With that coming from a corporate shark like you, I'm humbled."

Just as the moment turned warm again, the sound of a buzzer going off intruded.

Someone was at the back door downstairs. Kadin stood and went to the door. Down the stairs, he stopped at the back door. He always wore his guns, and if he didn't want to see whoever was at the door, then he wouldn't respond.

Peering out the window, he saw Lott and almost didn't answer.

"Open up, I know you're in there," Lott said in a raised voice.

Chuckling, Kadin opened the door. "What are you doing here?"

"You stood me up for our fishing date." He stepped inside.

"I called."

"Yeah, and gave me a work-related excuse. You know that doesn't fly with me."

Kadin didn't argue. He led Lott upstairs and into his apartment, where Penny still sat. She stood when she saw them.

"Hey, I remember you," Lott said, his gaze going all over her the way it had done when he first met her.

Kadin had warned Penny about his friend when he thought nothing would develop between them. While he still thought nothing would—or could—something in him rebelled against Lott staking any kind of claim on her.

"Is she a client of yours?" Lott asked him.

Kadin had no choice but to answer honestly. "Yes."

"I'm not paying him," Penny interjected with annoyance. "I gave him information. The only reason I'm here is someone is trying to kill me."

"Ah." Lott surveyed her again. "Then today is my lucky

day." He strode over to Penny, but then he stopped and turned to Kadin. "Unless…" He moved his index finger back and forth between the two of them.

"No," Kadin said, seeing Penny fume with anger as she glanced up at him.

What made her so mad? She was the one who didn't commit. Her words.

Lott sat down on the sofa and patted the space next to him. "Who's trying to kill you?"

"We can't discuss the details of the investigation," Kadin said a little too sharply, going over to sit beside Penny.

"Oh." Lott stared at him a long few seconds. Then he sat back. "Nice try, bro."

Penny turned her head from Lott to Kadin and back again.

"There *is* something going on between the two of you."

"No, there isn't," Penny retorted.

Lott glanced at her but kept his attention on Kadin. "Yeah, there is. You're different."

"Why are you here, Lott?"

His friend chuckled. "Okay, I won't make you uncomfortable. I met this girl."

"Another one?"

"Her brother was murdered ten years ago and the killer was never caught."

And he thought Kadin would solve her mystery?

"She'll pay you," Lott leaned to remove his wallet. "Here's her card. I said if you were interested that you'd be in touch to meet and discuss the case."

Kadin took the card. "Does this mean you're going to be my marketing director?"

Lott chuckled again. "I actually like the sound of that."

"I'll look into it and give her a call," Kadin said. But

he sensed the new case wasn't the only reason Lott had come to see him. "Okay, you could have called me with this. Why are you really here?"

Lott sat back. "Wow." He crossed one leg over the other and stretched an arm out across the back of the sofa, drawing a look from Penny. "You're good."

"I just know you. Talk to my mother again?"

"She called me. I'm never the one to call her. She said she's been trying to reach you."

His mother would ask how he was doing in that soft, sympathetic, sad voice and then she'd try to get him to talk about his tragedy.

"I'll call her." Maybe next year.

Lott frowned as he realized he'd get nowhere once again. He stood. "I'll tell her. But only because I consider you my friend." He turned to Penny with a slight bow. "Penny, if you weren't his, I'd ask you out on a date."

She smiled and laughed at Lott's easy charm. "I might have accepted the invitation."

"Might." He put a hand to his heart. "You wound me."

Still smiling, she said, "Something tells me that would take more than rejection."

Facing Kadin, who stood during the exchange, he shook his hand and gave him a firm pat. "Next time I come here, we're going fishing."

"Deal."

After Lott left, Kadin came back to the living room to find Penny drifted off in thought. Hearing him, she looked up at him.

"Why haven't you talked to your mother?" she asked.

That couldn't have been what had her thinking so intently. "I don't want to talk about Annabelle. My family talks about her and my wife whenever I'm around or on the phone."

"Have you told your mother that you don't want to talk about it?"

"Yes. A hundred times, but there's always her careful tone." He scowled. "She treats me like I'm different, like she pities me."

"You *are* different. No one could go through what you did and not change. And have you ever considered that she might be mourning the loss as a grandmother? You should support each other."

"I guess I can add you to the list of people who force me to talk about their deaths."

She put her hands up. "No forcing from me. And I don't pity you, either. In fact, I think you're being selfish."

"Selfish. That's great. So I suppose I deserved to have my daughter kidnapped and killed and my wife unable to live with it."

He heard her draw in a sharp breath the instant he realized he'd been unnecessarily cruel. "I didn't mean that." She stood up. "I do think you should talk about what happened, though, especially how you feel." She walked toward him. "Keeping that bottled up won't help you."

At the risk of saying something else he'd regret, Kadin turned and headed for the door. "I'll be downstairs."

If Kadin reacted that way to simple talk of his daughter, would he react the same if she told him she was pregnant? Again she clung to foolish hope that she wasn't having his baby. Finding herself next to the table where Kadin had worked on the files of the missing and murdered girls, she sat down and saw that he had some electronic files, as well. The one on Vanessa was open on the screen of his laptop.

Seeing the folder open where he stored everything, she gave in to curiosity and clicked to see the contents. One caught her eye right away, titled with the name, Penny

Darden. She opened that electronic folder and found it full of documents and correspondence from someone with the NYPD. As she went through some of them, the detailed information gathered seemed more appropriate for a security investigation.

She skimmed through some basic information that she'd expect from a background check. But then she came upon something unexpected. Another background on a man she didn't know. Alias Cochrane. He worked at an environmental engineering corporation and lived in Bismarck, North Dakota. Married with three kids. Two boys and a girl. Scout leader. Humane Society volunteer. Junior league baseball coach. Athletic.

She stared at pictures of Alias's kids and wife. And then came to one of him. Reddish-brown hair, hazel eyes, features that resembled hers.

With trembling fingers, she scanned through the document some more, finding a pedigree of Alias's ancestry, a pasted copy from a website. The time that the document had been saved coincided with the time Kadin would have received the background information. Listed at the bottom was Alias Cochrane, and beneath that were four names. Alias's three children…and hers.

Penny Darden.

Shock jolted her into numb disbelief. She let go of the mouse. Kadin had investigated her biological father? Why? And more important, why had he kept it a secret from her? She felt invaded, one of her most private struggles in life laid bare to a stranger's eyes.

She flipped to the next page, not caring that the one she held floated to the floor. A more detailed report of what had been itemized in the previous pages sliced her privacy into a gaping exposure.

Her father had a family, a good job and hobbies. He

seemed normal. Happy. Did a day pass when he thought of his other daughter? Didn't he care?

The shock began to lighten its icy grip and anger began to settle. How dare Kadin do this? Work history, home address and criminal background check she could understand, but details about her estranged father?

Penny dropped the report and marched out of the upper-level apartment. Down a narrow stairway, she pushed open the door leading to Kadin's office. He sat at his desk and turned when he heard her.

"Alias Cochrane?" she said.

He swiveled his chair and stood. "You went through my files?"

"If I hadn't, would you have told me what you discovered?" She walked to him, bursting with indignation.

"I asked you if you ever wanted to find him and you said no."

How unfair of him to use that lame excuse. "I might have changed my mind if you'd have told me you found him."

"You said you didn't want to find him."

"What are you, God? You know all about him. *Scout leader?*" She scoffed and folded her arms, feeling vulnerable. *Vulnerable.* Where had this insecurity come from? She'd never given her deserting father more than a fleeting thought and now suddenly it hurt that he existed and thrived in a family unit. He had multiple interests like her. She hated how that made her wonder if she'd taken after him that way. She hated wondering if she should try to meet him. Hated even more doubting that he'd want to see her.

"Penny…" Kadin said after a while. He reached for her hand. "I didn't think you'd—"

She swatted away his hand. "Do me a favor, let me do

my own thinking." Pivoting, she marched back up the stairs and would have slammed the apartment door shut if Kadin hadn't stealthily followed her and put his hand on the wood.

He stood close behind her and took in the anger radiating off her with a little too much amusement.

"There's *nothing* charming about this." She stepped into his apartment, going to the window overlooking the western town's main street. Clouds had rolled in and a light sprinkle had begun. The forecast called for rain.

"I'm sorry," he said thickly. "I asked and thought you didn't want to know anything about your father. I thought I'd impose on you if I did tell you."

As if digging deep into her personal affairs wasn't imposing enough?

He moved closer, too close for her frazzled emotions. When he put his hands on her shoulders, she sidled away and walked back across the open, high-ceiling room. The window off the dining room offered a view of a parking lot and another building.

"I would have told you if I'd have known it was this important to you."

She turned. "You found him. That forces me to care, Kadin. You shouldn't have looked. Not without asking me first."

His head bowed and he stuffed his hands into his jean pockets. "In my line of work, I look for character traits that might give me insight into a case, especially in relationships. Sometimes they're tied to the victim."

"You could have told me when the conversation came up."

He walked toward her. "Would that have changed your reaction?"

So much hurt coiled and twisted in her she could barely catch her breath. How could she have been so sure she preferred to never know her father? Maybe his abandonment had a lot to do with that, even though she hadn't felt *abandoned*. Feeling this emotionally unstable deviated far off her usual demeanor. Would Kadin's telling her what he'd learned changed anything?

She had to be honest and admit, at least to herself, that nothing would have changed. She still would have been upset, which boiled up more confusion. Decisiveness came easy to her, not this overwhelming sense of uncertainty. Penny voiced her next thought out loud. "You didn't have to pry to the extent you did."

"You're right. I did pry more than normal." He moved closer.

That he'd admitted such a thing impressed her and led to other curiosities.

"I thought you weren't interested in marriage and children," she said before thinking first.

Her loaded implication didn't pass by Kadin. Standing so close, he looked down her body. An involuntary action or had she tipped him off?

"I—I didn't mean," she stammered. "It's just that if you were that curious, it could…i-it could lead to…that." Damn, what was the matter with her? She never stuttered. She hung one arm down and rubbed up and down with her other hand, unable to hold his direct gaze. More dichotomies to her character.

Well, she reasoned, she'd never faced pregnancy before. Unplanned pregnancy. Secret pregnancy…

"Does that happen to you a lot?" she asked.

"Does what happen?"

"Curiosity."

"No," he admitted. "You're the first."

Really? Since his wife passed, no other woman had moved him to find out more about her?

"And it's not that I'm not interested…in those things. I just don't think I can invest in them again."

Hearing him essentially reiterate what he'd already told her, Penny grew disconcerted. They'd wandered into another area that had set her life off balance. Why did all these things have to come hailing down at her all at once? The Sara Wolfe case and Jax's involvement, this crazy attraction between her and Kadin, the prospect of being pregnant…

Give her numerous obstacles at work and she'd tackle them without faltering. But outside of that, a real hot mess had erupted.

Chapter 10

The next morning, Penny rolled over and the motion was enough to upset her system. She threw the covers off and ran to the bathroom, hanging onto the edge of the claw-foot tub as she bent over the toilet. Kadin's room was just down the hall. She hoped he didn't hear her retching. Only the outer wall was brick.

When the nausea eased, she sat against the bathroom wall and leaned her head back. She needed some distance from Kadin. Some time to sort her feelings out and her situation. Going back to Salt Lake City might be too dangerous, and Kadin would only follow. She could go home to see her mother, but she didn't want to lead any trouble there.

She could also go and see her father. He'd abandoned her so she felt no obligation to be sensitive to his feelings. Knowing about him and where he lived would plague her the rest of her life. He didn't deserve her sympathy.

Never the kind of woman who put off facing problems, Penny would resolve two of them right now. Getting up, she paused in the hall to make sure Kadin hadn't awakened and then went into the guest room to pack for a quick trip to Bismarck. He didn't need her to solve Sara Wolfe's case anyway, and they were still waiting on DNA results.

She snuck out of the apartment, down the stairs and out the back door. Walking through the warm summer sunrise to the street, she nodded a greeting to a man who'd just opened the doors to his hardware shop, sweeping the concrete in front. The town had a real western feel, taking her back in time, far away from big-city bustle.

A short walk later, she reached a small car rental office and waited until they opened. An hour later, she couldn't help worrying Kadin would catch up to her as she drove away. Not seeing him on her way out of town, she breathed a sigh of relief and drove ten miles an hour over the speed limit toward the next town.

There, she found a drugstore and went inside. Each step intensified her dread. Willpower kept her headed for the *special* products aisle. Once she was there, the row of shelves became a tunnel, sucking her in. No way back. Only forward to a potentially dreadful outcome.

At the pregnancy tests, she forced away her flightiness and picked up one. The package felt like lead in her hand all the way to the checkout counter. The girl glanced at her as she processed the purchase.

"Where is your restroom?"

The girl blinked and then pointed to a back corner.

Penny took the test there. After going into a stall and performing the task, she stared at the positive sign as it emerged, telling her what she already suspected but didn't want to believe.

Pregnant.

She would become a *mommy*?

A mommy without a daddy for her baby.

She saw herself advancing to upper executive management, making a name for herself, career-driven and socially active, not a mother by accident. This must have been how her own mother had gotten trapped. She'd carelessly had an affair with a man who didn't love her. Her mother could claim youth and stupidity. Penny should have known better.

Anyway. On to the next problem. If you could call it a problem. She'd been fine all these years without a father. Now that he had a face he felt real, not just a name her mother told her. Maybe she needed proof, to see him with her own eyes, a living, breathing being, the father who had discarded her but embraced three other children.

She shouldn't go there and put herself through the torment. But why would something torment her that hadn't mattered until now? She didn't have the answer to that. But she hoped to by the time she returned from North Dakota.

Kadin couldn't believe Penny left without him hearing a thing. He shrugged his gun holster over a short-sleeved button-up shirt and then hid the hardware with a light dress jacket. He'd tracked Penny to Bismarck. What the hell was she doing? Why did she have to pick now to go find her father? Grabbing his keys, he hurried down the stairs and into his office.

A man stood there. Tall, really tall, with a blond buzz cut that hinted to at least an affinity to military, his blue-gray eyes staring hard at him and his leather pants and jacket suggesting he rode a motorcycle. Kadin looked past him, through the office door and out the front window. Yes. A mean-looking one leaned on its stand.

Kadin had locked the building, but Penny must have left the front door unlocked. He went for one of his guns.

The man held up his hand. "I'm here for work."

Stepping farther into the office, Kadin took his hand off his pistol. "I'm on my way out. You'll have to come back."

"This won't take long. And I came here all the way from Montana."

Then why didn't he call first? Actually that seemed really strange. "What's in Montana?"

"Home."

The way he answered sounded too simple, as though there were so much more to it than that.

"How did you find out about me?" Kadin asked.

The grin that half formed looked more wry than amused. "You're something of a celebrity."

Not that much of one. People had to be looking to find him. "Not good enough."

"I'm available and your company needs me."

"Why you?"

"I was a marine for eight years before becoming a narcotics investigator and SWAT member."

Now they were getting somewhere. He certainly sounded as though he had the right background, but Kadin didn't have time for an interview. If it weren't for Penny running off...

"Look, I really have to go," Kadin said.

"Working a case?"

He leaned over his desk and picked up a business card. "Call me in a day or two."

The man took the card. "I hoped we'd get to know each other sooner than that."

Kadin began to look closer at the man. He'd seen eyes like that before, past haunts kept at bay by tough determination.

"Who are you?" he asked.

"Lucas Curran."

"You're part of a SWAT in Montana?"

"LAPD. I resigned a couple of years ago and moved to Montana."

That could be impressive, or not. "Why did you leave?"

"I got bored."

There was that grin again, and the simple response that held hidden meaning not divulged.

He couldn't afford to beat around the bush. Penny could be in danger. He had to get to her. *Now.* "I don't hire anyone who has something to hide."

The stranger leaned over the desk, his long fingers grasping a folder and sliding that toward Kadin. "Everything you need to know about me is in here. I'd be a great asset to this agency."

Kadin picked up the folder and put it in his leather briefcase that also had his ammo.

"And this agency will be an asset to me."

Kadin looked up at Lucas's pointed, suggestive look. What personal vendetta did he have? Kadin could understand the drive to fight back against injustice or to stop criminals from hurting anyone else. But a man looking for a cover to practice lawless revenge crossed a line.

"Why do you need my agency?" Kadin asked. "Why can't you work alone to do what you intend to do?"

"I intend to solve cold cases," Lucas said.

"Didn't you do that in LA?"

The man gestured to the briefcase. "Everything you need to know is in there."

He was sure full of himself. Or was that a smoke screen?

"Why do you want to work for me?"

"Same reason you opened an agency like this."

Kadin wondered if he could finish that sentence with a leading *except*. "You won't get a license to kill working for Dark Alley Investigations."

"I don't need one. I just need freedom and unconventional resources, which I am sure you understand."

That, Kadin couldn't argue with. But he wouldn't hire anyone he didn't check out, and this man seemed to be withholding something.

"I'll let you know."

The man reached out and shook his hand. "I'm looking forward to working for you."

Kadin watched Lucas leave, wondering how he could be so certain.

After his new pilot took him to Bismarck, Kadin waited outside the office building where Penny's father worked. He'd known the pilot since college and hired him as soon as he'd decided to open Dark Alley. He needed a plane so he could transport equipment and weapons without incident, and the small, private airstrip a few miles outside Rock Springs afforded him convenience and secrecy. The owner was another of the first friends Kadin had made when he moved.

Penny had been sickeningly easy to find. And she still hadn't noticed him parked across the street. She kept watching the front doors of the engineering company where Alias worked, sometimes biting her nail, other times checking her phone and sending text messages, working on the run. A woman like her would never be able to slow down enough to tolerate life in a small Wyoming town. Would she? Why did he even make the analogy? As if he wanted her to slow down enough to live in the same town as him.

Something in him had conjured the thought. Fantasizing she was that kind of woman, one who loved to fish and relished the quiet, unhurried pace of small towns. No chain coffee shops. No tight schedules. Just peace.

Manufactured peace.

He'd created this. He'd moved to Rock Springs to surround himself with the idea of peace and tranquility. But now he realized that everything he'd created for himself was just an illusion.

Just then Penny stared at the front door of the building. Kadin looked there and saw Alias Cochrane leaving work in business casual. He went to an Audi sedan and drove out of the parking space, family man on his way home. He glanced at Penny, who stared with fixed absorption, lips parted, unmoving, eyes hidden by sunglasses but he imagined them unblinking.

She began to follow her father as he left the lot. Kadin passed Penny and she didn't even notice him. If he were a killer, she'd be an easy target.

He passed Alias, not caring if he saw him. He wouldn't know who he was. Kadin already knew where he lived and wanted to get there first.

Was Penny going to introduce herself? Her boldness didn't surprise him, but her reaction did. He hadn't expected her to get so emotional over finding out her father's identity. He hadn't seen her this overwrought since he'd first met her. And come to think of it, he hadn't pinned her for an emotional woman then, either.

Fifteen minutes later, he parked on the opposite side of the street and waited until Alias drove into his driveway. Penny stayed in her car as her father finished gathering his things and climbed out of the car. The front door opened and three children came pouring out. His wife stood in the doorway with an adoring smile. Did they have to choose this day to look like a Hallmark family?

He checked Penny's reaction. Her lips weren't parted but she watched with a sort of stunned confusion. This could get bad.

Alias went into the house with his beautiful family, kissing his wife on the way inside with a loving hand on her waist. Even Kadin felt the sting of such perfection, uninterrupted by life's cruelty.

Penny got out of her car.

Yup. Things were going to get ugly. That perfection was about to receive a good dose of reality.

He couldn't watch her do this alone. Getting out of the rental, he walked across the street to intercept her. She saw him and stopped short.

"Kadin?"

He reached her and stopped. "What are you doing, Penny?"

"What are *you* doing? You actually followed me here?"

"You shouldn't have left without me. Someone is still trying to kill you." He put his hand on her shoulder. "Come on. There's a better way to do this."

"There was a better way for him to leave my mother, too," she snapped, shrugging him off.

"How did he leave her? Did she ever tell you?"

Penny lowered her head and then looked toward the house. Finally she turned back to him. "I'm going to meet him."

Kadin wasn't going to stop the inevitable. She'd made up her mind.

"Okay." He stepped aside to allow her room to pass on the sidewalk. "I'll go with you."

"No."

"I'm going with you." He walked beside her toward the curving path up to the front door of perfection.

She hesitated, knuckles poised before the door.

"It's not too late to leave. Spend some time thinking about this," he said.

"I've thought about this long enough." She pounded the door and then rang the doorbell once.

He half expected her to ring it over and over again.

Less than a minute later, the door opened and Alias's wife appeared.

"May I speak with Alias?" Penny said.

"Who may I say is calling?" the woman asked, soft spoken, polite, peaceful.

"His daughter," Penny said.

The woman tried to conceal a sharp breath, her eyes going wide and her exhale shaky. She didn't know.

Kadin had predicted this. Reality would come crashing down on the Hallmarks today.

"U-um…o-one moment, please." She left the door open and walked with her hand to her mouth into the kitchen, where Kadin heard the excited voices of kids blurting out the events of their day and Alias chuckling fondly.

"Kids, go wash up for dinner," the woman said. When she didn't get an immediate response, she demanded, "Now!"

"Honey," Alias protested.

She said something low that Kadin couldn't hear. But the kids scurried up the stairs and out of sight.

Alias approached the door, staring at Penny, while his wife trailed behind, hands clasped and face tight with distress. She didn't want to witness this, but the scandal of Alias's firstborn child at the door drew her.

Alias looked from Penny to Kadin and back to Penny. "Uh…h-how did you find me?"

Kadin felt like pinching the bridge of his nose. If Alias meant to make peace with his estranged daughter, he'd just gotten off to a rotten start.

"Do you know who I am?" she asked.

The disconcerted man nodded once. "You're my daughter."

"What's my name?"

Alias swallowed and ran his tongue over his lips. "Jenny."

"It's *Penny*."

"Penny. I knew that. I…" He rubbed his face briefly. "Y-you caught me off guard. My wife didn't know about you."

"Why didn't you tell her?" Penny asked.

His wife looked expectantly to her husband, obviously injured that he'd married her and started a family with her without being completely honest.

"I…" He looked at his wife. "Honey, I…" He reached for her hands, taking them in his.

"Daddy?"

Kadin saw the youngest of the three peek around the corner of the stairs.

"Go up to your room, sweetie," Alias said.

Alias's wife withdrew and stepped back. "I'll let you talk in private." With a look at Penny, she turned and went to the young girl at the foot of the stairs, ushering her up and out of sight.

"I can explain," Alias said to Penny. "You have to understand that your mother and I were very young when she got pregnant."

"So that made it all right to walk away and leave her with all the responsibility?" Penny looked up at the clean, fresh paint of the front porch and then beyond him. "So you could go on and have an easy life?"

"We were so young…"

"Did you ever care that you had another daughter?" Penny said, not in an emotional way. She asked out of pure curiosity, as though she sought understanding more than a father.

"Of course I did."

"You forgot my name."

Alias sighed and rubbed his face again. "I left before you were born. I went to college."

So, he'd forgotten?

Penny's eyebrows rose mockingly.

Had he not been caught unprepared, he might have remembered her actual name. Damn, this had to be rough on Penny.

"Your mother knew I had plans to go to college."

Penny folded her arms, turning the mocking into something even more cynical.

"Look, I'm sorry. I know I made a mistake. I was only thinking of myself. I was eighteen. What do you want from me? Can we talk tomorrow?" He glanced back. "You shouldn't have come here like this."

With a scoff, Penny said, "I wasn't going to come here. I wasn't even interested in who you were until I read about you in Kadin's background report."

Alias looked his way. "Wha—" He glanced back at her. "What background?"

Pivoting, Penny stepped down from the porch.

"Hey...wait! I do want to talk." Her father came after her.

Penny kept going.

"I have a security clearance," he said to Kadin. "Is she going to cause trouble?"

His long-lost daughter came to see him and all he could think about was what kind of trouble this would cause his clearance? Still selfish, it would appear.

"How could your own daughter cause you trouble with

that?" Kadin hissed, and then before waiting to hear his reply, he turned and left to go after Penny.

"I do care," Alias called. "I just didn't know how to approach her. After so many years had gone by, I thought it was too late."

Kadin didn't acknowledge him.

"I have thought of her!" Alias called again.

Penny had reached her car and spun a U-turn before Kadin could catch up to her, then sped off down the street. He cursed and ran to his own rental, racing after her.

Holding a fingernail polish brush, Penny drew stars on a napkin while she waited for her toenails to dry. She sat on the floor of her hotel suite, knees bent and cotton stuffed between her toes. The TV played a chick flick, she had the lights set dim. Today had accomplished nothing. Nothing but deeper confusion and stirred up angst. Rather than settle her down, seeing her flesh-and-blood father gave her silly thoughts that she hadn't been enough for him, he hadn't loved her. That was what had her painting stars on a hotel napkin. Of course his running away had nothing to do with her. He and her mother had been too young. Yes, he'd been a coward for running. A selfish one. But kids made mistakes. Sometimes really big ones.

Her cell vibrated again. If she could mute that, she would, but work might call. Kadin wouldn't stop calling. Why had he come here, anyway? He'd caused her enough turmoil.

A firm knock on her door announced his arrival. She'd been expecting him. A man like him would find her. He'd found her in North Dakota. Why not find her at her hotel?

She stood and walked on her heels to the door. Once she swung it open, his gaze ran down her body, pausing on her toes and then going back up bare legs to the bright, floral cotton nightie that hung to mid-thigh.

"It's comfortable," she said.

His gaze lifted from her breasts, eyes glowing beneath the brim of his hat. "Uh…" He cleared his throat. "May I come in?"

She extended her arm and moved aside, shoving aside the reminder of his image in that picture of him leaning on the tailgate of his truck. "Sure. Join the party." She waddled back over to her spa on a towel and sat, lifting her glass of pinot noir.

"Is this a pity party?" he asked, sitting down on the floor facing her.

She smiled at his crossed legs. "Would you like a glass of wine? There's other options in the fridge."

"No, thanks. What I want is for you to stop running from me."

"Don't ruin my mood. I've worked hard to get where I am right now." She sipped her wine, meeting his eyes as she did.

"Are you drunk?"

"Not yet. Here." She held up her hand and wiggled her fingers. "You can paint my nails." Giving him the nail polish, she felt more like herself.

He took the polish and twisted off the cap, eyeing her. "Is this typical?"

While he began to paint the first nail, she said. "This isn't a pity party, and no, not typical."

"Life's curveballs turn you into a girly girl, huh?"

Hmm. Apparently he knew her better than she thought. She didn't paint her nails. She wore minimal jewelry and dressed professionally.

"I wear dresses…"

"Business attire." He painted the next nail. He was

really pretty good. Steady hands. Hers began to tingle as she watched his manly fingers work.

"It's making me feel good." *He* was making her feel good.

He grinned as he finished her hand. "Put the wine down, Scarlett."

She laughed lightly and set the glass down on the towel. "Scarlett?"

"I'm waiting for you to hiccup."

"Scarlett drank brandy, didn't she?"

"Hold still."

She smothered her wine-enhanced humor but couldn't dim her big smile, especially as she continued to watch him. By the time he finished screwing on the cap to the polish, she no longer smiled. Warmth from more than the wine filled her. The sight of him, or just him in general, radiated heat.

"You make me feel good," she said, not caring how sultry she sounded.

His bold gaze met hers. "How much wine have you had?"

"Not enough to cloud my judgment." Leaning toward him, she looped her arms over his shoulders and felt his hands go to her waist. "You make me feel good." She tipped her head back, wanting him to kiss her.

"All I did was paint your nails."

"Not many men would do that." Only men sure of their masculinity would. Nothing threatened this guy's masculinity. Penny found that extremely sexy.

She watched his eyes begin to smolder, taking in her face as she held nothing back. He could see her desire.

"Kiss me," she said.

"Haven't I already made you feel good?"

"Yes, but you can make me feel even better. Kiss me."

Chuckling, he did as she asked. At first chaste, the passion between them broke free, flames hitting fuel and burning hotter. He joined her in her world of love, a barrier from the day.

His hands slid up her back, one going to her head, holding her firm as he delved in for more. She ran her fingers through his hair and felt the polish, not quite dry, smeared into the strands.

He moved back when she did.

"Oh." She looked at the ruined nails and then up at him. "Turn your head."

He did. She saw a small amount of polish stuck in his hair and began to laugh, covering her mouth.

Frowning his good-humored disapproval, he reached for a cotton ball and the nail polish remover.

"We should probably just cut it out," she said.

Laughing softly, she got up and went to the bathroom to retrieve a small facial hair scissors, coming back to kneel at his side and snip the red polish away, careful to keep her nails from touching him.

"There."

He turned his head and took in her happy face. And then he looked down. Kneeling so close as she was, her breasts brushed his arm as he moved his hand up and down her leg once. She flexed her fingers where they rested on his chest and dropped the scissors to the towel.

Lifting his hand, he cupped her face and hovered close to her mouth. "Don't touch me." Then he kissed her again.

Brushing the nail paraphernalia out of the way, he took her wrists and leaned forward over her until she lay on her back. Pinning her hands, he continued to kiss her, his weight coming down on her.

The smell of polish and wine and man mingled and then faded from her awareness when he moved against her. She tugged her hands, yearning to touch his hard body, but he wouldn't let her go.

"My nails are dry," she rasped.

"Yeah, but they made me want to do this." Raising the hem of her nightie, he pulled her underwear down one-handed. While she kicked out of them, he unzipped his jeans and pulled them down along with his boxers, just enough to expose himself.

Penny tugged her hands again, moaning in protest. He held her down with one strong hand and penetrated her warm, waiting center. She groaned from pure ecstasy now, loving the sweet torture.

He pressed his mouth to hers as he thrust in deep and withdrew slowly, raising his face to share an intimate look while he moved inside her. She peaked in record time, crying out and arching her back to the power and wonder of sensation only he could strum from her, and therein lay the problem. In the morning, how would she feel?

Chapter 11

Penny woke with a languorous stretch, smiling at the lovely morning, sunlight bathing her inner glow. She rolled to her side to see Kadin already awake and propped up on the bed, bare-chested and holding his phone. The tense crease and low slant of his brow indicated a much different mood than hers.

"Hey," she said, coaxing him not to go where she needed to avoid, lest all the unhappy things that had occurred over the last few days come rushing forth.

His brow smoothed and he smiled a little. "Good morning."

That was nice. But he seemed to have to force it.

"Are you okay?"

"Yeah."

Now *she* had to force it. "You're still safe, you know." Boy, was that ever a lie! How safe would he feel if she told him she was pregnant?

"Are you okay?" he asked rather than go there.

She propped herself up like him, tucking the covers to keep herself concealed. "Yeah."

"You don't sound very convincing. It must have been a shock to see him. Your dad."

There went her mood. "Yeah."

He put his phone aside. "Come here." He opened his arm to invite her closer.

She scooted over, rearranging the covers again as she did, until she cuddled against him. He stroked her arm, a sweet gesture, one she felt he truly meant.

"What bothers you so much about finding him?" he asked.

She shrugged one shoulder, not really knowing herself. But his asking broke some clarity free. "I guess…" She tipped her head to see him. "I guess…it's finding out he's real. Before…he was just a fact. A statistic. My mom got pregnant when she was young and the boy ran off. Who cares?" She blew out a frustrated breath. "He didn't care enough to find me or keep in touch or even later, when he matured and began to have more kids. I didn't matter to him, so why should he matter to me?"

"But it does matter."

"Yes. I've never worked through it before now. I just accepted that I didn't have a father and my mother never married." She felt liberated with that revelation.

"What if he meant that he thought it was too late to contact you?" he asked.

She shrugged one shoulder again, tucking her head on his shoulder. "I think it's too late for me. Why should I get to know my father now? After I had to be the one to find him? I'm fine without him and have been my whole life."

"No, you don't need him." He smiled slightly, more out of sympathy. "You don't need anyone."

"What's that supposed to mean?"

"Nothing bad. You were raised by an independent woman who taught you strength and the same independence. You don't have to settle for anyone. You don't mind being alone."

What he said ringing true but at the same time raising her defenses. "But…I don't want to be like my mother."

"What's wrong with being like her?"

"She puts on a good front, but…she's lonely. I think she actually loved Alias." Penny moved her head to see him briefly. "She surrounded herself with friends and community and kept busy with social activities. And…me." She'd always known that about her mother, but she'd never really thought of it in this light, how her mother's loneliness had transferred to her.

All the way back to Rock Springs, Kadin couldn't stop thinking about what Penny had said—that her mother had been lonely. She'd loved once in her life and hadn't remarried. The similarity to his own life situation struck a chord. Would he end up the same way? Ever since Arielle had died, he hadn't considered what he'd do with the rest of his life, not outside fighting crime, a fight that had turned personal after Annabelle's murder.

Even now he resisted contemplating his future. Maybe he wasn't ready. He didn't feel ready. And yet…

He glanced over at Penny as they headed for the back door of his office and apartment, unbelievably sexy in tight jeans and a scoop-necked white T-shirt and casual jewelry. Last night and this morning had been so easy. He'd felt a little unsteady this morning, as if he'd lost control and might be slipping back into that tortured state. Then as soon as he and Penny started talking, that had vanished and only their enigmatic connection remained.

Now he'd swung back to unsteady, uncertain where his future led, if he'd wind up lost again. Structure and single-minded focus had gotten him through that horrible time. He had to have structure. No structure came with a package like Penny. She kept reassuring him, but he sensed her reluctance. They had control issues in common. He needed control to protect himself from his past; she needed it to preserve her independence.

Because of that he felt awkward with her.

Inside the dark back entry, Kadin turned on a light as Penny passed him.

She put her hand up over her mouth and nose. "What's that smell?"

Kadin sniffed and didn't notice anything other than the smell of an old building being shut up for a couple of days. "I can't smell anything."

She turned the handle for the door leading up to his apartment and climbed the stairs. At the top, she hurried for the bathroom. Upstairs.

Kadin stood in the open area before the dining room, looking up to the loft and hallway. He heard water running and nothing else in the quiet. Passing the dining table and seating arrangement around a gas fireplace in the brick, he stopped in front of the windows, looking down on the street in the afternoon sun, wondering why Penny was still getting sick.

Hearing her come back downstairs, he turned. She went into the kitchen and retrieved a soda.

"Feeling all right?" he asked, going to the kitchen island.

"Yes. Just got a little queasy."

Why? he wanted to ask.

She sipped the soda, looking at him. "Must be my head."

She'd smelled something and that had triggered her nausea?

"I didn't feel well on the flight," she said. "All that movement…"

"Maybe you should go lie down." Maybe she should go see the doctor again.

"I'm fine." She drank more of her soda and wandered out from the kitchen, going into the living room.

His cell rang. Seeing her rub her forehead and wavering over the strange feeling he had, Kadin went to answer. Seeing the caller ID, he prepared himself for news.

"Tandy."

"Detective Cohen. Can you two meet me at Felicia's? It's down the street from Penny's apartment. I chose this location so it would be convenient for you."

Felicia's was a diner down the block. "Sure. Be there in five." He disconnected and turned to Penny, who didn't look enthused about going.

"Cohen has news. Maybe you should stay here and get some rest," he said. "You haven't slept enough." She'd been running all over the country.

She shook her head. "I'll go with you. I want to hear what he has to say." She headed for the door.

Kadin followed and they took the elevator to the main floor.

"Where are we meeting?" Penny asked.

"Felicia's." He held one of the front doors open for her.

She winced and then swallowed. "We haven't had dinner yet. Might as well eat there."

Was she going to be able to eat anything? As they walked along the street, he studied her. "Maybe you should go to the doctor."

"I'm fine. I feel better." She breathed in slowly. "The air is helping."

He supposed she might have nausea for a week or two after getting a concussion. Then, why did he get this strange, niggling feeling that she shouldn't be nauseated anymore?

At Felicia's, he held that door for her, too, and spotted Cohen at a booth table. He dismissed the hostess and went there with Penny in tow. After shaking the detective's hand, he let Penny sit down first and then sat down beside her.

"Did the fiber tests come back?" Kadin asked.

"Yes. The fiber from Sara Wolfe's crime scene were high-modulus polyester, or LCAP," he said. "That's liquid crystal aromatic polyester. They match the samples you gave me."

That was good news, but it wasn't enough to implicate Jax. Kadin noticed how Penny had tensed.

"The forensics team did an analysis on the dyes found in the samples," Cohen went on. "Those were a match, as well. We can be confident the fibers came from the same type of rope, but we can't prove they came from the same rope that the fiber found with Sara Wolfe came from."

"It doesn't place Jax at the scene," Kadin said, more for Penny's benefit.

"No, but it still implicates him, and gives me a good enough reason to keep interrogating him."

"What about the DNA?" Penny asked.

"Jax's DNA didn't match the DNA from the crime scene, and he passed the lie detector test."

Penny sat back. "He didn't do it." She glanced around the restaurant as she thought and then turned back to Kadin and the detective. "If he didn't, then who did? And what does the rope mean?"

"The previous owner of Jax's property?" Kadin suggested.

"He has an alibi for the time Sara Wolfe was abducted," Cohen said.

"When did you learn that?" Penny asked.

"Just yesterday. Sorry, I meant to tell you, but since it was another dead end, I didn't see the urgency." The detective looked at Kadin. "I've asked Jax to come in for more questioning tomorrow morning to see if he can reveal anything about the rope fiber. I don't want him to know you're there, but I'd like you to hear his statement." He turned to Penny. "Both of you."

"We'll be there."

Penny stood beside Kadin, waiting for Jax to be brought into the interrogation room. She still grappled with how Jax had been absolved of any connection to Sara's murder, but had rope fibers that matched those found at her crime scene.

Kadin startled her by asking, "How are you feeling today?"

A flash of alarm caused her hesitation. Was he getting suspicious? He'd seemed so yesterday. She couldn't blame her concussion for nine months.

"Mmm-hmm," she replied. "Yeah. Good."

He scrutinized her as the sound of Jax entering the interrogation room gave Penny a reprieve. Detective Cohen thanked him for coming in again.

"No problem. What can I do for you?" Jax sat down.

Cohen sat across from him. "We've had some developments in the investigation and I'd like to go over your whereabouts the day Sara Wolfe disappeared. Would that be all right with you?"

"Of course." Jax relaxed back against the chair, crossing his legs and folding his hands on his lap, all confident executive.

"Could you go over once again where you were that day? Let's begin with that morning."

"As I've said, I went to work that morning and left early to spend time with my son. Before I left, I noticed my truck missing."

"What time did you leave work?"

"I think it was about two."

"Last time you said it was one," Cohen remarked.

"One. Two. It was early afternoon."

Penny glanced at Kadin. Had Jax lied about the time he left work? Did he know something about the murder and had hidden it?

"After I went home to pack, I drove to Park City and went to a five o'clock movie with my son."

"Right. Okay. Did you stop anywhere on your way to pick up your son?"

"No. I didn't drive by Miller Elementary School. I've told you all this already."

Cohen nodded calmly. "Yes, and I appreciate you going over this again. I did check out your disgruntled employee. He had a solid alibi from the time you last saw your truck to when you noticed it missing the next morning."

"I didn't think a disgruntled employee would steal something from me," Jax said. "Why did you call me in here today?"

"We have evidence that connects you to Sara Wolfe's murder."

Jax uncrossed his legs and adjusted his posture on the chair. "What evidence?"

"Would you care to revise your previous statement?" The detective cleverly led Jax without telling him about the DNA test.

"What? I didn't kill Sara Wolfe. What evidence do you have? If you tell me, I might be able to help you."

"What happened from the time you left work the day of Sara Wolfe's disappearance and the time you went to the movie with your son?" Cohen asked.

The rope fibers linked him. That they matched couldn't be a coincidence.

"I drove to Park City. I don't understand why you don't believe me."

Detective Cohen merely looked at Jax for several seconds.

"I didn't see anything," Jax insisted.

"I didn't say you did."

Penny glanced at Kadin again and he briefly met her eyes. *Had* Jax seen something? Why would he say that so defensively if he hadn't?

"Did you see your brother before you picked up your son?" the detective asked.

Jax blinked a few times. "Dane?" He seemed surprised.

"Do you have any other brothers?"

Jax shook his head as though shaking off confusion. "No. I didn't see him."

The detective gave Jax another long look. "Mr. Ballard, we recovered evidence that may link you to Sara Wolfe's crime scene."

"DNA?" Jax asked, quick and full of anxiety.

The detective slowly shook his head. "No. Your DNA doesn't match that found in the scene."

Jax sat back, slumping in relief. "Of course it doesn't. I didn't kill her!"

"But we do have fibers from her crime scene that match some recovered from your home."

That bombshell caused Jax a few seconds of processing time. "From my home? You can't do that without a warrant."

"You're right, I can't."

As Jax stared at him and realization struck, he grew angry. "Did Penny give it to you?"

"I'm not at liberty to reveal my sources."

Jax cursed a few vulgar words, calling Penny names.

"Tell me again, Mr. Ballard. What happened after you left work and before you went to the movie?"

"We're finished talking." Jax rose to his feet. "You'll have to talk to my lawyer from here on out."

"Who are you protecting?" the detective asked.

"Protecting?" Jax scoffed, turning to face the detective at the door. "Nobody. Maybe you should bring my brother in here and ask him where he was that day."

Detective Cohen stood. "Why should I do that?"

Jax's mouth pressed tighter in his agitation. He seemed reluctant to reveal whatever he hid about Dane.

"What do you know about Dane that you haven't told me?" Cohen prodded.

"I didn't think it was significant. But now…" Jax turned toward the door. "You'll have to talk to my lawyer."

"Wait." Cohen put his hand on Jax's shoulder. "I know he's your brother, but you can tell me whatever you know. It won't leave this room unless I have proof of guilt."

Jax looked toward the one-way window, clearly doubting whatever he said would stay in that room. But he met the detective's face and then finally said, "I didn't keep climbing rope in my Park City house. Someone put it there."

"Climbing rope?" Detective Cohen said. "I didn't say it was climbing rope. I said *fiber*. I didn't say what kind of fiber."

"Like I said, you'll have to talk to my lawyer from now on." Jax tried the handle and found the door locked.

Detective Cohen knocked on the door and an officer opened it.

Before leaving, Jax looked back at Cohen. "My brother put the rope in my closet. I noticed it there yesterday. He's trying to set me up. He's the one you should be looking at, not me."

Jax didn't have a high regard for his brother. The two fought. Disagreed on business issues. Was Jax jealous of his brother or was his brother jealous of Jax?

Detective Cohen didn't say anything and Jax left. They'd get nothing out of him after this. But something still bothered Penny.

Why would Dane try to frame his own brother? Did it have something to do with his best friend's illegal embezzling?

After leaving the police station, Penny went with Kadin to talk to Vanessa's parents. She'd listened in when he called to let them know he'd taken over their daughter's missing person case but hadn't had to hear how thrilled the woman on the other end became. Detective Cohen had let her know prior to the call. The visit had been brief, with Kadin only informing them of the tattoo parlor and confirming what he'd already suspected. Vanessa had run away from a good home after falling into friendship with a misguided boy.

With the Sara Wolfe investigation once again at a standstill, Kadin had decided they needed to take a quick trip to Houston. Penny sensed the stout determination to find the missing girl and that doing so would bring him that much closer to healing, or at least coming to terms with his tragedy.

She just hoped she could keep from getting sick in front of him.

After landing, Cohen had called to report the results of his interview with Dane, who'd, of course, denied any connection to the stolen truck or the climbing rope. Cohen hadn't asked for DNA because Jax's had been so different from the crime scene sample. As Jax's brother, Dane would also have different DNA. Whoever had left the DNA was of no close relation to Jax or Dane.

The tattoo parlor looked as unkempt as the owner, a short, inked-up dark-haired man with a Fu Manchu mustache.

The man took one look at each of them and half grinned. "First time?"

Kadin took out a photo of Vanessa and showed it to the man. "This girl came here for a tattoo a few weeks ago."

"Yeah. I remember her. She got her first tattoo here, a real pretty one." He twisted and pointed to the middle of his lower back. "One of these."

"Was she with this boy?" Kadin showed him another photo.

"She did come here with someone. Yeah, that could be the guy. He didn't say much."

"Did they pay cash?"

"Yeah. I only take cash."

"Did Vanessa talk about anything while they were here?" Kadin asked.

The man's roughneck congeniality faded. "Is something the matter? You two cops or something?"

"Would it matter if we were?" Penny asked.

The man glanced at her and then did a visual inspection of Kadin's size and intimidating aura. "No, man. Just wondering. They in trouble or something?"

"Vanessa was reported missing almost a year ago and we think the boy she was with when she came here knows where we can find her."

Obviously, or he wouldn't have been with the girl while she got a tattoo.

"She mentioned being hungry and wanting to go to the hamburger place down on South Post Oak Road," he finally said. "They picked that place because it was close to their apartment. That's about it."

"Thanks. You've been a big help." Kadin gave the man a pat on his shoulder.

"I can give you two half off on a couple of tattoos," he said as they headed for the door.

Penny glanced back, surprised that the man would even ask, and then caught Kadin's cynical smile.

A few minutes later, they parked in front of the burger place. Penny followed Kadin's gaze and found herself looking at an apartment building down the street.

"Let's go talk to the landlord."

The landlord lived on the first floor. A heavyset woman with curly gray hair in a loose-fitting floral dress and socks answered the door, a television loud in the background.

"I only rent from ten to noon, Monday through Friday."

Nothing like a workaholic, Penny thought wryly, catching a glimpse of borderline hoarder piles scattered throughout her home.

"We're investigating the disappearance of a girl." Kadin showed her the photograph and told her the name.

"You're police?"

"Private investigator, but I'm working with the lead detective in her case."

"I can't give out personal information on my tenants." She looked back at her television, where a daytime drama played. She didn't welcome this intrusion.

"Then she does live here?" Kadin asked. "Just tell us which apartment and we'll be out of your hair."

The woman eyed him and then Penny. "Three-sixteen.

She lives there with her boyfriend. Looks young, if you ask me."

The boy must have false identification, or he'd gotten it for both of them. Didn't a person have to be eighteen to rent an apartment?

She and Kadin left and went to the apartment door, where Kadin knocked.

A few moments later, the door opened as far as the chain would allow and a young girl peered out at them, hazel eyes wary and medium brown hair in a ponytail. *Vanessa.*

"Hello, Vanessa. I'm private investigator Kadin Tandy. We'd—"

The girl started to push the door shut, but Kadin had already put his foot in the open space. She moved back from the door.

"She's going to run," Penny said. Then she heard Vanessa race through the apartment.

Kadin kicked the door free of the chain lock and entered before Penny. She saw the girl opening a window, ready to climb down the fire escape.

Kadin reached her before she made it through the window.

"Let go of me!" Vanessa struggled against Kadin's hold.

"Come over here and have a seat." Kadin guided her to the old, stained sofa. "Let's talk."

He plopped the girl down and when she began to rise, he put his hand on her shoulder and pushed her gently back down.

"We just want to talk to you."

The wild instinct to run softened in her young eyes and her body relaxed, indicating she'd cease fighting, at least for now.

"Your parents have been worried sick about you," he scolded.

To which Vanessa averted her head. From Penny's angle, she caught sight of something dark high on Vanessa's cheekbone, hidden by hair.

"Can you tell us why you ran away from a loving home?" Kadin asked, not having seen the same.

"It wasn't loving. My mom wouldn't let me do anything. She wouldn't let me be myself!"

Standing before the sofa, Kadin had a looming presence. To soften that, Penny sat down beside the girl.

"Are you an investigator, too?"

"No. I'm just with him." Penny reached over and took the girl's hand. "Your parents *are* very worried about you, Vanessa, and they don't understand why you left." With her other hand, she brushed the hair along the girl's cheek aside, revealing a small cut and nasty bruise.

Vanessa jerked away and would probably have bolted again if Penny hadn't held firm.

"Vanessa…" Penny began softly, looking up at Kadin, who stayed back, although his hands had fisted at his sides.

The girl bent her head again.

"When is he going to be back?" Penny asked, glad that Kadin had left this up to her.

She shrugged. "Sometime tonight."

"Do you want to stay with him?"

No response came from the girl. She must be terrified. She'd made a mistake running away with a boy she thought she could trust and now she felt like the walls were closing in.

"I read your case file," Penny went on. "Your boyfriend came from a pretty rough background. He's been arrested several times. Did you know that?"

"Arrested?"

She nodded. "And his parents have problems, too. They aren't like your parents."

As Vanessa stared at her, Penny realized she wasn't telling her anything she hadn't already figured out. She just hadn't admitted it to herself until now.

"Your parents love you," Penny said. "Your mother is so scared for you. She wants you to come home."

"She's going to be so mad at me." Some of the rebellious girl returned, the one who had led her to flee with a bad boy. "She'll ground me and yell all the time. Just like before."

Penny patted her hand, then let it go. "I bet if you stop hanging around boys like the one you came here with, she won't ground you anymore. And I also bet that she'll be so happy to see you that she won't ground you at all. Or be mad." She smiled encouragingly at Vanessa. "She'll want you to get past this phase in your life. To move on and have a bright, successful future."

Vanessa didn't seem to believe her at first. Her eyes didn't meet Penny's and she rolled her lower lip between her lips.

"Do you really never want to see your family again?" Penny asked softly.

The girl shrugged.

"Come with us, Vanessa. You don't have to live like this."

After a while, she lifted her head and then tears bloomed. "What about…what about…"

"He can't hurt you anymore," Kadin said. "I'll make sure of that."

Vanessa looked up at him, taking in his big, commanding form.

"Why don't you go and pack your things?" Penny said gently.

Glancing around, Vanessa looked toward the door and then up at Kadin again, and then finally back at Penny.

"It's okay. If you come with us, everything is going to be okay. I promise."

Blinking a few times and then letting out a tense breath, Vanessa stood and went into the only bedroom.

"Nicely done," Kadin said.

"Let's bring her back to her mother."

Kadin received a call later that day. He'd contacted the Houston police and informed them of the runaway boy. They'd subsequently intercepted him during a drug deal and he was now under arrest. Kadin found it difficult to feel sorry for the boy when he'd essentially abducted Vanessa and had nearly ruined her life. Kadin's only hope was that some time in jail and some therapy would steer him onto a better path.

Kadin had phoned Cohen, who'd notified Vanessa's parents that their daughter had been found safe and sound and would be brought home today.

"I'm nervous."

Kadin looked into the rearview mirror at Vanessa as he stopped the car in front of a house. Cleaned up in new clothes Penny had bought for her, she presented a picture of the girl she'd been before her terrible ordeal.

Her mother appeared on the front porch, her father behind her. Thin and fit, hair tidy. Her father, also thin and much taller, emerged tight-lipped and grim. Both had to be worried over what their daughter had suffered but tried to put on strong fronts.

Borders trimmed with flowers and a plush green lawn finished the perfect-family picture. She came bouncing down the steps and ran to the car, where Vanessa slowly climbed out of the back.

Crying—no, sobbing—Vanessa's mother took her into her arms. Her father came to stand near them, fighting emotion, stuffing his hands into his front pockets.

Kadin felt deep resonance of bittersweet regret open a hole in his chest. He got out of the car when Penny did, but couldn't make his feet move close to this happy reunion. What he wouldn't give to have had the same with Annabelle.

"All this time we thought…we thought you were… Oh…we were so scared and now we're just so happy you're back," Vanessa's mother cried as she continued to squeeze her in a heartfelt hug.

Vanessa's father put his hand on his wife's back and then an arm around his daughter. The three stayed that way, in a huddle, basking in joy.

"Mom…I'm so sorry."

"No, no. No apology. I'm just so grateful you're home." She leaned back, her husband doing the same and lowering his arms to his sides. "Never do this again."

Vanessa shook her head with remorse. "I thought he was a good person."

Her mother took her face between her hands. "I know. You're so young, honey. I love you. I'm so happy you're home."

"Me, too." Vanessa hugged her again and then moved to her father and embraced him, too.

That was when her mother turned to Kadin. While Vanessa and her father talked, she walked around the car to him. He felt like withdrawing, like running, like getting far away from here.

And then the woman took his hands in hers, and her teary eyes met his.

"I can never repay you for bringing her home."

"You just did," he said.

She breathed a laugh. "How did you know she ran away? We couldn't believe she'd do such a thing."

"I didn't believe it, either. That's how I found her."

The woman touched his face. "I wish you could have done the same for your little girl."

Why did she have to make this harder? He stepped back. "We should get going." He looked over the roof of the car at Vanessa, standing with her dad, arms around each other as they faced him with big, tremulous smiles.

Penny gave Vanessa a farewell hug and got into the car with Kadin. He looked back once to see the trio as a family, watching him go. Was this what he had to look forward to? He'd see other families joined together, alive and happy. He wouldn't see his.

He'd really like to be alone right now. The first time he returned a child to their mother, he thought he'd feel complete. Satisfied. Whole again. Instead, he felt…wretched.

Chapter 12

"Wait here."

Penny shot Kadin her best unappreciative look. When he saw that and ignored her, she glanced through all the car windows. Nothing stirred in the dark neighborhood, but she didn't relish the thought of sitting out here alone, not with Hoodie Man still on the loose.

"Thanks, but I think I'll go with you."

He'd been insufferable ever since they delivered Vanessa to her parents yesterday. He wouldn't let her out of her apartment without him, and he wouldn't talk about his daughter. She respected his needs, but tiptoeing around his manly emotions had begun to wear on her.

"You'll be safer here." Kadin finished organizing his break-in tools and stuffing a plastic bag inside the flexible container.

"I beg to differ." She got out of the car and slammed the door, tired of his surly attitude. He really needed to figure out how to move on.

He climbed out and joined her on the other side. "That was noisy."

She began to hurry up the sidewalk. "Good."

Taking her arm, he stopped her. "Hold on there, Neytiri. We can't go through the front door."

Now he compared her to a brave fictional character? She found that rather endearing and felt a tickle spark in her abdomen despite his frustrating distance. Did he picture her beautiful and lithe, carrying a bow and moving acrobatically into danger? Right through the front door? Something she supposed Scarlett O'Hara would do?

Her frustration returned when she realized how easily he aroused her. Why couldn't she shut off her reactions?

"Ever since you gave Vanessa back to her parents, you've been difficult. Snapping at me. Not saying much. I would think finding her alive would make you happy."

Surprise and confusion moved across his eyes. "I am happy."

What? "This is happy?" She swept her hand down his body.

Seeing where this topic was headed, he turned abruptly and strode onto the lawn toward the back of the house. She kept up beside him.

"You'll never be satisfied," she accused, talking her thoughts. As they reached the back patio and he went to work on the back garage door, she added, "No matter how many you save, they'll never be enough."

He sent a warning look back at her before entering the garage.

She followed him into the dark house. The new threat of discovery changed her focus. Before coming here, Penny had called Dane's assistant and gotten chummy enough with her to find out her boss had a dinner meeting tonight and his wife was visiting family out of state.

The house was more of an estate, a big, modern struc-ture with a cut roofline, beige stone accents and several arched, three-pane casement windows.

"What if he has security cameras?" Penny asked.

"I already checked for them. He only has an interior system, which I disabled remotely."

He'd done all that from the car? "How did you do that?"

"I jammed the signal to keep them from reaching the control box."

"Wow. You can hack, too?"

He didn't respond as he found Dane's office and searched in there for a while, including his computer, not the laptop Dane took to work every day. If he had any-thing to hide, he wouldn't use his work computer. They searched for almost an hour, ending in the basement. They came up empty. No emails. No rope matching what had been found in Jax's Park City house. No items that could be used in arson. No compulsive collections of damning information, like photos or details of Jax's whereabouts.

"Let's get out of here," Kadin finally said.

He began climbing up the stairs from the basement and Penny followed.

They'd head back to her apartment, where she'd have to put up with his mood again. She wasn't looking for-ward to that.

"If you don't face what happened, you'll never heal, Kadin."

"Do we have to talk about that now?"

Before she had his baby would be preferable. "You get annoyed every time someone brings up your loss."

"That's because I don't want to talk about it. You wouldn't, either." He reached the top of the stairs and emerged into a short hall.

Just then the sound of a door closing alerted them both.

Penny sucked in a startled breath and Kadin took her hand and pulled her back into the stairway. He peered out into the hall. The stair where they stood creaked.

Penny heard Dane put keys down and then he must have gone still with the sound.

Kadin put a finger to his lips, then pointed down the stairs. Penny stepped softly back down the staircase. At the bottom, they moved around the wall and waited.

She heard Dane coming down just before Kadin took her hand and tugged her through the lower level family room to a spare bedroom. Silence stretched on, Penny aware of every breath she took and the heavy pulse of her heart.

Kadin slid out a pistol and held it aimed up beside the door. When Dane didn't appear, he moved his head for a quick bob out into the family room. Then, with the sound of the stairs creaking, he took her hand again and led her slowly into the family room.

Checking the stairway, Kadin led her with his gun raised up the stairs, pausing to point at one of the steps and then showing her to skip it. How had he known that was the one that had creaked?

In stealthy silence, they made it to the top of the stairs. Penny heard Dane doing something in the kitchen. They had to cross the living room to get to the garage.

Penny peeked out into the living room around Kadin. Dane had his back to them, removing items from the refrigerator.

Kadin took her hand again and crouched, moving to the back of a sofa with a long table with a piece of art and a lamp along the back. He looked over the back and crouched again, shaking his head at Penny. Dane must be facing the living room. Penny listened to him mix a drink and then move out of the kitchen.

She shot a glance at Kadin. Would Dane walk by them? What would they do if he saw them? She looked at Kadin's gun. This could get bad.

The television went on and Dane sighed as he sat on a chair.

Great. How long would they be stuck here?

Several minutes passed before a ringing phone brought Dane to his feet. With a quick look, Kadin led Penny to the entry to the garage. Penny glanced back before going into the garage. Dane didn't appear as she feared and they left the house, running around the side toward the street.

Once on the sidewalk, they slowed to a walk and Penny caught her breath. "That was close."

"Yeah. You should have waited in the car."

Did he think she'd slowed him down? "We were in there too long."

He glanced at her, his surly self again.

"You're wrong, you know," she said, still not finished with their earlier confrontation.

"Wrong about what?" he almost snapped, glancing behind them toward Dane's house.

"That I wouldn't want to talk about losing two people I loved more than any other on the planet. I would. Maybe not at first, but after a few months or a year, I'd start to get pretty tired of myself."

"I'm not tired of myself." His strides lengthened.

"No?" She pictured herself losing what he had lost and feeling miserable all the time. "I would be. I'd be sick of feeling depressed and alone and irritated every time someone tried to help out by offering their support." She had to jog a few steps to keep up with him. "Look, I know it's hard, but you need to talk about what happened, Kadin."

He stopped at the car and turned on her. "Why? What

would I say? My daughter is dead. There's nothing anyone can do about that, and *sorry* doesn't change anything."

"That's a good start," she said softly.

"What?" He stomped around to the driver's side.

She got into the car. "Saying that *sorry* doesn't change anything," she said. "You're right—it doesn't. It's just a lame thing for people to say when there is nothing that can be said to ease the pain of loss." Just as she said that she didn't understand why she felt so compelled to help him. Only that the desire came from her heart. Maybe the impending day when he'd become the father of her living and breathing baby had something to do with that.

"They all mean well, though," she added.

He just shook his head and Penny sensed he'd taken all he could.

"Just know I'm here if you ever want to talk about it. I won't ask questions. I won't say I'm sorry. I'll just listen."

His rigid face told her how hard he tried to control the firestorm inside him. She sat back and looked ahead, just then seeing that they were following Dane.

"He left?"

"About the time you said you'd start to get pretty tired of yourself."

He'd just methodically gotten into the car and taken up a covert chase with her going on and on about his loss. She contemplated his rugged profile, thick black hair just messy enough, clean-shaven but strong-featured face, bright gray eyes reflecting light. She pictured him in an office somewhere, the leader of a corporation, and the image disintegrated into open space, a wild stream, mountains in the distance. But just as driven and smart as the corporate version. Maybe more so.

Passing a sign for Cottonwood Canyon, Penny wondered why Dane headed into the mountains. Where was he going? Shadows grew long and Kadin kept as much distance as he could on the winding highway.

When he slowed, she saw Dane turn onto a side road, this one unpaved. Dust billowed up and lowered visibility, but provided a trail for them to follow. Around a hairpin curve, they passed his car. He'd pulled off the side of the road.

"Did he see us?" she asked.

"Seems that way." He drove farther up the road, reaching a driveway. Kadin turned there.

The mountain home with a barn and corral at the end of the driveway struck her as familiar. Had she seen this place before? Yes, Jax's boarded-up house and barn. This did have a resemblance, only this one appeared in better shape. Slightly more maintained. And no boarded windows. As Kadin turned the car around, she noticed more details, and some differences between the two properties. Architecturally, this one leaned more toward Victorian, the roof having more angles and the windows less symmetrical.

"Something wrong?" Kadin asked.

"No. I just wish I knew where Dane was going."

"That makes two of us."

As they reached the pull-off where Dane had gone, Penny didn't see him. Had he gone back down the mountain?

"We have company."

Penny twisted and saw a black Jeep Wrangler come up behind them. Hoodie Man. Fading light and dust kept Penny from seeing him clearly, but she did see him move to lift a weapon.

"He has a gun!" she shouted.

Kadin reacted immediately. He stepped on the gas and

drove wildly around the next turn just as a bullet hit the passenger-side mirror.

"He's shooting at us!"

"Get down," Kadin ordered, maneuvering into the next curve.

Penny bent forward and braced herself against the console and grabbed hold of the door handle. A rapid succession of bullets pinged the outside of the car. One shattered the rear window.

Penny made sure Kadin hadn't been hit and then stole a quick look back. The driver reloaded.

"Take this." Penny saw the pistol Kadin handed her. "It's ready to fire." She took it from him and saw him retrieve his second gun, driving one-handed into another dusty turn. They were almost to the highway.

Twisting, she stayed as low as she could and aimed through the rear window. She'd fired guns before, but not often and certainly not enough to give her confidence. She got lucky enough to get close, though. The driver had to duck and veer to throw her off.

He finished reloading and started firing back.

Penny crouched low on her seat. A bullet hit the windshield and a spiderweb of cracks spread. Kadin skidded into the last curve on the dirt road, giving him an angle to shoot.

Penny looked back and saw the driver of the Jeep hold his shoulder and slow down. She fired the last of her bullets as Kadin reached the highway and swung the car out into traffic. A car honked as it passed, missing them by about twenty feet. Another car approaching the other direction had to slam on their brakes but couldn't stop in time. The car rear-ended them. Hard.

Penny felt the whiplash and could see little of what happened next as Kadin lost control and the car slid into a three-sixty and then rolled once. Disoriented, she blinked and shook her head and searched through the broken windows.

Kadin had already gotten out of the car. He yelled at the driver who'd rear-ended them to keep moving. Seeing his drawn gun, the driver of that car complied, squealing tires as he sped off.

Searching for the black Jeep, Penny spotted it still on the dirt road, door open and no sign of the driver. She opened the glove compartment and found two more clips there. Knowing Kadin, he probably had ammunition stored in many other places. She took one for him and got out of the passenger's side. The car had stopped upright and facing the right direction but it was in the gentle ditch along the road. A few feet off the road, rocks rose a few hundred feet. They were lucky not to have hit that.

Crouching low, she didn't hear Kadin firing anymore and, in the next instant, the Jeep driver fired back at him. Where was he firing from? She spotted movement on her side of the road. The gunman jogged in the trees, toward her.

Oh no. Was he coming after her?

She scrambled to the front of the car for cover and fired toward the man. He stopped his movement toward her and went behind a tree, peeking out to check Kadin's position.

Using the hood of Kadin's car, she aimed and fired, hitting the tree trunk and forcing the Jeep driver to duck.

As soon as he did, she stood up and threw the extra clip across the road. Kadin saw her. The clip dropped off the side of the road. Kadin pointed toward the other man with his gun.

She resumed her position over the hood and shot. Kadin retrieved the clip and reloaded his gun.

The Jeep driver fired, missing by far. He wasn't a good shot.

Penny fired back as he tried to make his way to her. He made it to the rock face, taking shelter behind a jutting boulder.

Fear threatened to overtake her adrenaline. He had good cover from Kadin now. Kadin must realize that, because he tried to leave his tree and come back to her. The Jeep driver shot his gun each time he tried.

Penny waited until the Jeep driver left the boulder and ran for the car. A bullet hit the fender as she went down.

Looking across the street, she met Kadin's intent face before hearing the other man shoot across the highway as he tried to reach her. Why was he coming after her? To use her to draw Kadin out and then kill them both?

She crawled to the rear of the car. Not hearing the man, she moved toward the other side of the car at the rear.

"Penny, no!" Kadin shouted.

Too late, she learned why. The Jeep driver had gone there, too, and now intercepted her. He aimed his gun at her. Up close, she saw that he wore a mask of a famous football quarterback. She wasn't into football and only recognized the face. His shoulder wound had soaked his light blue sweatshirt with blood but hadn't slowed him down much.

"Come here," he said.

She crawled with the barrel of his pistol to her forehead. "Stand up."

When she did, he held her in front of him, a barrier between him and Kadin. He sidestepped up the road, toward the Jeep. Penny watched Kadin try to step out from the tree.

Her captor fired at him.

Kadin moved to the other side of the tree and fired back, then came out from behind the tree and spent a second more to aim. The next time he shot, he hit the Jeep driver, who grunted and stumbled back. Penny rammed her elbow into his sternum. He fell onto his rear, holding his cheek where the bullet had grazed him, looking up at her and then at Kadin, who strode toward him. He stood up and started to raise his gun.

Penny kicked his arm, and the gun went sailing. Watching that instead of him, Penny wasn't ready for the blow the Jeep driver delivered to her head. She fell hard onto the gravelly side of the road. Her vision blurred and her head spun. She propped herself up with her hands, seeing the Jeep driver run past the rock outcrop and up into the trees.

Kadin fired several times, but when he reached her, he kneeled and grasped her shoulders, helping her sit upright.

"Are you okay?"

Holding her swimming head, she barely saw him clearly. Her head couldn't take any more blows.

"Go after him," she rasped, certain she'd almost been captured by Sara Wolfe's killer.

"He's gone and I'm out of bullets. Are you all right?"

She nodded. "I think so."

He looked up the highway. There was a line of three cars stopped. The first car moved forward, going slowly.

The driver looked dazed and frightened, an older man. He rolled his window down next to them.

"I called the police," he said.

As Penny wondered how he'd managed to get reception, Kadin lifted her onto his lap. She rested her head on his shoulder, wishing she could do this all the time—without the danger.

Kadin wouldn't let Penny up off the couch the next day. She reclined with her laptop and a glass of iced tea on the coffee table, the television playing a documentary about Yellowstone at a low volume. He'd picked out the program and Penny concentrated on keeping Mark calm and having a chat session with Jax on the next phase of the ad campaign. Her ex hadn't mentioned anything about Dane, so she didn't think he knew what had happened. He also behaved neutrally, very businesslike, professional. No personal feelings coming through or any mention of her taking rope fibers from his house. Well, she hadn't; Kadin had. But she wasn't going to enlighten him.

Is Dane in the office? she typed. They'd reached the end of their discussion.

No, why?

How are things between you?

He hasn't spoken with me. Why do you ask?

Detective Cohen is looking into him.

Several minutes went by before Jax responded. Anything Dane says is probably a lie. Detective Cohen will have to catch him doing something wrong.

As in, kidnapping another girl? Has he gone anywhere lately?

Not that I know of.

Has he been at work all week?

Is this where I tell you to talk to my attorney?

Penny expected him to back off as soon as the topic veered off work.

Sorry, she typed.

No. I want you to catch the man who killed the Wolfe girl.
I just have to be careful.

Not quite the response she expected. Rather than be defensive, he had a good reason for not talking to her about this. Anything he said could be used against him.

Her phone rang. She started to get up and Kadin held his hand up in a stop sign.

Sighing, Penny leaned back against her pile of pillows and waited while Kadin went to the phone. When he said, "Send him up," she knew the concierge had called with a visitor.

She sat up, swinging her feet to the floor. Detective Cohen had come to the car wreck site and been part of the investigation after she and Kadin had been ambushed. The police had tried to find the shooter with no luck.

When her apartment bell rang, Kadin let the detective in.

"Kadin," Cohen said.

"Detective." Kadin shut the door as the man walked in.

"Penny. Are you all right?"

"Yes, I'm fine." *Just pregnant and keeping that a secret.*

The two came to her. The detective sat on one of the chairs opposite her.

"Can I get you anything?" Kadin asked Cohen.

Penny found that odd but charming, since this was her apartment, not his.

"No. This won't take long. And I don't want to keep Penny from her rest."

"The only reason I'm on this couch is that Kadin is making me stay here." She smiled sweetly and earned an answering grin from Cohen. He glanced up at Kadin.

"You just might be what he needs. Someone to take care of."

Kadin's face froze with the innuendo. He had lost the family he'd cared for before meeting Penny.

"I'm not the *take care of* type," she said, mostly because that was true but also to spare Kadin the speculation that they were a couple. Still, the detective must have picked up on something.

"What brings you by?" Kadin asked. He had a way of doing that, bluntly steering the conversation right to the point.

Detective Cohen lost his sociable face and regarded them grimly. "Another girl has gone missing."

Oh no...

They hadn't caught the pedophile and he'd kidnapped another girl. Penny felt sick to her stomach and it had nothing to do with her pregnancy. Urgency to find the girl overwhelmed her. She saw Kadin go rigid with the news, no doubt picturing his daughter, and fearing as she did that they wouldn't find this new girl in time. He sat down next to Cohen.

"She was on her way to a friend's house. Her mother was the last to see her. She left the family home and rode her bike a route she'd taken numerous times before. Well lit. Populated. There's a park on the way that's heavily wooded. The entrance is open, but the bike trail through there is sheltered for a short stretch. That's where we found her bike."

And where she'd been taken.

"The subject must have gotten her to stop," Cohen continued. "The ground is disturbed near her bike, suggesting she was forced into the trees. He could have gotten her to his vehicle in the parking area."

"Out in the open?" Penny asked.

"It was after dinner last night. The park empties at that

time. We're talking to neighbors and anyone who may have driven by at that time."

Gathering statements would take time.

Kadin stood up and swore as he walked away, across her living room to the balcony doors. Penny knew that deep down he blamed himself for this. He thought he should have caught the killer by now, and feared he wouldn't be able to save this next girl. "Her name is Makayla Moore," Cohen added. "Thirteen years old. Artistic. She draws animals, her mother says. Does good in school. She has lots of friends in the neighborhood. Her mother says she even knows the geriatrics. Brings an old woman cookies every once in a while."

"She sounds like a sweet girl," Penny said.

Kadin kept his back to them. This had to be so hard for him.

"Her mother said Makayla had a strange incident a few weeks ago at the Cottonwood Tiny Town up Highway 190."

That brought Kadin turning to face them. "Highway 190?"

"Yeah, that sprang out at me, too," the detective said.

The Cottonwood Tiny Town was a popular attraction, with small versions of town buildings, like giant dollhouses set up to resemble a town. Kids could play in the stores and houses that were sized just for them. There was a train that circled the town that people could ride and enjoy the views of both the town and the surrounding mountains.

"What strange incident?" Kadin prodded.

"She couldn't say. Makayla wouldn't elaborate. Just said she came home early because the place freaked her out."

Something had scared her. What had that something been? A man?

"We should concentrate the search there," Kadin said.

Cohen nodded. "Already have teams combing the area."

Penny watched Kadin and didn't have to be inside his head. He wouldn't leave the search up to others. He'd conduct his own.

"We talked to one of her friends, but she wouldn't give us anything. I think she was afraid." Cohen handed Kadin a small note paper page with the girl's name and address. "Maybe you'll have better luck."

Something told Penny that he would. Sheer will and determination would make it so.

Chapter 13

"You're going to frighten her with those guns," Penny said as Kadin parked in front of a beige and white tri-level.

He reached in the back for his leather jacket and then got out, donning the jacket as Penny came around and took hold of the open sides, tugging down to straighten and check.

"All hidden?" he asked, unable to keep affection from his tone.

She looked up with a responding, flirty grin. "Looking good, cowboy." She pushed the rim of his hat up and rose to plant a kiss on his mouth.

Damn.

He almost drew her against him, but she moved back and the heels of her boots clicked on the sidewalk. In another pair of sexy jeans and a bodice-fitting blouse that dipped just enough to get his blood warming, he watched her a moment before catching up.

The young girl's mother let them inside and went to sit next to her daughter and clasped her hand with hers. Something had this family spooked and he had a sneaking suspicion that it was merely the parents being paranoid. Nobody wanted to be involved in a major crime.

"You don't have to be afraid," Penny said kindly. "This man is only trying to help. He's just going to ask you a few questions, okay?"

The girl nodded tentatively.

Her mother bent her head to study her face. "Honey, if you know something, tell this man. He needs to find that missing girl."

The girl looked sheepishly at her mother. "But...I don't want to get Michael in trouble."

"Michael?" Her mother looked up at them. "That's my son."

"Where is your brother?" Kadin asked, growing impatient.

"He and his father went to the store," the mother said. "They should be home any moment. I should warn you... my husband is sensitive about police coming to our house asking questions about a possible murder victim. He thinks our justice system convicts too many innocent people." She then turned to her daughter. "Tell us what you know, honey. It's all right. No one's going to arrest Michael."

Penny glanced at Kadin, who met her questioning look and confirmed what he thought. Michael would be in trouble if he had anything to do with Makayla's disappearance.

"Makayla is his friend." Those young, shy eyes slid up to Kadin. "He was supposed to meet her at their favorite place. That golf place. He said he was scared, after she went missing, that her parents would think he did something."

"There's a fun center with games and go carts and putt-

putt golf near Old Miner's Park where her bike was found," the girl's mom said. "It's on the way to the fun center, a shortcut."

"She could have lied about going to her friend's house," Penny said to Kadin.

"Did Michael ever mention his relationship with Makayla and her family?"

The mother shook her head. "He's two years older than Makayla. I suppose her parents might have restricted her, but he never told me."

Kadin looked at the daughter. "What about you? Did Michael ever say anything to you?"

"He called her mom a bad word." The girl's face turned bashful.

"Did he see Makayla the night she disappeared?" Kadin asked.

The girl shook her head. "She didn't show up at the fun center."

"But he talked to her."

The girl turned to her mother, who said, "It's okay, tell them."

Facing Kadin, she said, "Yes. I heard him. Then he said for me to tell Mommy where he was going."

"Did you?" Kadin asked.

"No."

"By the time I got home from work, Makayla had already gone missing."

"Michael told me he was afraid," the girl said.

"You did the right thing by telling me this," Kadin said. "You've been a big help."

The girl smiled, her timidity fading.

Just then the front door opened and father and son appeared, the father's laughter stopping short when he saw

Kadin and Penny. Michael looked at his little sister as though she'd betrayed him.

"Come on, pumpkin." The girl's mother took her hand and led her from the couch to go up the bi-level stairs, pausing to say something low to her husband.

The man looked at Kadin as the mother and daughter went upstairs.

Kadin went to offer his hand in greeting. "Kadin Tandy. And this is—"

"I know who you are. We heard about you on the news. Are you working with the police? Because we already talked to them."

Protective dad. Penny gave Kadin a look, indicating she'd let him handle this delicate situation.

"Michael, I'm not a policeman. I help parents find their missing children. Your sister told me that you're friends with a girl I'm trying to find. Makayla Moore?"

The boy, who was nearly as tall as his dad but skinny, looked up at his father.

"Like I said, we already talked to the police, so unless we need to hire an attorney, I'm going to ask you to leave," the man said.

Why wouldn't they want to help? Kadin understood Michael fearing the appearance of guilt, but he looked guiltier by not talking.

"Please." Kadin ignored the man. "If there's anything you know. Your sister said you were supposed to meet her at a fun center the day she went missing, but she didn't show up."

"His sister is just a young girl. Now, Mr. Tandy—"

Tired of him getting in the way just because he was paranoid about the legal system, Kadin stepped in front of the man, taller by a good three inches and in much better shape. He wore his cowboy hat today, and the gentleman gave him a wary look.

"Let the boy talk."

"He's my son!"

"I'm not a cop, Michael." Kadin paid no attention to the father. "You won't be in any trouble. As long as you had nothing to do with Makayla's disappearance, no one's going to hurt you. But if you refuse to talk to me, I'm going to have to report to the lead detective that I believe you did have something to do with her disappearance because you seem to be hiding something."

"I don't have nothing to hide," the boy shot back, frightened. Had his parents frightened him into not talking? Why? Overly overprotective? Kadin had never been that way with Annabelle. He'd wanted her to feel free to explore any adventure, as long as it wasn't life-threatening. She'd been well on her way to discoveries when she'd gone missing.

"You're scaring him," the father said.

"He should be scared. If he knows something, he should do the right thing and tell me." Kadin put his hands on the boy's shoulders. "I need to find Makayla. We don't have much time."

"I told the police all I know," Michael insisted.

"Did you? Did you really?"

The boy could see he'd caught on to the lie.

Kadin decided to push. "Did you go to the Cottonwood Tiny Town with Makayla Moore?"

Michael tried to step past him. "I told you all I know!"

Kadin took his arm and brought his face down over Michael's. "Your parents have you scared, Michael. Just tell me if you were there with her."

"We went there a lot."

"What happened the last time you were there?"

"Nothing!"

"Did she see someone? A man?"

The boy's mouth fell open and he glanced at his dad, who'd stopped protecting him, seeming surprised that his son might know more.

"Go on," the dad said, "tell him."

Michael slowly looked up at Kadin. "She said there was a boy watching her. He scared her because he wore a sweatshirt with the hood up over his head. He stood there just staring at her."

That sounded like their man. Kadin kept his excitement from showing. "Did you see the boy?"

Michael nodded. "There was something weird about him. The way he stared. But when we noticed, he turned and walked away."

Kadin let go of his arm. "Why do you think he was a boy?"

Michael shrugged. "He was tall, not curvy. I didn't really get a good look at him. He could have been a man."

A man, not a boy. That perception intrigued Kadin. His phone rang and he answered, mouthing, *Cohen* to Penny. He moved away from Michael and his father.

"Kadin. You're going to want to meet me just past mile marker twelve. Dane Ballard was killed this afternoon."

Kadin parked on the side of the highway, not far from where he'd wrecked his Charger. He got out of the car, Penny after him, seeing Dane's Mercedes upside down on the banks of the stream, at the base of a steep slope. He walked toward Detective Cohen, who stood with other officers on the side of the road.

"How'd he end up down there?" Kadin asked as he shook the detective's hand.

"A witness saw a black Jeep behind the Mercedes just before he went over," Cohen said.

"He was driven off the road?" Kadin asked.

"Looks that way. The witness said he had to veer out of the way. The Mercedes was ahead of the Jeep and they were driving fast. The witness came around the turn back there and saw the Mercedes in the ravine. He stopped and called 911."

"Did he get a look at the Jeep driver?"

"No. but he did get a plate number, and we just learned the Jeep was reported stolen."

"Not Jax's?"

"No," Cohen said. "Definitely wasn't his."

Kadin tapped a finger against his chin, thinking. The killer had stolen Jax's vehicle in Sara Wolfe's case. Fibers matched those found in Jax's home. Whoever had done this knew the Ballard family, and maybe had it out for them. Or had Dane begun to get too close to figuring out why Jax's truck had been burned in the barn? He'd driven up here before. Where had he been headed?

"Dane's wife couldn't say why her husband decided to drive up this highway tonight," Cohen added. "He usually takes I-80 when he goes to see his brother in Park City."

"This is not adding up," Penny said, looking up the highway and then down at Dane's Mercedes. "There has to be something off this highway."

"We're looking into that."

But were they looking close enough? Kadin stared up the highway as Penny had done. What if Makayla was here somewhere? They could be so close and not know. She could be suffering and they could save her...if they only knew where to find her. A familiar wave of helplessness came over him. So many similarities between the past and the present. The way Annabelle had vanished so close to home…all of that unspeakable violence being carried out while he'd searched blindly for her. Lack of knowledge had cost him her life. Hiding information had been her killer's powerful secret weapon.

More than anything, Kadin wanted to take that power away from Sara Wolfe's kidnapper.

There had to be something. Some clue that would open this case wider. Lead them to a demented killer. Save a child.

No, there was something he wanted more than taking power away from a dangerously warped criminal. He wanted to save Makayla. He *needed* to save her. No more children could die on his watch.

"What about the previous owner of Jax's property?" Kadin said.

"I'm not following you. What would he have to do with this?" Cohen asked, lifting an inquisitive brow. "We checked him out. He doesn't live here anymore."

"He didn't move far. Fifty miles from here." Kadin began to organize his thoughts.

While he did, Cohen studied him as though impressed. "You've been conducting your own investigation."

Of course he had. That was why Cohen had welcomed him onto his team. That was why Sara Wolfe's parents had asked for him by name. He respected Cohen and his ability as a detective, but he wouldn't stand idly by and wait for the law to deliver him clues. He'd investigated the previous owner of Jax's property as soon as suspicion turned toward him. While nothing he found implicated the man, he had never been far from his persons of interest list.

"What makes him suspicious to you?" Cohen asked.

"Jax's stolen truck, the trapdoor in the abandoned house. What if he initially used the basement for the girls?"

Detective Cohen pondered that a moment, rocking on

his heels with his hands on his hips. Then he nodded. "Okay. I'd buy that theory. He used his old house and when Jax bought it, got mad and stole his truck. He wouldn't care if Jax was implicated in the crime."

"And now he's had to find a new location."

Penny put her finger to her mouth and then wagged it as a thought came. "But that was a trapdoor in the kitchen floor. If he already had the girl under his control, why the need for a trapdoor?"

"The cuts did look new in the floor," Kadin said.

Detective Cohen looked from Penny to Kadin. "We'll take a closer look at the previous owner. Locate him. Have him watched."

Good. While he did that, he and Penny could concentrate on Jax.

Penny's phone went off. She had a text message. Kadin saw her hand tremble as she read and he grew alert.

"What is it?" he asked.

She showed him the message.

You're next if you don't back off.

"May I?" Cohen took the phone and, after reading the message, handed it to one of his other detectives. "See if you can trace that call."

"Yes, sir." The man took the phone and went over to a windowless van.

Kadin followed with Penny at his side.

The detective opened the side door and revealed a state-of-the-art crime scene van. The office area behind the driver's cab could also function as a command center, with all the latest communications equipment. He climbed inside where two other officers sat before laptops. Kadin stepped up into the large van as well, taking Penny's hand to help her up.

She eyed him as though his act of chivalry had warmed her. For a tough businesswoman, she sure could be soft with him. He tried to deny how much he liked that.

Behind the office area, a sliding-glass door separated a more spacious work area with coin-style flooring and several shelves and bins to store evidence. A fume hood with an exhaust fan had been installed above the long, stainless steel countertop for working with chemicals. There were other items as well—a portable generator, refrigerator and sink, even a small bathroom.

He'd gotten well acquainted with the crime scene van for his daughter, and it hadn't been as swanky as this. The detectives hadn't allowed him to participate in much of the processing, naturally, but he'd insisted on studying the evidence. A year later and Kadin had tracked down her killer. Six men had to stop him from killing the man.

"Kadin?"

He turned to Penny, aware that he'd drifted off into memory and that he'd been staring aimlessly at the evidence bins.

"Are you all right?"

"Fine," he replied curtly. He'd gotten good at pushing the worst thoughts back to the dark pits of his mind.

The detective had handed one of the officers Penny's phone, and that one worked away on his laptop. The screen ran text and switched to a new display.

"Must have been one of those disposable phones. Bet he tossed it after sending the text."

"Find out who sells disposable phones in the area and then look for anyone who's bought one in the last week," Kadin said.

Detective Cohen nodded his consent to the men in the van.

"We'll go try to find Jax," Kadin said. "Clearly his brother isn't the one trying to frame him."

"Maybe no one is trying to frame him," Penny said.

No, Kadin thought to himself, he had a niggling feeling that Jax knew more than he'd let on. He'd had that feeling all along.

"Be careful with him," Cohen said to Kadin.

Kadin needed no warning. He could handle Ballard and any danger he kept hidden. Jax's DNA didn't match what had been recovered from Sara Wolfe's crime scene, but he had to be connected somehow, whether through the previous owner of his property or not.

Unable to locate Jax, Kadin took Penny back to her apartment. What she didn't expect to find waiting for her was her father. That came as quite a shock. The sputtering deadbeat dad she'd met in North Dakota seemed more the type to hide in his perfect life. But he hadn't. The concierge had allowed him to sit in the lobby until they arrived. Now, late at night, she could see him in the small sitting area, looking right at her.

Penny stopped walking. "Did you…"

"I didn't arrange this, no," Kadin said, standing beside her and placing his hand on her shoulder.

Her father stood and after a few seconds of hesitation, he stepped nervously toward her.

"Kadin gave me your contact information," he said.

When had he done that? She sent him a glare.

"I emailed it to him before we left North Dakota," Kadin explained.

Another thing he'd neglected to tell her? She didn't reprimand him now, not in front of her father.

"I hope you don't mind me coming here unannounced," Alias said. "After you left, I've thought of nothing else but you. Can we talk?"

He wanted to talk? *Now*…after all these years? Her anger sprang from her core, sensitivity she normally didn't have making her vulnerable. She didn't know what to do with it, this foreign feeling of insecurity. Why did she feel this way? She'd never been insecure before. What had shifted inside of her?

Traitorous thoughts ran back to when Kadin had asked her if she'd moved to Salt Lake City to get away from her mother. She'd said no, but now she wondered if that was completely true. Why had she left her hometown? Why, really?

To get away from her mother? Or to avoid this? She may have told herself she didn't want to know about her father, but she did. She didn't want to know about why he left, why she hadn't been important enough to keep in his life.

She feared attempting to start a family because of that. And now she was pregnant and afraid of what Kadin would do.

He wasn't a good choice for a family man. He was what her mother called a *runner*.

"Maybe now isn't a good time," her father said in her lengthy silence.

"No." Her hurt came from insecurity and she'd not allow that to dictate her actions. "Come up to my apartment. I'm glad you came to see me."

She must have shocked both men. Kadin did a double take and her father's face went slack in surprise.

"This won't be easy on you," she said to her father and then looked pointedly at Kadin. "Either of you." When Kadin grinned at the fiery woman he recognized, she headed for the elevator.

Up in her apartment, she sat her father at the kitchen island and went about getting them water. Kadin left them alone, going into the guest room with his laptop. She felt incredibly awkward as she put two glasses down on the island counter. Moments later, she found the courage to look at him, his face, his features, trying to determine which resembled hers. Not much. She resembled her mother more.

Seeing that he'd done the same with her, she breathed a laugh and took a sip of water.

"Are you sure you're my daughter?" he asked, breaking the tension.

"Are you sure you're my dad?"

With that, his joking faded and he became serious. "Penny, I want to explain."

"You already did."

"That I was young, yes. But I was wrong for not coming to see you sooner. During college. After. Definitely before I met my wife and had kids."

Not able to disagree, she didn't respond.

"I was a coward. I also knew how your mother felt about me, or thought she did."

"You don't think she loved you?"

He shook his head. "No, I know she did love me, the way any seventeen-year-old loves. But I don't believe she loved me like two people should when they get married and have kids."

She couldn't argue with that. "Sometimes I think she still loves you."

"She has the idea that she does, or that she did." He drank some water and pressed his hands together, his forearms on the island counter. "You see, your mother is a feisty, fun-loving, independent woman."

She smiled. "Boy, you have that right."

"She was always that way. Fiercely independent. We

would argue about everything. I had to give in or she wouldn't give up. She had to live her own way."

That sounded familiar. Penny stopped smiling. He'd just described her.

"I'm not saying that's bad, but if you ever wonder why your mom never married, that's why. She doesn't need a man in her life."

"I think she does."

"She may fancy the idea of being able to have one in her life, but she doesn't want one, Penny." His hands came apart as he spoke with them.

How did he know so much about her when he'd only been with her a few years when they were so young?

"That's why I left," he confessed. "Not just because I felt, in my selfish young head, that she'd rob me of college and the future I dreamed of by tying me down with a baby. Not just because having you to take care of terrified me. She didn't want me. She wanted the *idea* of me. Does that make sense?"

Penny had to nod.

"I'm not trying to justify my actions. I should not have left your mother with the sole responsibility of raising you. And I damn sure should have contacted you long before now. It should have been me who came to find you. For that, I'm deeply sorry."

What was she supposed to say to that? She didn't feel forgiveness. She felt angry and hurt that he hadn't. But she did feel capable of forgiveness…someday.

"Why do you think my mother could never live with a man?" she finally asked. Although she had never really fully analyzed that, she did wonder.

"She blamed me. She contacted me from time to time up until you were about three, claiming she loved me and that I ruined her life."

Deep down, that was what her mother believed. Maybe having a daughter made it harder for her to find another man. Maybe she had feared the rejection. Her mother fearing anything didn't jibe. Unless she'd gotten good at putting on a face. That notion saddened Penny. Was her mother unhappy? She sometimes mentioned that maybe she should have tried harder to find someone, but then she'd be off on her way to a book club meeting or a lunch with friends or a new volunteer job. Her mother had never spent much time sitting around at home.

"She isn't interested in sharing her life," Penny finally said.

"Except with you."

"Kids are different. She could tell me what to do."

He chuckled. "You came out all right. Kadin told me all about you. You're successful. And you got out of Michigan."

"Kadin stuck his nose where it didn't belong."

Her father swatted the air with his hand. "Aw, he meant well. Don't punish him for something I did wrong."

Don't punish him when it had been her father who'd abandoned her and hadn't had the courage to confront her.

"Besides," her estranged father said, "he did it for you."

"What?" What was he talking about?

Her father glanced over toward the hallway and the closed guest room door. Then, leaning forward over the island counter, he said in a low tone, "Kadin didn't just email me. He called and we spoke awhile. He said he found me when he did a background check on you and that you weren't happy he kept that fact from you. You had told him you didn't want to find me."

"Yes, I did." Funny, how finding out anyway changed how she felt.

"He cares a great deal for you. I may be a nerdy engineer, but I can tell when someone has feelings for another person. That man does, for you. Is there something going on between the two of you?"

Penny's face blanched. Confiding in her father about her pregnancy seemed highly inappropriate at this early stage of their reunion. "Nothing…nothing yet."

"I would have come no matter how important it was to him. In fact, I was going to reach out to Kadin when he called."

Penny didn't engage further. Talking to Alias as though he'd been a real father since her birth felt too awkward.

He must have seen that in her, because he leaned back and studied her thoughtfully. "What would you like to do going forward, Penny?"

"What would *you* like to do?"

"Well, I'd like to do the right thing. My wife isn't speaking to me and we've told the kids they have a half sister. We're all in a bit of an upheaval at the moment. But I'd like to plan a get-together some time."

Penny didn't think she wanted to pursue a family-type relationship with him or his wife and kids. "I'd be open to a meeting. Beyond that, I'm not sure getting to know each other makes much sense at this point."

She could tell from his shocked expression that he hadn't expected her to respond that way. "All right. We all need time to adjust…"

"No, I mean, I don't think we need to be a family. I can be friends but not family."

After staring at her for several long moments, he said, "You are your mother's daughter."

"What?" Should she be insulted?

"Penny, I'd like us to get together as a family someday. I'd like to welcome you into mine. Don't shut us out the way your mother shuts everyone out."

"My mother doesn't shut *everyone* out. Only those who betray her."

Her father raised his hand to stop her outburst. "I didn't mean it like that. I only meant that being independent is good up until it costs you loving relationships."

That might as well have been a slap to her face. Would her independence cost her a loving relationship with Kadin? Her way of relating became suddenly crystal clear. Her mother carried her independence too far and Penny was on her way to doing exactly the same. The way she was with men proved it. Kadin was the first man who ever made her feel out of control. And she was ready to walk away from him.

Chapter 14

Penny woke to her phone ringing. Groaning, she rolled to her side and reached for her cell, lifting it as her stomach lurched with nausea.

Jax.

Sitting up, she answered.

"I need you to meet me," he said.

Meet him. Why? "Jax…I'm so sorry about Dane. Do you know who ran him off the road?"

"Yes. And I'll tell you if you meet me. But you have to come alone."

Alone? Why alone? "I can't come alone, Jax."

"You will or I won't tell you who killed my brother, and who kidnapped those girls. I also know where Makayla Moore is. Meet me."

He knew?

"Get a pen."

She opened her side table drawer and wrote down an address—one off Highway 190.

"Jax, how do you know who killed your brother. Why was he killed?"

"Meet me and I'll tell you. And, Penny…"

"Yes?"

"There's another reason I want to meet."

She waited.

"You. I want to put all this behind us and pick up where we left off. We had a good thing going."

She and Jax had had a good thing going before Kadin had come into her life, but she heard insincerity in his tone. He worried how much Kadin had ruined them and now may be looking to do damage control. But little did he know there was nothing he could do about her pregnancy. That changed everything, regardless of Kadin's reaction to knowing.

Her stomach put off a wave of nausea she wouldn't be able to ignore. "When?"

"Tonight. Eight o'clock. And, Penny?"

"Yes?"

"I mean it about you coming alone. If I see you with anyone else, I'll leave."

"Why is it so important that I come alone?" He gave her an uneasy feeling, putting so much emphasis on that.

"Because the only other person who'll accompany you is Kadin Tandy. He's not man enough for you, Penny. You need someone like me."

She didn't tell him that she no longer felt anything for him, and that she felt so much more for Kadin—the soon-to-be father of her child. Keeping that to herself, she agreed to meet him. Anything to find out who preyed on girls.

And save Makayla Moore.

But if Jax knew the killer…

The rope fibers tied him to the crimes. He might not have committed them, but he knew of them.

After hanging up, Penny found herself out in the hall to a more urgent roll in her stomach. She saw Kadin walking toward her from the living room, showered and dressed for a casual, laid-back day. He made casual look sophisticated and for once didn't wear his hat or guns.

"I heard you on the phone."

Penny glanced at the bathroom as she passed, wondering how long she could hold off vomiting. She swallowed hard, and then again, stopping before him.

"Jax called."

"Jax?"

She hadn't sounded as monumental as that revelation warranted. She swallowed again and breathed deeply, blowing out.

"Are you all right?" He eyed her strangely.

The nausea rose and there would be no holding back. A projectile of her minimal stomach contents came up and out, splashing Kadin's chest.

He looked down in surprise and she in horror, but only for a second. Another rise of nausea would not be kept at bay.

She covered her mouth and darted into the bathroom, not sparing the time to close the door. She threw up for several minutes.

At last, when the first wave of sickness passed, she rinsed her mouth out and brushed her teeth. When she finished and put her brush back in the holder, she looked in the mirror at Kadin, who'd dampened a hand towel and wiped his chest.

"You've been getting sick a lot," he said, tossing the towel down.

She put her hand to her forehead. "Must be my head."

He turned on the faucet and washed his hands. "You've been getting sick almost every morning."

Penny braced herself with her hand on the counter, feeling the illness abate. "I still get a little dizzy in the morning."

"In the *morning*."

The way he looked, so apprehensive, stirred her anxiety. A smart detective such as himself would be able to figure this out. Perhaps he already had done so.

Suddenly she couldn't meet his eyes. He would not be happy to learn her news.

"Penny…"

Why did she have to feel cowed? He'd gotten her pregnant. Turning, she leaned against the bathroom counter.

"Please tell me you aren't—"

Planting her hands on his chest, she shoved him back and marched out of the bathroom. In the kitchen, she searched for something to calm her stomach, which had renewed its roiling.

"Penny…are you…"

She poured herself a glass of orange juice, stalling. She sipped some juice and set the glass down on the snack bar.

Kadin flattened his hands there and leaned toward her. "Are you?"

She took in his fierce gray eyes and the twitch of muscles as he ground his teeth. "Uh…"

He slapped the counter with one hand. "You are? How long have you known?"

"I…uh…" She couldn't find her tongue. How to tell him, a man so tortured by loss? She felt empathy and also resentment that she should have to carry this burden alone.

"When were you planning on telling me? Or were you?"

"Kadin—"

He pushed off the counter and straightened, stark-faced with apprehension, his worst nightmare coming true. Penny couldn't bear the sight and in that instant realized she secretly didn't disagree to having a baby with him. The lack of planning made for bad timing, sure, but the idea of something so intimate with him warmed rather than chilled. That he felt the opposite punched her soul, leaving her completely unprepared. "I thought… I assumed…" he stammered.

Kadin at a loss for words hammered down just how disagreeable he regarded having a baby. With her. With anyone. She could be any other woman on the planet right now. The threat came in the form of a child. A family. She could see instant replays of his life with the family he lost flash through the stark gleam in his eyes.

"I normally rely on condoms." To her own ears she sounded matter-of-fact, contradicting the obliteration going on inside, where he couldn't see. Both pride and a sensitivity for his past kept her together.

"You could have said something." He raked his fingers through his hair.

"When?" When had there been an appropriate time to bring that up? The first time they'd slept together hadn't been planned. No romantic dinner. No official date to precede such a responsible conversation. Their night of passion had nothing to do with responsibility.

None of the starkness left his gaze as he searched hers for something, and Penny wondered what he looked for. An answer to this *problem*? A solution. Way out. Escape. Place to run. She saw and felt his wild, desperate energy.

"I'm not getting an abortion," she said.

"I wasn't…" He lifted his arms, hands open as he faltered with what to say and how to say it, a man riddled with confusion.

"No?" Even in a state of chaos, she wouldn't have expected him to go there, to that extreme in order to spare himself the agony of making another family, of risking another terrible heartache.

"The thought crossed my mind, but I'd never ask you to do that. I'm against abortion."

Except in this situation? Penny felt something slip into place, a defensive wall. If he could even contemplate abortion, she lost a giant chunk of respect for him.

"I am," he insisted, seeing her reaction. The haunted wildness eased from him. "I just… I wasn't prepared for this. I didn't see it coming."

"You should have."

"Did you?"

Folding her arms, she walked to the big, white-framed casement window in her living room, not really seeing the view. There had been too much going on to pay attention to the potential consequences of sleeping together. Neither of them had.

This resembled what her mother had gone through. Her mother had been young, but the result would be the same. The man couldn't handle having a baby. He didn't feel enough for the mother and couldn't take on the responsibility, couldn't allow this to alter his course…his mission in life. Her father had college as his excuse. Kadin had saving the world from predators like the one that had taken his daughter. And, eventually, his wife.

"I'm not going to end up like my mother," she said aloud.

Turning, she saw Kadin standing across the room, with his hands in his pockets.

Whether with him or someone else, she refused to raise a child fatherless. But she'd be careful who she chose. She didn't have to love a man for him to be a good father.

This had become a business deal the moment she realized Kadin would not be there for her.

~~Because she loved Kadin. Finding that kind of love~~ now, with a baby on the way, reduced her options. She wouldn't wait the way her mother had. Wait until too much time passed, until she convinced herself no other man would give her love. That only Kadin could. Deep in her heart, she felt truth in that, an awful truth. She might never feel for another man the way she felt for Kadin. Her mother had faced the same truth, except she'd grown to believe her love had come and gone forever and had chosen a life without any man, believing she'd settle.

Penny wouldn't settle, but neither would she stop searching for a good father for her baby. She would not be alone. She would have a family.

"I need some time to think about this," Kadin finally said.

"Take all the time you need. Just do it away from me." She would not be tortured by his presence, his lack of joy over the news that Penny would have his baby. That came as another jolting revelation, that he lacked joy. Whereas she had tremendous joy. She hadn't recognized that sentiment until now.

"I can't leave until the killer is caught," he gritted out.

The tigress businesswoman in her emerged, her trusted strength. "Oh yes, you can. And you will. I don't want you in my house anymore."

Removing his hands from his pockets, he began to approach. "Penny…"

She unfolded her arms and held her hand up. "I understand why you're so repulsed. But you need to understand how I feel."

"I'm not repulsed."

"You're not happy."

He stopped a few feet from her, just when she would have moved away. "Are you happy? About...this?" He indicated her stomach with his hand.

She put her hand protectively over her stomach. "Yes."

"Then...why didn't you tell me as soon as you knew?"

"Why, indeed." She stomped over to the door. "Get your things and leave."

He didn't move. "It's dangerous for me to leave. You'll be in danger."

"I don't need you. I'm sorry for all you've been through, Kadin, but I have to think of myself right now. So, please. Get your things and leave."

Her tone must have told him she meant business. Without further argument, he went into the guest room. Her heart shattered with each second she waited for him. He would actually walk away. Just like her father. When he appeared with his bag, she opened her apartment door.

He stopped there.

Penny held on to the threads of her resolve. She did this for herself. For self-respect. And to let Kadin know that even though he had a terrible burden to overcome, he had to make a decision.

That night, Penny drove to meet Jax at the address he'd provided, downtrodden with thoughts of Kadin. That he'd walked away. That he hadn't been happy. But most of all, that he robbed her of her own happiness. The two of them had potential. Didn't he see that? The timing wasn't ideal, but news of a baby should be joyous. A time for celebration.

She supposed that only worked when both parents loved each other. Kadin didn't love her. He probably couldn't love anyone.

Turning onto the road Jax had given her in his directions, Penny realized she'd been here before. The dirt driveway ended at a Victorian-style home with a barn and corral that resembled his boarded-up house and barn. She stopped the car and debated whether to turn around. This had to be the reason Dane had driven up Highway 190.

She checked her cell phone. No service.

When she looked up, Jax had emerged from the house, his son behind him. That relaxed her a bit. He'd brought Quinten with him. But…

She looked toward the house and barn. Why hadn't he told her about this property?

Jax leaned down with a smile. Penny had the window down on this warm, pretty summer day.

"You going to come in?" he asked.

Penny felt she didn't have much choice. Taking her purse and dropping her cell inside, she turned off her car and got out.

"What is this place?"

"Dane's," Jax said.

Dane's. Penny looked at the house again. Of course. She'd seen this in Jax's digital picture display.

"What happened to Dane?" she asked before they reached the front steps.

"That's what I asked you here to tell you."

She was glad when he stopped on the front porch. She didn't want to go inside.

"Dane killed that girl."

"Sara Wolfe?"

"Yes. I found rope at his house. And I found clothing that belonged to her, at least we think it belonged to her. I tried to confront him, but he fought me and then ran. I chased him up the highway and he lost control of his car and wrecked. I'm sure you've heard by now?"

Penny nodded. "Did you call the police so they can process the evidence?"

"Not yet. I wanted to tell you first."

Why her? Penny's bad feeling began to expand. She looked at Quinten and noticed the shirt he wore. Pieces of that photo from Jax's digital display popped out at her. Quinten had worn the same exact shirt. He'd stood in front of this mountain home. And, most disturbing, there had been a white pickup truck there in the background. For the first time, she noticed his blank eyes. They watched her like a predator's.

He opened the front door.

Jax put his hand on her lower back. "Let's go inside."

Penny resisted. "No." She jerked her arm free and spun to run down the steps.

Jax caught her arm again and yanked her back around. Quinten had drawn a gun.

Penny looked from Quinten to Jax, who still maintained that innocent face she'd seen him put on for her.

"We'll go inside and talk this through," he said.

Talk?

How much talking would he do before he let his son kill her? Jax guided her firmly into the house, Quinten taking up the rear, his wordless, triumphant look the last she saw before facing the richly appointed house. Her gaze landed on a familiar sweatshirt draped over a kitchen chair.

Dane must have figured out what he'd done and tried to intervene, just like Jax. Only Jax had tried to cover up for his son.

Quinten had met his father in Park City the night Sara Wolfe had disappeared. He would have had ample time to kidnap her and take her here and then drive the back way to his dad's house on Highway 190. He'd been at his dad's mountain home the morning she went there and she and

Jax had walked to the burned barn, the day she fell through the trapdoor. He hadn't left. He'd stayed long enough to try to capture her. Jax had coaxed her inside. What would he have done if Kadin hadn't been there to rescue her?

What he'd do now that he'd lured her here…

Penny turned to Jax. "You knew."

He looked confused. "What? Knew what?"

"You've been protecting him."

"Dane kidnapped those girls. I was afraid you'd react this way, what with my pickup truck and rope found on my property. My brother hated me. He set me up."

"So…you asked me here to convince me?"

"Yes." He took both her hands and held them like a lover about to propose, making her sick. "Penny, I want us to be together. That can't happen if you keep thinking I had anything to do with Sara Wolfe's kidnapping and death. I didn't do it. Dane did."

Did he not know about the others? "When did you realize your son was a pedophile?"

Quinten scoffed. "Pedophile. Shut her up."

"You're not listening," Jax said. "It was Dane." His brow lowered and he took on a desperate frown. "Penny, we can be together. We can have a great life. I run Ballard's now. We can finish the ad campaign. Get married. Have kids. It will be wonderful."

Oh dear God, the man had gone off into la-la land. Delusional. Insane.

"There are other girls who've gone missing, Jax. Do you know about them?"

He flinched before he recovered, glancing over at an aloof Quinten. "Can the police prove Dane kidnapped them?"

"Don't you mean Quinten?"

"Quinten didn't do it." Denial based on blind love drove

Jax. He did not want to believe his son could do such a thing. "Dane planted the rope."

Penny saw how smug Quinten looked. "What about the DNA? It won't match Dane's." And she'd also received that threatening text *after* Dane had been driven off the road.

"He planted that, too, then. Penny, it was Dane, *not* my son."

What was the matter with him? Why did he protect his son this way? He loved Quinten, and quite possibly would do anything to protect him...including from charges of murder.

"No, Jax, Quinten kidnapped Sara Wolfe and now Makayla Moore." He had to know that by now. "It may not be too late for her." She searched the house. "Is she here?" Walking past them, she came to a closed door and would have opened it if Quinten didn't grab her arm and pull her back so hard she stumbled and fell onto her rear.

"We have to kill her, Dad."

Moving to stand in front of Penny, Jax held up his hands. "No, son. We don't have to."

"Yes, we do. Bring her downstairs and you'll see why."

Jax stood fixed for seconds, staring in disbelief at his son. "You didn't. It isn't true. What Penny said. You didn't take another girl."

"Bring her, or I'll shoot you both." Quinten wagged his gun impatiently. "She'll lure that hero cop here and once they're both gone, Detective Cohen will believe our story. Dane did everything."

"Dane can't kill her and Kadin," Jax said. "Dane is dead, remember? The detective will know one of us killed them."

"Then I'll tell them you did."

"You'd—" Jax stammered and couldn't find words fast enough. "I'm your father."

Penny realized how all this fell into place. "But he's not, is he?" When she had both men's attention, she said, "He isn't your real father." The DNA found on Sara Wolfe would have been a closer match to Jax's. That would have raised a big red flag and changed the course of the investigation.

"I adopted him after his mother left." Jax sounded near defeat.

He was her only way out of this. Jax wanted a life with her, even though somewhere in a rational part of his mind he had to know the police would figure out Dane hadn't done any of this. He'd tried to stop them both, and for that had lost his life. Dane, protector of his best friend, Mark, had even wanted to save his brother. Because Dane hadn't put the rope in Jax's closet. He also hadn't put the truck in the barn. Quinten had. Hoodie Man.

"Son…" Jax sounded pleading. Not a good sign.

The sign of weakness only gave Quinten more power. "You were never around for me," he said, sneering. "You cared more about Dane and that business than me. You were always trying to win his approval."

"That isn't true. I've protected you. Through all of this."

"I don't need protection."

He needed to go to prison, that was what he needed. Penny searched for a weapon. She still had her purse over her shoulder.

"I found out who my real father was. He died in Iraq. My mother was a piece of garbage and he was killed. You were never my dad. You could never be a hero like my real dad."

"Jax, don't let him do this," Penny said. "Quinten kidnapped and killed Sara Wolfe and the other girls. He also kidnapped Makayla Moore, and she's here."

"Take her downstairs," Quinten said.

Jax looked at the gun and then Penny.

She stood up and went to him. "We have to free that girl, Jax. You have to turn Quinten in to the police. And you have to tell them everything." When he only stared into her eyes with indecision, she said, "You have to realize your plan won't work. The evidence won't point to Dane. They have DNA from Sara and the other girl. Who do you think is going to be found guilty? Not Dane. Quinten will. And you'll go to prison for conspiring to help him. For hiding evidence."

"Dane planted the evidence."

Penny shook her head. "You know that isn't true." She put her hand on his upper arm. "I'm sorry, Jax."

"I burned the barn because Dane used my truck to kidnap Sara Wolfe."

That was what Quinten had told him. "Quinten stole your truck. Quinten put the rope in your closet. *Think*, Jax. He's your son, I understand that. But you have to face the truth now."

"Take her downstairs," Quinten demanded. "Shut her up."

Penny went to him and, with Jax watching, pressed Quinten's shoulder where the Hoodie Man had been shot.

Quinten winced and stepped back. "Get downstairs or I'll shoot you."

Seeing blood soak through Quinten's T-shirt, she faced Jax. "He chased us after we followed Dane up here. Kadin shot him."

Jax stared at Quinten, at the quarter-sized stain slowly growing on his shirt. He needed medical attention and hadn't gotten any. Jax went to Quinten.

His son pointed the gun at Jax now. "Stay back! I said get her downstairs. Now do it!"

Afraid that Quinten would fire his gun and fighting to

remain calm and clear-headed, Penny walked to the basement door on her own. At last, Jax followed. She took the
steps down to an unfinished open space. At the far end,
Quinten had framed in a rough wood room. No drywall.
The plywood door had a locked latch.

"Unlock it." Quinten gave his dad a key.

Jax took it numbly and unlocked the door. As he pushed
it open, a young girl cowered against the wall.

Penny turned to Jax, furious that he'd allow this to go
on. Maybe he hadn't known about the others, only Sara,
but he knew now.

"If you don't do something to help us, I'll kill you myself," she hissed, leaning close to his face.

He blinked a few times, seeming to come out of his
stupor. But he said nothing as Quinten gave her a shove
and she stumbled into the room.

"No," the girl wailed.

Penny forgot all of her own troubles and went to her,
taking her into her arms. "It's all right now, sweetie. You're
going to be all right."

The girl only cried against her shoulder.

"Did he hurt you?"

Makayla rolled her head in negation. "He scares me. He
made me come here and locked me in here." She leaned
her teary face back. "I want to go home. I want to see my
mom."

"You will. I'm going to get you out of here."

The girl clung to her and Penny hoped she could make
her promise come true.

Chapter 15

While the knowledge of Penny's pregnancy crushed him, Kadin had stayed close to her and had seen her drive into the mountains. All the way to the dirt road where she turned, he fought between confound over her decision to go here alone and dread over the impeding birth of their baby. *His* baby. His second baby. By the time he parked along the highway, he realized loving another child wasn't the crux of his issue. Fear of loving the second baby more was. He still struggled with so much guilt over not being able to save his little girl. He feared forgetting her, loving her less or not revering her enough.

The thought of holding a baby in his arms, a different baby, sent him into a cold sweat. Love and family. Could he love Penny? Did he already?

Could he love another child?

Imagining Penny's stomach growing, how beautiful she'd be, Kadin felt the tug of something other than fear.

Their baby had no face yet, but he could see Penny holding him or her, a tiny bundle. When he again thought of holding a baby—their baby, he felt the promise of love. But then his dead daughter's face materialized and he had to withdraw.

Frustrated, Kadin got out of his car and hiked through the trees along the dirt road. At a clearing, he saw a house but no sign of Penny's car. No sign of the black Jeep, either. There was no other way off this property other than the driveway. Had the cars been put inside the detached garage? Was Penny inside? Was the missing girl in there, too? He had to stop himself from going in alone.

Detective Cohen was on his way with more cops, but Kadin would not wait. If Penny and the child were inside this cabin, he'd do all he could to save them. But first he had to know more about this cabin and what he'd be charging into.

Back at his car, he used his satellite internet Wi-Fi hotspot to look up property records on his laptop. This house belonged to Dane Ballard. Jax had lured Penny here. Why do that? His DNA didn't match the killer's and he'd passed the lie detector test. He must be protecting someone. Dane? Dane was dead. Did he mean to draw Kadin here as well and kill them both? Kadin had to make sure he didn't succeed.

Just when Kadin would have returned to the cabin, the detective arrived, driving up in the crime scene van and parking in the dirt driveway, blocking any exit or entry. Another van, this one black, parked behind that. As a SWAT team filed out armed with black-layered polymer and ammo, Kadin got out of his rental and approached the crime scene van, where Cohen had opened the side door. The cabin wasn't visible from here. The driveway curved up into the trees, hiding them from sight.

"We're going to surround the place," Cohen said. "Let's talk strategy from there."

Kadin stepped up inside while the SWAT team jogged through the woods.

"I didn't have time to get intelligence," Cohen said with a frown.

"That's all right. I did." He explained what he'd learned.

"I suspected you would." Cohen moved closer to the counter where another detective had booted up a laptop. "Jax is in there now?"

"He must have a strong motivation to be involved," Kadin said. "I think he's protecting someone close to him."

"It can't be his brother," Cohen said. "The DNA isn't a close match to his."

There was only one other person who could motivate Jax that powerfully.

Cohen leaned over the countertop to navigate the laptop through some satellite images. "What are you thinking?"

"That Jax would only protect his son. He's a selfish guy, except when it comes to Quinten."

Cohen straightened to pin Kadin with a deeply thoughtful look.

One of the other detectives returned from outside to sit before a laptop.

"The perimeter is secure, sir," he said with his back to them.

"Look up Quinten Ballard," Kadin said to the man. "Find out if Jax Ballard is his biological father."

Quinten's mother had abandoned him, and Jax had raised the boy. Had Jax adopted Quinten? That would explain why the DNA didn't resemble Jax's.

The man at the laptop glanced back as though needing confirmation. A young adult deviating into child crimes did seem shocking, if not a stretch.

"Do it," Kadin said.

The man looked at Cohen, who nodded and then faced his laptop. Within minutes they had a copy of an adoption paper in front of them.

"I'll be damned," Cohen marveled, looking up at Kadin. "You're brilliant."

That was what losing your family to reprobates like this did to a man. Made him strive to be smarter and then to *be* smarter than the criminals. Always get a few steps ahead of them.

Quinten Ballard had used his father's truck, had stored rope in the closet, had killed Sara Wolfe and had abducted Makayla.

"Take a look at this," the detective in front of the laptop said.

Kadin and Detective Cohen moved to see the screen better. Quinten had been sent to a private school his last year of high school. A boarding school for troubled teenagers. Quinten didn't have a juvenile record, but Jax had sent him, anyway. He'd been having problems with the boy. Must have been having problems for a while.

"And this." The detective brought up an old news article about a complaint from a neighbor, who claimed Jax's son had taken and mutilated their cat. There had been no proof and the matter had been dropped.

"Penny never mentioned anything unusual about Quinten," Kadin said.

"Killers like this can put on a normal face when they have to," Cohen said, stating the obvious.

Quinten had played the role of a together kid, happy with his loving father, on his way to college and a promising future. But inside, he hid a monster.

"Jax didn't know about Sara Wolfe until her body was found." Kadin spoke his unraveling thoughts aloud. "He must have been shocked and in denial that his son could have done it."

Cohen nodded. "But he also had to have a good idea that his son could be the one responsible. The truck. The fire…"

"The rope," Kadin added.

Cohen nodded, meeting his gaze and then taking in the rest of his face. "Nothing surprises you anymore."

Unfortunately truer words were never spoken. What could shock him more than losing his daughter and wife to violence?

"Let me go in first," Kadin said, without acknowledging the observation. "Jax might let me in and keep Quinten subdued long enough for me to find Penny and Makayla. Once I confirm they're either there or not, then we move in for an arrest."

Kadin stepped out of the van. The property ran up a steep rock outcrop in back, and the SWAT team had already disbursed into the woods to surround the house and barn.

While that would ensure Quinten's capture, there would be no guarantee Penny would make it out of there alive. Penny, and most likely Makayla. Would he reach them in time? Penny—pregnant with his child. He didn't have one child to save. He had two. He dared not let the fear of failing interfere now. He had to succeed. His entire being vibrated with determination. And to see their abductor punished. Especially if he thought he could get away with murder. The face or identity of the killer didn't matter to Kadin, boy or man. The fact that he preyed on innocent children did.

"How do you know he'll let you in?" Cohen asked.

"Follow me."

He led Cohen to his car and used his cell to return the call he'd ignored while waiting for Cohen.

Jax answered.

"Am I invited to the party?" Kadin asked, watching Cohen go tense with uncertainty.

"Penny's here. We need to talk about my brother."

"So you arrange for us both to meet you here?"

After a lengthy pause, Jax said, "You're here already?"

"You didn't think I would be?" Kadin saw Cohen relax when he saw that Kadin had this under control.

"Well...good. Come on up, then. We're waiting for you."

Jax, Penny...and Quinten. What was Jax thinking? He'd go to prison for conspiracy if he helped his son cover up a crime.

"I'm only giving you fifteen minutes," Cohen said.

"Done." He'd do this in five.

Kadin drove up the dirt driveway, the van moved out of the way enough to allow him passage. Parking next to Penny's car, he got out, tempted to remove one of his pistols.

The door opened and Jax greeted him with a smile, a practiced smile, one he often wore and one that Kadin recognized as false. He stepped up the stairs and entered the house.

The first thing he saw was Quinten, and no sign of Penny. The bloody T-shirt explained enough. He noticed other things, like the rich furnishings in a spacious great room marred by used frozen dinner packages, crumbled paper towels, quarter-full glasses of curdling milk, empty bottles of beer and dirty dishes piled high in the sink. He couldn't tell which smelled worse. Maybe all of it combined to foul up the air. Someone had been living here awhile, and it hadn't been Jax.

"Where's Penny?" Kadin asked Jax, feigning nonchalance so that Quinten wouldn't be alerted to all he knew.

Quinten began to move his hand toward the back of his pants. Kadin put his hand on his left-side pistol.

"Wait!" Jax said.

"You shouldn't even be here, Dad," Quinten said to him.

"Why are you?" Kadin asked.

Jax turned from his son and his struggle for what to say fluttered across his face, eyes blinking, mouth open and forming words that wouldn't come out.

"She's downstairs," Jax said. "She's fine. Safe."

"Well, that's good, Jax. Is there a reason why she wouldn't be safe?"

Quinten's hand lowered to his side, and smugness curled up one side of his mouth.

"N-no." Jax eyed his son, clearly confused over how to handle his lunatic son.

"I know about Dane." Kadin went on with his ruse. "Is this where he brought Makayla Moore?" He started toward the basement door.

Quinten didn't stop him from opening the door, which clued Kadin into enough. When he reached the top stair, he pivoted and stuck his foot in the opening just as Quinten tried to close the door. Then, drawing his pistol and firing, he shot Quinten in his knee.

With a guttural shout, the boy dropped, falling backward, his gun sliding across the wood floor.

Kadin stood over him, having drawn his second pistol and aiming it at Jax while he aimed the other between Quinten's eyes.

"Quinten." Jax began to cry, an ordinarily together man crumbling, finally realizing there was nothing else he could do to save the only son he'd ever had.

"I want you alive to stand trial and go to prison for what you did," Kadin said to Quinten.

Stepping over him, he kicked the fallen pistol across the room, where it slid underneath the trash-cluttered sofa.

Tucking one of his pistols away, he kept his aim on Jax. "Down the stairs."

Ballard wiped his eyes and went to the basement door. Before following, Kadin shot the lock mechanism.

"Kadin!" he heard Penny yell.

At the bottom of the stairs, he shoved Jax back and went to the enclosed room.

"Stand back!" he shouted. Allowing a few seconds, he shot out the padlock and swung the door open.

Penny crouched with her arm around Makayla, who was crying against her shoulder.

"It's okay, you're safe now," Penny said to her, rubbing her arm. "Come on." She coaxed the girl to leave the cell.

Kadin's insides ripped and pulled with the emotion racing through him, relief, bittersweet triumph and anger. Yes, anger. Fury consumed him that he couldn't have done this for his daughter.

Penny screamed just before his distraction cost him Jax's attempt to hit him over the head with something. He stuck out his arm to block most of the blow but had to stagger to collect himself.

Penny charged out of the room, grabbing Jax's arm when he would have tried to strike Kadin again.

"You can't have her!" Jax shouted.

From the stairway, Quinten appeared, hanging on to the railing, knee soaking his jeans with blood, hand trembling as he held his pistol.

Kadin wanted to kill him so badly he could taste the tinny sting in his mouth.

Jax moved in front of Kadin's pistol just as he would

have fired to immobilize Quinten once again. But Quinten shot and the bullet hit Jax, going all the way through him and plugging a hole into the plywood as Kadin leaped out of the way, landing on his side as Jax's surprised eyes went wide and he put his hand over the gush of red on his chest.

Kadin checked on Penny and the girl. Penny had taken hold of Makayla and moved them behind the plywood wall, craning her neck to see Kadin and Jax.

"No!" Quinten wailed, his true feelings for the only person who'd ever cared for him coming out in wrenching breaths. He fell to the floor and crawled toward Jax, unable to use his injured shoulder. Jax had trouble breathing at this point.

Kadin rose to his feet, gun ready as the SWAT swarmed the basement. He held his hand up for them to stop. In a half circle around Jax and Quinten, they did.

Quinten held Jax's head on his arm and Jax looked up at him.

"I'm sorry," Quinten cried.

"I...love...you," Jax barely got out. Then he gurgled and could take no more breaths. He died in his son's arms, Quinten sobbing with his forehead against his dad's.

Kadin crouched and took hold of the gun Quinten still held, easily removing it. Handing that to one of the SWAT men, Kadin tapped Quinten's cheek with his pistol.

With pain from more than his gunshot wound contorting his face, the eighteen-year-old looked at Kadin.

"Why?" Kadin asked. He just wanted to know. Why had Quinten done this? Kidnap and kill Sara Wolfe. Attempt to do the same with Makayla.

"Why?" he repeated.

Quinten's eyes squeezed shut. "I couldn't help it," he wailed some more. "I don't know. I didn't want to." He sobbed more. "I didn't want to."

But he had. The evil monster inside had made him.

"People like you have to be stopped," Kadin said grimly. Then looked up at the nearest SWAT cop. "Arrest him."

Standing, he went to Penny and the girl, who'd both moved out of the room, Penny covering the girl's eyes as she held her against her.

Kadin put his hand on the back of Penny's head and leaned to kiss her hard. She took the kiss and gave back, her arm sliding around his neck. Her breath came with a mix of passion and relief. She kissed his mouth several times before he drew back, aware of the young girl below who still cried.

"I'm glad to see you," she said.

A surge of love overcame him. "I'm glad to see you, too." She had no idea. Or maybe she did.

He caressed her cheek with his thumb and then knelt before the girl, gently taking her hand when Penny let her go.

Her crying eased as she looked at him.

"Are you all right?" he asked.

She nodded unsteadily.

"These policemen are going to take you to your mom now." Where she belonged. Where she should never have been taken from.

With two great gulps of air and a giant sob of gladness, Makayla threw her little arms around his shoulders and didn't let go. She squeezed him as though he were her lifeline, as though she understood that he had just freed her from horror, that he would see that she'd be returned to her sheltered, innocent life. Dolls awaited her. Birthday parties. Sleepovers. Princess socks and comforters. Prom. Graduation. All of it.

Her soft crying came from relief, from returning to the arms of love.

Having to fight the burn of his own tears, Kadin stood with her, holding her carefully so as not to disturb her liberating float back to innocence. He caught Penny's streaming eyes before he took the girl upstairs. She knew what this meant to him.

He wanted to kiss her again.

Detective Cohen waited outside. Kadin didn't want to let the girl go. He felt as though she could be his daughter, alive and well. Saved.

Penny watched Kadin the whole time the police took Makayla into their care, how he hadn't wanted to let her go, how his eyes misted as they drove her away. She watched him as officers put Quinten in the back of a police car and how the kid looked through the window at him. Kadin hadn't seemed satisfied, only weary after a finished job. A duty. One more bad seed removed from society. Quinten looked like a defeated young man who'd just lost a battle with a formidable foe. And lost a father he'd mistakenly believed didn't love him, one who'd given his life trying to stop him from destruction.

Now, with the action winding down except for officers processing the crime scene, they had nothing else to do but go home. Where was home? Rock Springs didn't feel like home. Her apartment in Salt Lake City didn't, either.

Penny realized she had some choices to make, some big ones. Her career at Avenue One would be difficult to maintain with an infant. And, incredibly, she no longer felt as though that was so important. What had driven her to succeed but also had driven her onto a wayward course, a misguided course. She'd made her career too important. What she needed was what her mother had avoided.

She looked away from the last police car as it disappeared into the trees on the dirt driveway, seeing Kadin do the same. Their gazes met.

~~The way he'd kissed her in the cabin had her reign-ing in hope.~~

Her dream of love and family couldn't be realized with him, so why did she still feel this strong tug in that direction? She released a deep, quivering breath. He was just too afraid to start over. One thing she'd learned from her mother was that you couldn't fix a man to have him. He had to be whole on his own. Kadin was not whole, by no fault of his own. He hadn't chosen to have his wife and child taken from him so violently. That would rip any decent man's heart out. There was nothing she could do but leave him to figure out his future himself, with or without her and their baby.

"I'm going home." She started walking toward the detached garage that the police had opened.

"Penny." He caught up to her, taking her arm and stopping her.

Then he had no words. How could he explain the state of his heart?

She believed that he felt something for her and that their baby would, too, once he had time to sort everything out.

He couldn't kiss her the way he had after rescuing her and not feel passion for her. This wasn't about the way they made each other feel. The chemistry was there and the love would come, but only if he could get past his tragedy.

"It's all right, Kadin," she said. "Take some time to think. Let me take some time, too. We both need to think things through."

The turmoil in his eyes eased, hurting her because she'd just enabled him to leave her.

"I need to get a few things I forgot," he said, his gaze

going down over her body, this time not to see if she was unharmed.

"Stop by then. I'll meet you there." She walked toward the garage again, feeling him watch her awhile before hearing his feet step on the gravel.

At her car, she stole a look at him. He walked with long, strong strides down the road toward the highway. Seeing how easily he walked away, Penny embraced a steely resolve. Her disappointment in him angered her. But she'd do what had to be done.

By the time Kadin reached Penny's apartment building, he felt more settled. Maybe saving Makayla and the way she'd clung to him had shown him the light. He would always mourn his daughter. She would always be his first-born. He would always love her and feel the loss of her. That didn't mean he couldn't give this new child the same love. He'd have his struggles, but he now realized he had to stand up and be a man. He had to stand by Penny.

He'd do whatever she needed him to. Marry. Not marry. Either way, he'd be with her.

Maybe he could convince her to move to Rock Springs. She'd probably want to stay home with the baby, anyway.

Penny let him inside her apartment, walking away and ignoring him, going about her business as though he didn't matter. She expected him to get his things and leave. He almost chuckled. She had no idea what conclusion he'd just come to.

"We need to talk," he said.

She put a glass down hard on the countertop and flashed hot sea-green eyes at him. "What's there to talk about?"

Undaunted, he went to the counter.

"There's plenty. You and me. The baby. We need to decide how we're going to handle this."

"This? Do you mean our baby?"

She deliberately goaded him, thinking he would abandon her.

"We can get married," he said.

Her jaw went slack and she stared at him, clearly not seeing that coming. "What?"

"Married." He felt awkward, a little hesitant, but sure at the same time. "You and me."

"Y-you're asking me to marry you?"

"Yes." He understood why she had doubts.

She gave him another slack-jawed stare. "Why?"

"Because…" He thought of all the times they'd been together, how she'd threaded her way into his heart, undetected and unexpected. Unplanned. The way she made him feel made him believe in love again. That scared him, but he refused to let fear stop him. "I think I love you."

She closed her mouth with that avowal. Her head sort of jerked back.

"You're asking me because you feel obligated."

She didn't believe him. "Yes… No. I mean, I feel obligated, but I also…feel…something…for you."

"Something?"

Was she getting mad again? "Yes. Something big. Love." Boy was he botching this or what? Fear did that to a man. "Penny…"

She leaned forward over the counter. "I don't need a roommate. I need a father for my baby."

"You wouldn't be—"

"I need a husband."

"I'd be that—"

"A real husband. That means a man who really loves me."

He said nothing. Did he love her? What he felt consumed him and might even be stronger than anything he'd experienced.

Instead of giving in to fear, he plunged ahead. "I do love you."

"You're just saying that because I'm pregnant. You're only doing what you think you have to do."

"No." The more he talked and denied her accusations, the more he knew he spoke the truth.

She resisted believing him. She didn't trust him, and her determination not to end up lonely like her mother drove her now. "Please go," she said, folding her arms protectively in front of her, holding in the pain.

"Penny. Listen to me. I didn't see this coming, but somewhere along the way, somewhere between meeting you and now, I fell in love with you. I ignored it until now."

She stared at him, contemplating. He could see her go over what stood in his way of love. His past. He would have hard times ahead. His loss wouldn't go away just because he claimed to love her.

And she didn't believe him. She didn't believe he loved her.

Kadin decided to let her think over what he'd said today.

"I need you to leave now." She moved around the kitchen counter. "I'd rather end up like my mother than live with a man who doesn't want to love me and my baby."

Doesn't want to love...

"I do love you." He followed her to the door, which she jerked open.

Before doing as she asked, he faced her in the doorway. "Think about what I've said."

"Just, please, go." She blinked away the moisture gathering in her eyes.

"I'll call you," he said, and then left, expecting to hear the door slam. When it didn't, he looked back.

Penny stood in the doorway, looking flustered and as

though already thinking about what he'd said. She hadn't expected him to declare his love and now that he had, she was afraid to trust him.

Chapter 16

Penny ignored Kadin's calls for a week. His words kept repeating in her mind. *Somewhere along the way, somewhere between meeting you and now, I fell in love with you.* Did he? He'd gone from keeping her at a distance to all-out love. What if she let him back into her life and he ran after the baby was born? For the first time in her life a man had gotten to her. Luckily she'd been busy at work. Mark had been arrested for embezzlement and she'd been named acting CEO. The trust the board of directors had placed in her went a long way in soothing her feelings—and doubts.

If she were honest with herself, she'd admit that Kadin's pledge of love terrified her. She feared believing him. How could he know he loved her? He hadn't gotten over his past. Or had he? Had he healed enough to make room for her in his life?

And then, of course, the matter of the tiny life growing

inside her. He could have told her he loved her to make her marry him. But that was not Kadin. He was not a man who'd say what he didn't mean.

That left her issue with being alone to blame. If she didn't change, she'd end up like her mother. Ever since she'd left Michigan, she'd thought dating and working put her on the right track. In the back of her mind she'd thought she'd eventually get married and have kids, but she'd never considered it seriously. Afraid of ending up like her mother, she never put herself in a position to try not to—by starting her own family.

Kadin's declaration of love had forced her to face that. She should answer one of his calls and go with him to Rock Springs.

Her office phone rang and after a jolt, she pressed Speaker.

"Kadin Tandy again," Jordan said.

"Cancel all my meetings for the rest of the week. I'm going out of town."

"What should I tell Kadin?"

"Tell him I'm going to see my mother."

Penny's mom trotted out to the driveway as the dark sedan pulled to a stop, her long gray hair dyed golden blond and hanging loose, half tied white bow blouse flowing over the waist of dark blue jeans. The driver got out and went to get her bag from the trunk while Penny stood and received her mother's exuberant hug.

"Oh, look at you! You're so successful. Why have you been away so long? You should have come home sooner." She hooked Penny's arm and led her to the house.

The driver deposited her luggage on the entry floor, and Penny thanked him. He'd be back in two days to pick her up. Penny figured two days would be all she could take of her single mom, which hit her as strange, since she'd never thought of her mother that way. They'd always been so close. But now Penny saw how she'd turned a blind eye to her mother's loneliness, believing that Katherine had made a personal choice to be alone and lived blissfully happy.

"You're different."

Penny put her purse on the entry table. An archway gave a glimpse of a modern living room in the early 1900s Victorian-style house. Her mother kept the place updated and well maintained, doing most of the work herself.

"How so?"

Her mother surveyed her. "You met a man."

"I'm pregnant, Mom. And the man isn't interested. So take cheer. I'll be just like you." She hadn't meant to be so blunt and biting. The words had tumbled out without giving them a sensitivity check.

After a brief moment of shock, her mother took no offense. "Come here. There's someone I want you to meet."

Penny followed her mother into the kitchen, where a man stood before the stove, cooking something that smelled rich and tasty. He turned to reveal a white chef apron covering a golf shirt and part of his jeans.

"This my daughter, Penny. Penny, this is—"

"Stewart." The mayor of Cheboygan. Her mother had been friends with him for years.

"He moved in earlier this year."

Moved in? Penny rounded on her mother. "Why didn't you tell me?"

"You've been avoiding me. I've tried calling you several times and you haven't called me back." She took her arm and guided her back into the living room. "You can talk to him later."

Penny sat down on the sofa and her mother settled beside her.

"What's all this about being pregnant?"

Penny regretted telling her. "How long have you been seeing him?"

"We've been in a relationship for a year now."

And friends long before that. Penny was chagrined that she hadn't taken that into consideration. Her mother hadn't been nearly as lonely as she'd thought.

"Why do you say you'll end up like me, Penny?"

She lowered her head, wondering where she'd gotten so confused over her mother. "You're alone. You've always been alone."

Her mom put her hand on Penny's knee. "Honey, I've never been alone. I have friends, and most important, I have you."

"I mean with men. You loved my dad and never got over him."

Her mother laughed softly. "He called, you know." When Penny lifted her head, she said, "He told me you went to see him and that he talked to you. I always knew you would find him someday." She patted her knee. "Good for you."

"You always said you were happy," Penny said.

"Of course I am. Why would you think I wasn't? Because I've been alone?" Dawning drew a grunt out of her mother. "Penny," she protested. "It wasn't because of your father that I never married. I loved him in my adolescent mind, but the truth is, he wasn't the right one for me. My life was full with you and my friends and my activities, and I made a promise to myself to never settle for any man. If I were to ever marry, I'd have to meet someone I truly loved."

Penny realized her mother had never said outright that she'd never marry again. Penny had drawn her own conclusion there.

"Tell me about this man." Her mother sat back, getting comfortable, ready for a story.

Penny felt reluctant to share until she recognized why. Fear. Fear of losing Kadin. Fear of never having him in the first place. But he must be just as afraid, for different reasons.

Seeing a tablet on the big, square white coffee table, she picked it up and navigated to web browsing, then found the article on Kadin Tandy. Then she handed it to her mother, who took it and read. When she finished, she spent some time studying his photo.

Then she lowered the tablet to her lap and looked at Penny. "You have to go after him."

That her mother would say that, of all the other things she could have said, made Penny smile.

"He's different than your other boyfriends, Penny," her mother said. "You have to give him time. Patience. You can't discard him the way you have the others. He's had something tragic happen to him. You can't walk away without giving him a good chance."

"I know." Now she did. Now that she understood her mother better and why she'd discarded so many boyfriends, everything made sense. She didn't have to be afraid.

Kadin would have to get used to having an assistant sitting in the front lobby answering phone calls and handling the administration of his company. He'd received a package this morning that contained a file on a ten-year-old cold case. That made four cases, and from the sound of his busy new assistant, more were pouring in. He read an email from Lucas Curran asking him if he'd had a chance to look at his case.

Even the new cases and Lucas Curran's mystery weren't

enough to distract him from Penny. Why wouldn't she answer his calls?

~~Marriage and all that entailed still gave him cold feet,~~ but not when he thought of Penny. With her, he believed in the possibility of having a family. Burning hope began as a tiny pinhole and had mushroomed into a volcano. Hope. Sweet hope.

He hadn't liked the way she'd kicked him out of her apartment, as though she'd kicked him out of her life the way she did all her old boyfriends.

Lucas. Back to that…

Kadin focused on the Lucas Curran file. He needed another investigator. He needed two or three. Lucas was his best candidate. Well, only candidate. He had no homicide investigation background. He had earned a college degree in criminal science while in the military, where he'd learned to become a sniper. Those skills had led to the LAPD and the SWAT. The file only said that he'd resigned. *Early retirement.*

As Kadin read the personal information, his eyes zeroed in on a name.

He pushed some papers out of the way on his desk and found the package that had come in this morning. He'd skimmed through the contents of the ten-year-old case.

The woman was Lucas Curran's sister.

He had intended to tell Kadin without words that he could solve this case, not only that he had a personal reason for wanting to, but that he might also have key information that would lead to solving the case, and that he wouldn't hand over the information unless Kadin hired him. Lucas might not be an experienced investigator, but he had enough to buy him a beginning.

That type of tiptoeing around the truth didn't curry favor with Kadin. Lucas Curran obviously had a bone to pick with whoever had killed his sister. Who wouldn't? That alone wasn't significant. What grabbed Kadin and wouldn't let go was that he suspected Lucas could put a name to the killer. That by itself tempted Kadin enough. He hadn't formed Dark Alley Investigations to go by the book, not completely. As long as his team followed his moral code, he'd let just about anything go. And if this mysterious Lucas Curran's personal vengeance brought information to the table, Kadin would give him at least a start of a chance. Kadin's business centered on solving cold cases. This was as cold as they got.

He picked up the phone and called Lucas.

"Curran."

"I've read your file."

After a brief pause, Lucas said, "Then I'm hired?"

"I'd like to meet in person again. Sort of a formal interview for HR purposes." And to make sure the man was legitimate.

"Just say when."

Kadin set up a time. As he disconnected, he looked up and saw Penny standing in the doorway.

He stood.

"Hi," she said.

She didn't seem so distant now. In fact, she seemed like herself again. Feisty Penny. And beautiful and radiant in a yellow dress.

"Hi."

She stepped into his office and closed the door. When she faced him, she said point-blank in true Penny fashion, "I'm going to have a baby. Our baby."

"Yes, I've thought of little else since coming home." Actually that wasn't completely factual. He'd thought of her right along with the baby.

She moved toward him, walking around the desk to

stand before him, where she slid her hands up his chest and turned churning apprehension into the ignition of passion.

"~~I went to visit my mother,~~" she said, ~~hardly the come~~-hither he expected her to deliver.

"Yeah?"

"Turns out she was waiting for Mr. Right all along."

He wasn't sure what that meant. "She found Mr. Right?"

"I was wrong about her. I was wrong about me, too."

"You?"

She pressed her body against his and hooked her arms over his shoulders. "I thought ending up like my mother was a bad thing. Turns out, I'm going to end up like her and I'm going to be happy."

"How's that?" He slid his hands around her waist and held her, grinning and going along with her.

"My mother waited for the right man to come along."

"She found someone?"

Penny nodded in her sultry way. "Mmm-hmm."

"And…so have you?" he guessed.

"Right again, cowboy." She poked the brim of his hat to move it up his forehead a bit. Then she traced her forefinger down the left side of his brow and cheek and then followed the crease beside his mouth.

"We'll take it slow, okay?" She rose and pressed a kiss to his mouth. "We don't have to do this the way everyone else does. We can be unconventional. Live together. Take one day at a time."

Kadin put his hands on her shoulders and set her back a bit.

"No, Penny. We won't take this slow. I meant it when I said I loved you and that I want to marry you."

"But…you don't have to prove anything to me."

"This isn't about proving anything. This is about meeting a woman I didn't expect to fall in love with. Now we're going to have a baby." He couldn't stop a beaming smile. "It's a miracle, one I didn't recognize until I saved you. The idea of losing you shook me. And then everything became suddenly so clear. You." He brought her closer again, his arms sliding around her waist. "The baby."

After a while where she registered what he said, tears moistened her eyes. "You're not...?"

"Full of dread and regret?" He shook his head. "No. I'm full of hope. I know I'll have bad days and moments when I'll wish Annabelle was alive, but the other moments, the ones with you and our child—our new family—will overshadow that. I'll be able to hang onto the good memories I have and be grateful for the new ones we make."

"Oh, Kadin!" She leaped up with a soft sob, hugging him tightly.

He lifted her off her feet and held her, feeling her warmth and smelling her sweetness, closing his eyes to it all because he finally knew he had her.

She was his. They were a family.

"What about your job?" he asked. He wouldn't take her career from her.

Back on her feet, she kept her arms looped around him, sniffling back happy tears. "I'm going to consult for Avenue One until I decide what I want to do after the baby is born."

He'd be all right with anything she decided, as long as she stayed near him. She pecked his mouth with a kiss. "I might want to stay home with the baby, though."

"Whatever you decide, I support. Except moving from Rock Springs."

"I would never ask that of you." He received another kiss. "I love you too much, and I know what this place means to you."

"Thank you." Reminded of another step toward healing

he'd achieved, he said, "I talked to my mother. We had a good conversation."

"The man comes full circle," Penny said, truly happy for him. "I'm glad."

"I told her about you. And the baby."

"Wow. A real milestone."

"She said I could bring you when we were ready."

"Great. Then we'll go next week." She smiled as she joked.

"Okay."

Her smile fled. "Really?"

"Yeah. I want you to meet them. And them to meet you. Before the baby is born."

Penny kissed him again. "You are on the mend, Kadin Tandy."

"Not quite."

She leaned back and looked for signs of teasing. What did he mean?

"You haven't told me you're going to marry me yet."

Relaxing, she smiled softly. "Oh…that."

He grinned at her teasing.

She laughed and kissed him. He kissed her back, taking over, softening the touch and then deepening the intimacy.

"I'll marry you, Kadin Tandy, my lover. Protector of the innocent. I'll be your wife and mother to your children. We'll grow old together. Hold hands in public. Laugh and love."

"I like your optimism."

"Get used to it, Detective."

Finally, something he could look forward to. He lifted her into his arms and carried her toward the stairs to his upper level apartment. "We're going to need a bigger house," he said as he climbed.

"Much bigger. You're going to give me more than one baby."

He'd enjoy every moment of obliging her. "We'll start looking tomorrow."

Tomorrow...

Instead of gloom, tomorrow held the promise of love and happiness again. He'd spend the rest of his life cherishing that. And Penny.

* * * * *

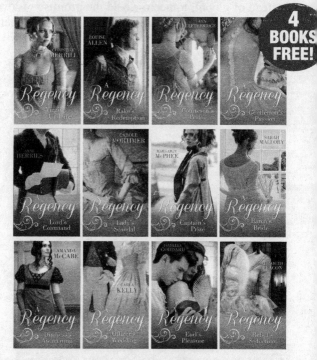

MILLS & BOON®

Want to get more from Mills & Boon?

Here's what's available to you if you join the exclusive **Mills & Boon eBook Club** today:

✦ *Convenience – choose your books each month*
✦ *Exclusive – receive your books a month before anywhere else*
✦ *Flexibility – change your subscription at any time*
✦ *Variety – gain access to eBook-only series*
✦ *Value – subscriptions from just £3.99 a month*

So visit **www.millsandboon.co.uk/esubs** today to be a part of this exclusive eBook Club!

MILLS & BOON®
INTRIGUE
Romantic Suspense

A SEDUCTIVE COMBINATION OF DANGER AND DESIRE